Her Family's Secrets

Her Family's Secrets

Joanne C. Parsons

ISBN: 978-1-7349436-2-7
eISBN: 978-1-7349436-3-4

Acknowledgments

I'm fortunate to have had a group of individuals who provided valuable feedback, suggestions, and advice as I wrote **Her Family's Secrets.** Thank you, Tom Hannon, Chris Melchior, my sisters, Fran Boyle and Connie Burgess, and daughter, Alison Elhilow. With your help, **Her Family's Secrets** matured from an unfinished manuscript to a story I am proud of.

And to Jim Berg, my patient husband and often the planter of the seed for a story, my special thanks.

Let me know what you think - jgparsons921@gmail.com

Please leave a review on Amazon.com

Invite me to your book club, library, or Zoom gathering.

Read my other books:

Kitchen Canary

Through the Open Door

Predator in the House

Table of Contents

I

Change in Plans

Boston, Massachusetts
March 2018

Andrea Birch Rossi sat tapping her foot and watching the door. She stood when the doctor walked in and shot her husband a look as he rushed in behind him. Will Rossi shrugged and took a seat.

She turned. "Why are you so far back? Move up with me."

He folded his arms across his chest. "I'm fine."

Andrea extended her hand. "Dr. Sherman…" He gestured for her to sit.

The fertility specialist leaned against the front of his desk, facing Andrea, and crossed one leg over the other. "You're one of those unique cases." He paused and opened her record.

Andrea slumped in her chair.

"We can't find any anatomical or gynecological issues. You ovulate each month, your eggs are healthy… They fertilize in the dish…" He looked at Will. "Mr. Rossi is fine."

"There's nothing more you can do, like test for a rare condition or something?" She turned toward Will, who was checking his watch.

"I could, Mrs. Rossi." He looked at Andrea. "After three rounds of IVF, when we have two healthy individuals in their early thirties, we sometimes conclude, well, we need to reassess." His tone turned condescending. "Take a break from all these tests and hormone shots. Relax a little." He emphasized 'relax.'

She nodded. "I know where you're going with this, Doctor. But I'm not an anxious person. I work in advertising and I'm used to deadlines hanging over my head. I don't stress." Andrea softened her tone. "If I had my way, I'd be teaching children's art or painting for a living, but the job in advertising pays the bills."

Will spoke for the first time. "If it's about learning to relax, she can take yoga classes or something. No way she's quitting her job."

Dr. Sherman looked toward Will when he made the comment, then back to Andrea. "Again, Mr. and Mrs. Rossi." He held both hands out to them. "Only you can make the decision to change your lifestyle. I can only advise." He stopped leaning on the desk and stood. "Set up an appointment for six months from now. We'll see how you're doing then."

—∞—

Andrea and Will stood shivering outside the office building on busy Boylston Street in Boston's medical district. Dwarfed by red brick hospitals stretching for blocks in either direction, and looming parking garages, Andrea shouted above the noise of screeching ambulances and gridlocked traffic. "Time for a new doctor. I'm not settling for a diagnosis of 'relax.'"

Will put his hand behind his ear. "I can't hear you. Told you this was a big waste of time." He flagged down a cab. "I have to get to work."

Andrea took off her sunglasses and moved closer to her husband. The two-inch heels on her leather boots brought her height to five feet, nine inches and eye to eye with her husband. "Wait. It's late. I thought we could catch dinner and process all this. Plus, we still have to discuss the letter."

Will opened the cab door. "Take the car home. I forgot to tell you I extended our hours on Fridays. We close at ten now."

Exhausted after a long day at work and the disappointing doctor's visit, Andrea arrived home and walked to the bedroom to change from her work clothes. Following her boss, Liz's, instructions, she dressed so as not to distract clients from their ad campaigns or presentations.

Her boss often cautioned, "Wear a blazer if the office seems too cold," adding, "Keep the attention on your work, not your nipples."

Andrea hung the black linen pants, white cotton blouse, and blazer on the side of the closet reserved for the size ten clothes she bought after gaining weight from the fertility hormones. She stored her size six wardrobe on the closet's far end. She pinned up her shoulder-length hair, took a shower, and wrapped herself in a warm robe. After pouring a glass of her favorite Italian red, she held it up and spoke out loud to the empty room. "Nothing like a glass of vino to calm the anxious non-pregnant girl down." Andrea didn't cry, she'd spent a torrid of tears over the months of infertility treatments. This night, she bristled as she let the rich warm wine roll down her throat. The doctor's words echoed in her head. 'We need to reassess.'

Her feet propped on the glass and stainless-steel coffee table, she looked around their eight hundred square foot condo. It was everything her husband wanted. They were on the fifth floor of a renovated brownstone in Boston's North End. Will chose the modern amenities, state-of-the-art appliances, a wine cooler, parquet floors, and a roof deck. The floor-to-ceiling windows faced rows of other rehabbed brownstones and offered a view of a narrow street below. Only the living room reflected Andrea. Ten of her best watercolor paintings hung on the walls, each piece initialed *AB* in delicate crimson red paint. She raised her glass. "And to you, Will Rossi. Yoga, my ass."

Andrea set the alarm on her cell phone. Her workday began in less than twelve hours. That it was a Saturday didn't matter. As she told the doctor, she was used to deadlines looming over her head. She poured another glass of wine and made a plate of cheese and crackers and retreated to her bed. Will wouldn't be home for two hours, which gave her enough time to clear any evidence she ate in their bed. She reached for the certified letter, notifying her she'd inherited a house and land on Cape Cod, and read it again.

II

The Chasm

The arguing began within hours of the letter's arrival. She picked it up at the post office, a letter from a Boston law firm, read it as she walked home, and again when she settled onto the sofa. "Oh my God. Will, I'm inheriting an old homestead on Cape Cod. I love Seahaven."

"From who? I thought you didn't have any relatives."

"Evidently, I do, or did, but the letter doesn't go into detail."

Will stood in front of the television watching the news. "Where's Seahaven?"

"It's a little seaside town on the edge of the world. Look." She passed him the letter.

He read through it and handed it back to his wife, turning his attention back to the television. "Sell it." He grabbed the remote control and turned up the volume.

Andrea stood in front of the television, facing her husband. "Sell it? We haven't even seen it yet. It might be charming. According to this, the house is one hundred and fifty years old and comes with a barn and sixty acres."

Will walked away. He poured himself a finger of Chivas. "I'll call Rick and have him check it out and give us a price."

She turned off the TV. "You will not call a realtor. In case you didn't notice when you scanned the letter, I inherited the homestead, not you." Her cheeks burned red. "Give a little for once in your life, Will. We're in this overpriced condo because you had to live in the North End. It wasn't my idea to live in the city."

"I thought you loved the character of the North End."

She shot back. "No, Will. I don't like crowded, noisy streets. You grew up here, remember? Not me. You get to walk to work, run the family store. Buying this place was all about you."

Will mumbled something about community property and walked from the living room. "I'll call Rick tomorrow."

"Don't you dare."

Will didn't mention the realtor again. There was little conversation between them until Andrea broke the silence the following Friday. "I'm driving to Cape Cod on Sunday to check out the property. I'd like you to come."

—⁕—

It was a rare sunny day for March. Once they got onto the highway, Andrea broke the silence. "I looked up the route, shouldn't take more than two hours, tops." When Will didn't reply, she turned to see him leaning his head against the headrest, eyes closed, earbuds in. "Thanks for the company, Will," she mumbled, knowing he wouldn't hear her.

Andrea followed the voice of the GPS, taking a right turn off the Seahaven exit, and traveling two more miles. When the GPS instructed, "turn right," Andrea hit the brake, maneuvering an unexpected sharp turn. A mile down the road, she turned into a half-hidden path and the GPS announced, "You have arrived at your destination."

The house at the end of the rutted driveway looked all of one hundred and fifty years old. Andrea stared straight ahead. "Are you getting out?"

Will opened the passenger side door of the Prius. "So, this is Seahaven. A sad little town with bumpy dirt roads, scraggly dead trees, and rundown houses. No wonder I never heard of it."

"You haven't heard of it because your family never left Boston. Most folks from New England, and New York, for that matter, know about the quaint towns on the tip of Cape Cod."

He slammed the car door. "You holding it against me because my parents worked hard?"

"Not my point."

Will wrapped his arms around his parka. "I wasn't lucky enough to have a daddy to pay my way through graduate school. I earned what I have."

"Oh, here we go. Poor Will, came up from nothing."

"It's the truth."

"Will, you pull this every time you want sympathy. It's like your badge of honor. Your father worked eighty hours a week scratching out a living in his grocery story. I know it by heart."

"It is a badge of honor. What I have, I got by myself. You think it was easy being the first in the family to go to college? Convert my dad's store to a pharmacy? I didn't get any handouts, Andrea. I did it all myself."

"Honest, Will. I don't even know how this got started." She stood in front of the house, blocking the sun with her hand, and staring at the black tar paper covering parts of a sagging roof that sloped from two stories in the front to one in the back. She walked on a carpet of frosted brown pine needles toward the house. After testing the rickety step leading to the porch, she tiptoed between the missing floorboards to the narrow front door.

Andrea turned to Will as she inhaled and spread her arms. "Isn't it wonderful?"

"This old place?"

"No. The salt air." She inhaled again. "So fresh, so clean."

"Air's air. You going in or what?"

"You coming?"

He stood, earmuffs, parka, and gloves, with arms still crossed over his chest, resting on the belly he'd grown over the past couple of years. "Look at this." Will pointed to scattered fractured bricks on the ground. "That's your chimney laying in the bushes."

"I said, you coming?"

"You first. See if it's safe. Check for signs that say, 'Do Not Enter. Property Condemned.'" Will laughed at his own response.

Andrea found the key under the porch doormat, just as the attorney promised. It wasn't necessary. When she pressed one hand on the wooden front door, it creaked open.

She stepped into a darkened room. "It's colder in here than it is out." Heavy window drapes blocked any outside light. She turned to her husband. "Leave the door open."

Will followed Andrea, finding his way with a flashlight. "Switch on the lights."

"There's been no power since Catherine Birch went into the nursing home. Sad, really. She was there two years before she passed. If I knew about her, I would have visited."

Will didn't respond. He maneuvered between a stuffed sofa and armchair and pointed his flashlight toward a splintered ceiling beam encased in cobwebs. "I knew it before I walked through the door. The place is a dump. Did you see the shingles? They're so dried up they're curling."

Andrea covered her mouth and nose and yanked a heavy drape off a window. Sunlight highlighted the dust particles floating about the room. She moved beyond the bulky furniture and pulled another set of drapes from an east facing window. "Look, already I see potential." She turned her flashlight toward the center of the room and moved it from floor to ceiling. "Will, it's a fieldstone fireplace. Have you ever seen such a piece of craftsmanship?"

"Yeah, the granite countertops and inlaid hardwood floors in our condo."

Andrea spoke, but more to herself than her husband. "This place is a diamond in the rough. A treasure."

"It's a treasure, all right. Andrea, think about how our lives can change if we sell this? A developer would tear this and the barn down and use the sixty acres to build condominiums. We'd be in the clear financially with money to spare." He shined his flashlight on her face, and spoke in a low, creepy tone. "You must sell this haunted house."

Andrea stared into the light. "Not funny, and I'm not selling the only piece of family history I have. I'm bringing it back to life."

III

The Storm

Seahaven, Massachusetts
October 1841

Abigale Birch was orphaned the day she was born. Her mother, Martha, bled to death, causing her father, Samuel, to withdraw from life. People in Seahaven thought God punished Samuel for the death of his brother, Roger, at sea.

—∿—

October 2, 1841... The storm hit with no warning. Samuel Birch and his crew made it through the night, but the next day, the storm intensified. More than fifty fishing and shipping boats off the coast of Cape Cod pitched and tumbled, leaving splintered pieces scattered in the sea. Some floated bottom up, their crews trapped in watery graves. On shore, furious waves seized barns and homes, washing them out to sea, bashing them about like matchsticks.

Samuel shouted to God as the gusting winds and lashing rain tore the foresail and mainsail to ribbons. He and his brother, Roger, clung to the ropes as the ship lurched violently, until monstrous black waves emerged from out of the darkness and consumed the vessel. When it righted, Roger was gone, claimed by the angry sea.

Women and children walked the beaches for the next days, collecting the bodies of their brothers, husbands, and fathers. Seahaven was a town of widows, with more than a hundred men dead and dozens of others swallowed up by the sea.

The town's few surviving men gathered in the tavern, dulling the memory of the storm with whiskey. Some told their stories; Samuel Birch was among them.

"My fleet broke up like tinderboxes, every boat." The men nodded in agreement. He'd describe the moment his brother, Roger, was lost. "A mountain high wave, black as the night, appeared. We had no warning before it was on us. It slammed us down into the fierce waves. I thought it was the end, until the boat righted." He'd bow his head, "Roger was gone." A few men, red-eyed from drink, raised their glasses to Samuel's telling of that night, others refrained, having heard a different account of Roger's death from his crew.

—⚬—

Samuel Birch turned his back on the sea after the storm, his six-foot, five-inch frame bent forward from the heavy weight of grief and loss. He stood with his son, Caleb, and Roger's widow, Martha, among the ruins of the home they once shared, now destroyed by the gales. "We'll build again, but not on this hill facing the sea. This place is only meant for the family cemetery, not the living."

He settled fifteen-year-old Caleb and Martha in the barn on the south side of the land and built a modest home, salvaging cedar shingles, pine floorboards, and fieldstone from the house on the hill. Samuel apologized to Caleb and Martha. "It's not the house my father built. I'm not a rich man. It's only the land I have left now."

There was gossip in the town when Samuel married his brother's widow. He took Caleb aside, "Now we only got two bedrooms. It's practical that Martha and I marry. We'll share one, and you'll have the other."

Caleb didn't protest, but his father continued. "Your own mother's been dead and gone for seven years, and Martha's good to you."

Again, Caleb, not one to raise objections, nodded.

A renewed sense of hope and faith took hold of Samuel that first year. Although Martha never bore children for Samuel's brother, she was pregnant six months after the marriage. The joy of the new home and life as a family was short lived when Martha died giving birth to infant Abigale.

Retreating into a state of despair, Samuel withdrew from life after Martha died. Some wondered if it was God's justice.

At sixteen, Caleb became the man of the family. Women from the church offered help, one even wanted to adopt the infant, but Caleb refused. "Abigale's family. I keep her clean and warm. That's all she needs."

The women protested, but he prevailed, rising each morning, tending to the baby's needs. The wife of a farmhand wet nursed Abigale during the day. Caleb worked the farm until dark, caring for the animals and seeing to the gardens. After several years of failed crops, he learned the good draining, sweet, sandy soil on his farm worked magic on turnip. He perfected his system and walked the fields instructing older, more experienced farmhands. "We harvest the crop and bury the best in a hole under the frost line after we cover them with sand and seaweed." In spring, he'd tell the men, "Dig up the turnip and plant them." When the flowering stems grew, the farmhands harvested the seeds for the next year's planting.

Young and industrious, Caleb planted asparagus, which after two years thrived in the acidic, sandy soil. Both crops were in high demand on the mainland. "Asparagus for the English, turnip for the Irish," he often declared. In the years he grew from a boy to a man, Caleb spent each day tending to his despondent father, raising Abigale, and farming his crops. A man of few words, but measured actions, he provided for and protected his family and farm.

—◊◊◊—

1858... Fifteen years after giving up on living, Samuel Birch stopped breathing. Caleb was thirty-two when he put his father in the grave. He kept Abigale, now fifteen, from the cemetery. "Nothin' but sadness up there. You don't need to be around the dead."

Relieved of his father's care, Caleb looked beyond the house and farm for companionship. He told Abigale, "It's a part of nature for a man to be with a woman. It's time for me now. I didn't take a woman into the home when Father was alive, and you were so young."

When Caleb decided to find a wife, the petite teenager confessed. "Like you, Caleb, I've been bound to this house. I have an interest in going into town."

Caleb's response was quick. "There's nothing for you beyond this house. I gave up my youth to protect you. You're a child and will stay one until I say you're not." In the beginning, Abigale didn't resist her brother's control. She remained at home while Caleb pursued women he thought suited life on the farm, but none returned his interest. He eased the sting of rejection and loneliness, making whiskey his only companion. He became resentful and more rigid over the years, even insisting Abigale sew her clothes 'dark and modest.' He often warned, "People out there have nothing good to say about us. We're better off to keep to ourselves."

Unwilling to defy her brother and risk his wrath, Abigale settled for life limited to home, school, and church. Except for casual acquaintances at church, she and Caleb spent the next ten years as each other's only company.

IV

The Contract

Seahaven, Massachusetts
November 1868

Abigale stirred the pot of chicken vegetable soup heating over the fire. She tasted it. "Ahh, good and hot." She used the ladle to spoon the soup for her brother. "Wake up, now. You need to eat some."

At forty-two, and after years of working the farm and soaking his soul in whiskey, Caleb's skin yellowed and belly swelled. He slept most of the day away, sometimes, when he woke, not recognizing his own sister.

When he was still able, Caleb saw to it Abigale would be cared for after he passed. He made arrangements with the neighbor, George Smythe. He found Smythe in his barn, boots sunken in three inches of pig slop. "My sister's a spinster. She'll be the sole owner of the house, barn, and forty acres of land after I go. It's yours, provided you marry her."

George Smythe was handsome, hardworking, and shrewd at twenty-two years old. He arrived in America a young boy, when London shipped their street orphans to work as farmhands in Western Massachusetts. The Civil War was his escape from indentured servitude. He wiped his forehead with a muddied hand. "I saved every cent for two years to buy these twenty acres."

"And you done a good job, I been watchin'. That's why I picked you."

George was one of a few available bachelors in town. He had plans to court Sarah, the pretty daughter of the man who owned the mercantile.

Caleb's offer of forty acres was an unexpected windfall for ambitious George Smythe. He wouldn't lust for Abigale Birch like he did for Sarah, but she didn't come with forty acres of land.

Caleb Birch set the terms. "Now, I could live for years. Fact is, I don't think I will the way I been feeling. I'm the last of the Birch men."

George eyed the belly protruding from the unhitched pants of this tall man, now stooped from his rounded spine.

"It's not till I die this deal is true. You get my house and land, but you got to marry my sister and guarantee her a home for life."

"You know, Caleb, law says she's allowed to own land on her own."

"I do. But she's not strong. Needs a man."

Smythe nodded. "I'll wait till after you're gone."

Not one to linger, Caleb walked from George Smythe's barn. "You make up the paper. We'll both put our names to it." He turned, "No need for Abigale to know any of this now."

"Understood."

"Once I'm dead, just show her the paper. She won't put up a fuss. Never had much of a mind of her own."

George Smythe wiped his right hand on his pants and the two men shook on the agreement.

V

The Rejection

Seahaven, Massachusetts
December 1868

Abigale Birch stood over her brother Caleb's grave in the family cemetery. The winds whipping from the ocean numbed her face. The last of the Birch family, she was responsible for managing the farm.

At the end of the day, the oldest farmhand, Jason, came to Abigale. "Miss Birch, no need to fret. The crops have been harvested and sent to market. The men buried the best of the turnip."

"You put my mind to rest." She hesitated. "Are you up to running the farm?"

Jason tugged at his hat. "No disrespect to the dead, ma'am, but I been doin' it for the past years." He covered his mouth and mumbled. "Since the drink got to Caleb."

Abigale nodded. "Thank you, Jason."

—ɯ—

Released from Caleb's tight control, Abigale made changes to the home. Cooking in a cast iron pot in the hearth was burdensome in summer when the heat became unbearable. Caleb never allowed a modern cooking stove, but now she ordered one from the Chattanooga Stove Company. To her surprise, the monstrosity took up most of the far wall near the door to the root cellar. Having no other option, Abigale enlisted the help of the Irish carpenter and his son from town.

"It's so much bigger than I expected. I didn't know I had to vent it."

The carpenter made a suggestion. "Miss Birch. You'll need an ell built onto the house, about six feet out. Let me make it so you can add a sink," he paused, "you might even be wantin' a pantry." Abigale offered a stern look, and the carpenter retreated. "Or now I'm thinkin' just enough space for the stove will do ya."

"Make it so I can have a hot cup of tea and maybe soup."

Once the stove was properly installed, the carpenter fired it up and instructed Abigale. "This here handle turns to the right when you want to cook. Don't forget, turn it to the right."

Abigale let the stove sit untouched, instead studying the cookbook that came with it. After a month, she dared try to boil water. She turned the handle to the left and to the right, then left again, but the wood wouldn't catch. She cursed, "Ignorant Irishman." Discouraged, Abigale let the stove sit cold and idle, and continued to make stew in the pot over the hearth.

Abandoning her dream of cooking, Abigale sharpened her seamstress skills. She'd handsewn her own clothes as a child, not having a mother to do it. Caleb bought her homespun and wool, always brown or black. He denied her when she begged, "Please, a few colored buttons, or perhaps a bit of ribbon or lace."

With him gone, she gathered her courage and went to the dry goods store in town. Overwhelmed by the choices, she purchased colorful textiles, buttons, and ribbons. Basking in her newfound freedom, she stopped at the General Store and treated herself to a few fashion magazines and romance novels.

Her days now free from caring for Caleb, Abigale studied the styles in her New York fashion publications. Using her new textiles, she created a hat for herself to wear to church. It was early spring, so she chose a navy-blue linen to cover the cap and brim. She wrapped light blue lace around the cap and tied a bow in the back. She attended services on the next Sunday, taking a seat in the back of the church.

Abigale didn't anticipate the enthusiasm for her hat by other church goers. Unaccustomed to such attention, she at first recoiled at their questions and compliments. Once home and alone, she savored the recognition, studied the fashion magazines made more hats. She swayed the dry goods shop owner to sell them on consignment. "Styles are changing. I've learned bonnets are no longer in vogue." She presented her creations. "Modern women are piling their hair on the back of their heads." She leaned in toward the store owner and whispered, "The oversized bonnets you have are out of style."

The shop proprietor walked away to assist a customer. Abigale took the moment to lay her latest edition of *Harper's Bazar* on the store counter. Several ladies took notice. She planted a hat on one of the women. "Look, I've copied the latest fashions. My hats sit flat on the head." She compared her hats to the magazine pictures. "There's a puff at the crown. It's all the rage." By the time the shop owner turned her attention back to Abigale, three women were wearing her hats and admiring their reflections. Abigale displayed the hats on the store counter. "I've added a jeweled headband on this one, and silk flowers here, just like the hats in *Harper's.*" She pulled another from her bag. "And for the ladies who prefer to keep their prominent noses and twin chins to themselves, a three-inch veil of tulle or lace."

The shop owner agreed to take them all.

—∾—

Unaccustomed to asserting herself, the occasional visits to town to sell her hats sapped Abigale's energy. She much preferred the solitude of reading romance novels by the light from the fire. It was her secret pleasure to imagine herself the object of a handsome man's affection. Books were her company, and their characters, her companions. Abigale read *The Scarlet Letter* three times. Although she never had a lover, and ascribed to Puritan views on adultery, she idolized Hester Prynne. She didn't consider herself beautiful like Hester, but thought they shared the characteristics of self-reliance and dignity. She so admired Hester, forced to wear an embroidered scarlet *A* on her chest after being accused of adultery, Abigale imitated her, using fine, crimson-colored thread to embroider an elaborate *AB* on every hat she created.

Abigale continued to improve her living conditions, putting in hours each day, lugging stacks of magazines, books, and newspapers to the half second floor of the old house. She swept out dirt and sand and after that, scrubbed years of tracked mud from the wide pine floors. She admired pictures of painted pine floors in magazines and created a stencil of a favorite textile pattern. It took her weeks on bended knees to paint a plaid floor three feet around every angle of the center fireplace. After beating years of dust from the heavy drapes, she used vinegar, heated water, and old newspapers to wipe away layers of tobacco and soot from the glass windowpanes. She was pleased with herself and content, as the old, dark homestead took on the look of a home, a woman's home.

—∽∾—

George Smythe fantasized about Sarah Marchant, the mercantile's young daughter, but after the agreement with Caleb Birch, abandoned the dream of courting her. Three months after Caleb's death, George approached Spinster Birch. After a hard day tending his crops and animals, and a gulp of whiskey, he knocked on Abigale's door, paper in hand. George stood in the doorway suffering the bitter March winds. The foul stench of pig excrement caused Abigale to stagger when she opened the door.

George removed his hat, revealing a head matted with dirty, blonde hair. "Ma'am, I have a paper your brother Caleb signed."

Abigale stood just inside the door, staring at the young stranger. She hid her romance novel in the folds of her skirt and spoke without looking at the document. "My brother didn't read or write. I don't believe he made up any paper."

A shivering George Smythe offered it to her. "I gave him a hand with it, ma'am. But it's his name on it." He pointed to an x. The printing was primitive, with misspelled words, but the message was clear.

Abigale spoke, delivering a stony stare at George. "My brother, Caleb, gave his farm, land, and buildings to you, along with me, as a wife?"

George moved back a step. His thoughts wandered to Sarah, the young beauty he was giving up. The woman in front of him was plain, with hair pulled back tight, and frail enough for a good wind to take her away. "Yes," he whispered.

She squinted at him with small, close-set eyes atop a nose that overshadowed her tiny chin. This filthy farmer, hat in hand at her door, had orders from the grave that she commit her home and herself to him.

The strong voice belied her bird-like frame. "Mr. Smythe. I, Abigale Birch, am the owner of this home and land. Caleb Birch had no right to delude you into thinking he could bequeath it and me to you." She tore the paper in half. "Now, get off my property."

George Smythe bowed in reply to the swift rejection, replaced his hat, and backed off the porch. "Good day to you, ma'am."

Abigale closed the front door. The brisk winds left the house cold. She went to her brother's bedroom and took the half empty bottle of whiskey from his shelf and poured a glass. After a few hard pokes at the fire, she crumpled the pieces of paper and tossed them into the flames. She rocked in her chair, welcoming the heat, her chest heaving with each breath.

Abigale downed a mouthful of the burning liquid and muttered. "There'll be no marriage."

VI

The Conflict

Boston, Massachusetts
March 2018

"Hon, this is our dream come true. Think about it. We sell this place and the land, and a bundle of money comes pouring into our hands. You can quit your job and paint all you want. Andrea, you won't have to work." He pointed a finger at her. "No stress equals baby, remember what the doctor said?"

Andrea was driving but turned her head to her husband. "Now you want to talk? First of all, I happen to like my job. Second, don't play the baby card, Will, I see right through you."

"I'm thinking about you, really. I'll always keep the store. The family would never forgive me if I gave it up after three generations."

"And therein lies the problem, Will. You have a family, a big family. Sisters, brothers-in-law, nieces, nephews, aunts, great aunts, cousins, and on and on. What do I have? Huh? Both my parents are dead. Neither had anyone close. It's just me, Will."

"Why are you mad at me?"

"Because you're missing the point. I inherited this house from a family member, someone related to my father, way back. It's family, Will. My connection to people related to me. Get it?"

"Sure, I get it. But what about us? We can make a family of our own. You're always talking about how much you want a baby."

"Like that's ever going to happen. You don't get it."

"Slow down. Why are you speeding?"

"Pissed off, I guess."

Andrea backed off the accelerator. "Are you happy...I mean, in our marriage? Tell the truth."

"The truth? It's hard to be happy with a wife who's always pissed at me."

Her cheeks flared red. "So, it's my fault?"

Andrea knew he was partly right. She wasn't as much pissed at Will as just not into him.

"What about you?"

"What about me?"

"Are you happy? Do I make you happy? Somehow, I don't think I measure up to your expectations of a husband."

Will was right again. After Andrea lost the love of her life, Paul, she compared every man to him.

"It's not about measuring up, Will." She sorted her words. "It's more about give and take. I think we want different things in life."

The conversation ended, leaving Andrea to her own thoughts. Will's sister, an intern at the ad agency, talked her into going on a date with him, her first in years. They had drinks and chatted. He boasted that he put himself through college.

"The first in my family." He raised a glass to himself.

Andrea spent that first date comparing Will to Paul, who was tall and thin, with light hair and blue eyes. Will stood an inch or two taller than she and had a teddy bearish build. She and Paul lived together for three years after college and planned to move to the West Coast for his graduate degree. When her dad suffered a devasting heart attack, Andrea left her teaching job and abandoned her plans to go to Oregon with Paul.

Will broke the silence. "What do you mean by give and take?"

"Oh, I don't know, Will." She emphasized his name. "Maybe because you always get your way in this relationship, and now you're giving me crap over this house."

"As in how do I always get my way, please?"

"How about railroading me into spending two hundred thousand dollars of my trust fund to buy the condo, and now we're stuck with a huge mortgage. Oh, and there's the thirty thousand dollars of debt you dropped on me when we applied for the mortgage, thank you. That was a surprise wedding gift, I suppose?"

"You should thank me for loosening you up. Your trust fund is for you to enjoy life. You'd rather live in your parents' old house than spend a little and live in one of the best neighborhoods in Boston."

Andrea had more to say. "Don't think I didn't notice you were more interested in picking out the granite for the kitchen counters and the type of wood floors you wanted than you were in our fertility treatments. That hurt, Will."

They pulled into a parking space outside their condo. "Nicely played, Andrea. Anything else you want to throw at me?"

VII

Tom Whelan

The day trip to Cape Cod left Andrea filled with anxiety. She tried to sleep, but tossed and turned, her mind busy imagining the house scrubbed clean, opened to the sun, with its character restored. Will's snoring incensed her. She resented him for his lack of understanding about the house and her need to connect with family history. She was outright angry that he let her endure all the fertility treatments alone, always finding reasons to miss them. It was hard to remember what she liked about Will.

At two a.m., she gave up on sleep and slipped out of bed. Using her cell phone flashlight, she poked around her dresser and found heavy socks, sweatshirts, and jeans. She crept into the living room and called her boss, whispering a voicemail message. "Hey Liz, I'm all caught up at work and need a few days to take care of personal business. Call if you need me."

She scribbled a note to Will. "Couldn't sleep. Too much on my mind. Gone to Seahaven."

An hour into the ride, the ring of the cell phone broke her concentration. Deep in thought about their relationship, she didn't pick up Will's call. His uncaring, indifferent attitude made her question if she wanted to stay married. From their first meeting she sensed a darkness about him, maybe pessimism, but agreed to a second date. He brought her to the pharmacy he owned, showing her a wall covered in vintage photos. He pointed to a black and white picture of a heavyset man standing beside a seated woman in a gray dress.

"My Nonno, he came over from Italy and bought this storefront. He sold fruits and vegetables from his own garden in the summer. He and my grandmother lived in the apartment upstairs. Actually, it's a room."

Andrea pointed out the positive. "And two generations later you went to college and converted the grocery store to a pharmacy. Outstanding achievement."

Will didn't seem as pleased with himself. "When my old man took over, he worked himself into an early grave trying to keep the store going." He took a framed photo off the wall and stared at it. "Foolish man. Didn't change with the times."

"Will, that's the past. You can't hold a grudge against him for trying."

"But I do. We were dirt poor and didn't have to be. We lived in my grandfather's three family house. After my grandparents died, my old man rented out the other two apartments to relatives coming over from Italy. He charged them almost nothing." He put the photo back on the wall. "And then he kept trying to sell tomatoes in his corner shop. The big grocery chains were popping up left and right, but he wouldn't give it up. Killed him, and my mother in the end."

Will ran an emotional marathon from pride in his immigrant grand-parents to resentment toward his own father. It wasn't attractive to Andrea. She challenged him. "What about you, Will? How long can a neighbor-hood pharmacy survive with CVS and Walgreens on every corner?"

Without responding, he ushered Andrea out the door of the store and locked up. "Let's eat. I picked out a restaurant only the neighbors know about."

Remembering those first dates made Andrea wonder why she went out with this sad sack a third time. He spent the evening venting his anger. "My father didn't pay a penny for my college. You'd think he'd help the first one in the family to get a degree." He went on, complaining the pharmacy didn't make much profit. She remembered suggesting he sell it. "I won't be the one in my family to throw in the towel." She thought his response revealed a disinterest in advancing his career.

As she passed the sign for Cape Cod, she remembered comparing Will to Paul, an eternal optimist who saw the glass half full. But Will persisted, turning up his positive attitude and romancing her. The morning after that third date, Andrea received a dozen red roses and a sweet note. "I can do better." Knowing Paul was out of her reach, she gave Will another chance and worked to overlook his moods.

—∽—

It was close to five a.m. when Andrea arrived in Seahaven. She took the time to explore, walking east, up a hill, inhaling the cold salty air, and admiring the panoramic view of the peaceful waters of the Atlantic. There, on a glorious morning she watched the orange sun lift from the horizon. Looking around, she realized she was standing in a cemetery. She stepped between half buried grave markers and engraved stones, disrupted by frost heaves, and tried to read the etchings worn by years of salt and wind.

With hours before the rest of the world woke up, she drove to the center of town and stood at the door of a coffee shop and watched as a woman flipped the sign from Closed to Open and unlocked the door.

"Mornin'. First customer of the day. Just put on a pot of French roast. Be a minute."

"Thank you." Andrea took a seat on a wooden stool at a bar. "Hmm. Fresh baked goods?"

"Just out of the oven." The woman, dressed in jeans and a True Brew T-shirt and cap, lingered. "You visiting town?" Before Andrea answered, she left.

"Here you go." The woman returned and poured a steaming cup of dark coffee for Andrea. She asked again. "Visiting?"

Andrea eyed a row of colored glass cake stands on the bar. "Those are beautiful. Very unique."

The waitress, whose nametag said she was Kay, picked the glass dome off one. "Depression era colored glass. I collect them. How about a raspberry scone? Still warm."

"Yes, please. It's hard to choose." She looked at the variety of scones, danish pastry, and donuts on each of the cake plates.

"There's a massive flea market on the town green every Memorial Day. That's where I get a lot of this stuff." She gestured around to the glass shelves behind her. "I got Jasperware, Wedgwood, all kinds of antique tea pots, china cups and plates." She placed the plated scone in front of Andrea. "Royal Albert Old Country Roses."

Andrea sipped her coffee, "Very cool. When did you say the flea market is?"

"Memorial Day. Think you'll be around?"

The question brought Andrea back to the business at hand. "Could be. Right now, I need a place to stay. Temporarily."

Kay nodded toward the front window. "If you don't mind the musty smell. Can't really get away from it on Cape Cod."

"The Seahaven Inn. Hmm. You recommend it?"

"It's the best in town." She paused. "That's a townie joke. It's the only place in town to stay."

"Good one, Kay. I'll remember that."

—⁂—

Andrea opened the heavy wooden door and entered the dark lobby of the Seahaven Inn just before seven a.m. "Good morning."

The innkeeper, a gentleman who looked all of eighty years old, answered back. "Early bird, aren't ya?" He pulled the chain on a rusted gooseneck lamp and leaned forward over the reception desk. "There you are. What can I do for you?"

Andrea sniffed, trying to identify the odor. "I'll be staying in town for a few days, maybe a week."

The old man nodded. "Welcome."

Andrea reminded herself she wasn't at the Copley Plaza in Boston and decided to be more specific. She spoke up as she walked toward him. "I would like to rent a room, in this inn."

He turned and slid a key off a hook. "This way."

Andrea followed the doddering, bowlegged man down a narrow dark hall, floorboards creaking with every step, the strange odor growing stronger.

"Here you go." The man opened a door to a small room with a vintage dresser and bed covered by a faded red and blue patchwork quilt.

Andrea remarked, "Nice bedspread."

The man nodded. "Reversible."

The waitress at the True Brew was right about the musty smell. "This inn must be quite old."

"Original to the town. Goes back to the seventeen hundreds." He handed her the key. "Don't be taking long showers." He lumbered toward the door.

She didn't ask why and suppressed the urge to ask if the stained flowered wallpaper was original. "Do you want me to pay? How much is it, by the way?"

He shook his head. "Oh, I don't get involved in that stuff. I'm just the night clerk. Take it up with Mercy. She'll be in soon." He checked his watch. "Seven o'clock on the nose."

—⚏—

Mercy proved to be a wealth of knowledge. "I know the house you're talkin' about. The Birches lived there for years."

"That's my understanding. I'm not sure where to begin. I'm thinking of renovating it."

Mercy wrote a few numbers down and handed Andrea a card. "Call Cape Electric, get your power turned on first. Can't really see much without light. And this other number is for Tom Whelan."

"And who is he?"

"Tom's been around for years. Renovated a number of historic homes on this end of the Cape. He'll set you straight."

Andrea went back to the coffee shop, and after two phone calls, more coffee, and a blueberry muffin, had the power turned on and an appointment to meet Tom Whelan at the house at eleven that morning.

—⚏—

She sat in her car with the heat on trying not to think about the possibility the house was beyond repair. She watched as a man in a pickup pulled into the driveway, got out and started walking around.

Andrea approached him. She extended her hand. "I'm Andrea…"

"What you got here is a saltbox." The man stood in front of the house. A worn cap covered his head almost to his eyes.

"You mean the house?"

"Called a saltbox because the roof slopes like an old salt box."

"An old box of salt?"

Tom sighed. "In Colonial days, salt was stored in a wood box, hung near the fireplace for cooking and to keep it dry." He gestured toward the roof of the house. "The salt box had a sloping lid."

He puffed his pipe. "Pine shingles gotta go. Chimney's leanin'." He gestured to the bricks scattered about and glanced at her high heel boots. "Watch yourself, there." He crumpled a few pieces in his hands. "Bricks are brittle."

Andrea moved closer, getting a better look at a face, weathered by the sun and half covered with a white beard growing in all directions. "What else do you see that needs fixing?"

"You got months, maybe a year's work here, if it can have a life at all."

Her heart sank.

He waved a hand around. "These Rhododendron bushes are so close to the house they're adding to the rot on the shingles." He poked a branch in the thicket. "You got overgrown holly bushes, wintergreen, grapevines. All this'll come out, been growing wild for years. You're lucky this stuff didn't cover the front door altogether."

She looked around at the brush, towering four feet, entangled, and encroaching the house on all sides. A trellis leaned against the side of the house, covered with layers of woven ivy vines, now browned by winter.

Tom poked a cluster of vines. "Wild raspberry." He exposed a bit of softness, looking at Andrea for the first time. "These old homesteads need attention and care. I'm not blamin' you, but this poor lady hasn't been loved in years." He shook his head as if concerned for the house. "Let's go inside and see how much lovin' it's gonna need to bring back her beauty."

Now cautiously optimistic, Andrea followed Tom. The house looked more decrepit with the lights on. The living space consisted of one room with a massive hearth in the center. "Kinda weird putting a fireplace in the middle of a room."

She was learning Tom was a man of few words. "Needed it for heat, light, and cooking. Had to be central."

She peeked into two small bedrooms to find stained, curled wallpaper hanging from every wall, and looked up at peeling ceilings. The uneven wooden floors were blackened with age. "I think I liked the house better without lights." She took two steps into the room. "It looks like someone left in a hurry. Look, there's a pair of slippers by the bed." Andrea opened a small closet. "There's clothes here, too." She turned to Tom. "What's that odor?"

"Could be anything. House's been closed up for a while. Mold, mildew, dead mice, cats."

"Oh God, cats?"

"We'll get it all cleaned up in due time. First things first."

"Okay."

Tom nodded. "Yup. We'll get my engineer out to determine if the place is structurally sound." He walked about, hitting walls and poking beams. He pointed, "You got some low ceilings."

Andrea looked up.

"'Cept for that second floor. Families used the extra space for bedrooms. In your case, just a place to put junk."

"It's like a big, open attic."

"I'll tell you why. The British taxed the colonists based on the number of stories in their homes, so they built these saltboxes and argued that since the roof sloped from two stories in the front to one story in the back, they only owed taxes for a one-story house." Tom walked to the back of the house. Andrea followed, all ears. "You've got what we call a Cape Cod cellar."

"There's a basement?"

"It's a dug out hole. A circular pit lined with stone or brick. It's where the root vegetables get stored in winter."

Andrea brushed the hair from her face. She hadn't been able to color it during the fertility treatments and made a mental note to find a hairstylist in town to cover her mix of mousey brown and strands of gray. "I'm overwhelmed. There's so much I didn't consider. Is there a bathroom? Oh, God, is it an outhouse?"

He walked through the front room to a bumped-out section of the house. "This is an add on. One of your ancestors saw the necessity for a functional kitchen," he paused, "a stove and sink." A brown-stained soapstone sink stood against a wall. He opened a door next to it. "This is your bathroom."

Andrea peered into a room measuring four feet by four feet to see a small porcelain sink and a stained toilet. A chain hung from a wooden water tank mounted above it. "Shower?"

Tom winked. "Maybe outdoors."

She smiled for the first time. "I suppose it would be foolish of me to ask about a washer and dryer."

"Let's get out of here and talk this over."

They sat in Tom's truck, warmed by the heat. "So, what do you think?"

Tom responded, "Well, Andrea, the real question is, what do you think?" He didn't wait for an answer. "Let me sum it up. You've got about nine hundred square feet of space. The two bedrooms are small, there's no walk-in closets, not a sign of a bathtub, much less one with jets or one of them rainfall shower heads that's all the rage these days."

Andrea nodded as Tom spoke. She released a hearty laugh at the mention of a rainfall shower. "Yes, yes, what do I think? Well, I'm pretty sure I'll be living here alone. So, the small space doesn't bother me. Other than that…"

Tom interrupted, "Tell you what. It's kinda hard making decisions until we get more information. Let me get an engineer to give us a report. If the house is sound, I'll spend some real time here, come up with a basic plan to make it livable."

"And a quote for the cost?"

He nodded. "And a quote for the cost."

"Sounds good."

"First thing we gotta do is get the hearth working for the heat. If you want a hot tub, master suite with bathroom, skylights, any of that fancy stuff, we'll try to work that in after we get the cost of the basics settled."

"Great plan. And Tom, I haven't given this a lot of thought, but I know one thing. I'd like to preserve as much of the original house as I can. I love the wide pine floors and double pane wavy glass windows. But more importantly, my ancestors walked these rooms, raised children here, and lived off the land. I want to honor their legacy, to preserve the imprint they made on their homestead."

The man of few words had the last one. "Okay, but you're thinkin' about honoring a legacy you don't know nothin' about. Just sayin'."

VIII

Courting Sarah

Seahaven, Massachusetts
March 1869

George Smythe's moment of disappointment was fleeting after Abigale Birch ripped up the paper bequeathing her and promising the Birch homestead to him. "Damn the land," he shouted as he made his way through the biting March winds. He was free to pursue the woman who held his heart, Sarah Marchant.

George tested Sarah's interest rather than risk another rejection. He walked with her from church services on Sunday. He softened his gruff cockney accent and summoned what he thought were the words of a gentleman. "Miss Marchant, you look like a spring flower this day." Sarah's practiced blush encouraged him. "May I offer you a carriage ride home?"

She quickened her pace and dropped her eyes, avoiding his. For months he imagined her voice as the soulful sound of the gentle stroke of a bow over the delicate strings of the finest violin, and now heard it for the first time, and it did not disappoint.

"Mr. Smythe, I'm sure my father would find the idea improper." She emphasized, 'improper.'

Her words floated into his ears and danced about brain. He inhaled to catch her scent, a bouquet of roses and violets. George stopped and bowed from the waist. "My apologies. A humble rancher, I beg your forgiveness for my lack of gallantry."

Sarah returned the slightest bow. She offered a suggestion to her awkward, but handsome suitor. "Perhaps another time, with my father's permission."

"Yes, my intention. I shall seek his permission this week." George bowed again as he backed away, his lips sealed to avoid exposing missing teeth. "Good day, Miss Marchant."

George Smythe spent the next three evenings putting himself to sleep recreating the interaction with Sarah. He imagined her alluring voice and seductive fragrance, and the glimpse of the light green eyes he caught when she offered a brief view of her full face. He summoned his courage to address Mr. Marchant and stopped by the store.

"Sir," he removed his hat. "You know me as George Smythe, a pig farmer. I'm not a rich man. I work hard for what I have." Mr. Marchant didn't respond. "Sir, I'm twenty-three years old and ambitious. You can say that about me."

Mr. Marchant had entertained many suitors for his daughter. "Get to it, son. I don't have all day."

George sorted his words. "Sir, would you be allowin' me to court your daughter?" He practiced that morning as he heaved pig slop into the pen. Without waiting for a response, he continued. "I'll be respectful, of course. You set the terms."

The mercantile stared at the nervous young man, standing hat in hand. "My Sarah is a strong-minded woman. She chooses her own suitors, with my blessing, of course."

Salty sweat dripped from George's thick blonde hair. "Yes, sir."

"You may sit on our porch this evening until sunset. Come after supper."

It wasn't summer, but George Smythe filled an old whiskey barrel and braved the cold water to bathe. He ducked his head, soaping his hair for the first time in months. His only presentable clothes, church clothes, were clean enough. At six-thirty p.m., he approached the home of Sarah Marchant.

At once intimidated, George stopped at the front of the Cape Cod-style house. It was the first time he'd been this close to such a grand home.

He marveled at the cedar shingles, aged by weather. Without knowing the terms, he admired the cornerstones and dentil molding. He stretched his neck to view the weathervane, topped with a great horned owl. Just as the thought of fleeing crossed his mind, Sarah's father opened the door and greeted him.

His mouth so dry, he uttered a brief reply in a hoarse voice. "Sir."

As Sarah walked through the door, George's heart fluttered, and thoughts of running off dissipated. Having never courted a woman, he was clueless of the proper etiquette. Sarah, however, took the lead, inviting him to sit on the side porch. George contented himself with rocking and staring at Sarah's lovely face. He assessed each feature from her almond-shaped eyes to her sloping, perfect nose, and heart-shaped lips. He lost himself in the fantasy of closing his eyes and kissing those lips. Sarah's delicate voice drew him from his illusion.

"Tell me about your ranch, Mr. Smythe."

George pictured the one room shack where he lived, and the image of Sarah bathing in the wooden barrel behind the barn flashed before him. "I'm planning on building a house on the south side, away from the wind."

"And you have how many acres?"

Exaggerating wouldn't serve George well. He told the truth. "Twenty." And then he added, "I'll be buyin' more." She stared back at him. "Soon."

Sarah stayed silent. It was George's turn. His mind was blank. He sputtered, "I raise pigs."

A stilted conversation filled the hour. When Mr. Marchant appeared without a word, George stood to leave. Again, not familiar with courting rituals, and self-conscious about his accent, he bowed and backed off the porch. Sarah's parting words gave him hope. "Call again, now."

IX

Leaving Sarah

George called on Sarah again and again. Mr. Marchant didn't exact tight control and allowed the two to take walks unchaperoned. Sarah took charge of the courtship, planning picnics on the beach and inviting George to attend church with her on Sundays. They spent most evenings on the porch, or in the parlor, if weather drove them inside. Mrs. Marchant, a very hospitable woman, invited George to dinner each Sunday, and sent him home with leftovers. Mr. Marchant boosted George's confidence and put his mind at ease when he took to calling him 'son.'

Sarah offered suggestions to George on how he could better himself. "Always remove your cap when in a lady's presence." When he remembered, she reminded, "A gentleman must have clean, neatly arranged hair."

George gratefully accepted the tips. His clothes were beyond the condition of benefiting from washing, so he purchased outfits he thought suitable for Sarah's company.

She encouraged him. "In the future, I will select your clothes." She corrected his English. "Isn't, not ain't," and suggested a visit to a dentist, "or perhaps dentures."

Realizing a woman of Sarah's stature deserved more than his shack, he researched the cost of building a home on his land.

Sarah expressed her pleasure at George's ambition. "I prefer the Cape Cod style home, with a proper kitchen, of course." If George had a moment's concern about his level of enchantment with the beautiful

Sarah, it left when she reminded him of her remarkable talent. "I'm an excellent cook." Each evening, Sarah pored through print portfolios, books, and journals, marking which stove, sink, carpets, draperies, even toilet, she required in a home. "I've been told I have exquisite taste." She sketched a house with blue shutters, a post and rail fence, and flower gardens, and used terms like cabriole legs, tufted upholstery, and marble tabletops. "Once the home is ready, we'll go to New York to choose our furnishings. I prefer light woods over ghastly mahogany."

George had yet to propose marriage. "Sarah, I'm not a rich man. I raise pigs and chickens for the market."

"But you have land, dear." Her voice no longer sounded like the sweet stroke of violin strings, but urgent, almost commanding. "Cattle. My father knows best. Cattle will make us money."

George bristled at Sarah's use of 'us,' but smiled at the prospect of making money. He asked to meet with Mr. Marchant.

They sat in the formal parlor. Mrs. Marchant brought tea. Her husband raised a finger. "Perhaps a drink more suitable for the occasion, dear." George twisted in the wing chair, upholstered in blue and gold brocade. "Be at ease, son." He passed George a cut crystal glass with an inch of brown liquid. "Drink up." He finished his in one swallow. "Young man, you've taken enough time courting my daughter. I expect you are here to declare your intentions."

"Sir, until I can offer a woman a proper home, I cannot ask for her hand." George played him. "If there are other men who want to court Sarah..." George heard rumors. "Perhaps men her age..."

Mr. Marchant cleared his throat. "Indeed, however my daughter prefers to spend her time with you. It is I, and her mother, who are protective of her." He got back to business. "Your intentions?"

"Sir, I live in a humble shack. I won't keep your daughter in a home less lovely than yours." He looked about the room. "The furnishings, plush carpets, gardens, and carriages. I have none."

Mr. Marchant didn't respond.

George continued. "Cattle, Mr. Marchant. Sarah tells me you have advice about raising cattle. If such an endeavor allowed me to become a suitable husband and provider..."

A light brightened Mr. Marchant's glum face. "Yes, of course, George. I, too, am concerned about how you will offer Sarah all she has grown accustomed to." He lowered his voice, "Perhaps, Mrs. Marchant and I gave her too much. She's our only child."

"About the cattle."

"Yes. I'm acquainted with a man who has an ambitious business plan. He, himself, lives in New York."

George leaned forward. "New York?"

"I'm to refer him to small cattle ranchers. He requires his ranchers to raise, feed, and breed the cows by his specifications. Only he can buy them back and will pay a premium price. He ships them to New York." Mr. Marchant looked around as if about to disclose a closely kept secret. "Edgewater Trading Post, Manhattan."

George whispered, "And?"

"New fancy resort catering to the wealthy and politicians. They offer an exclusive cut of beef, the finest quality tenderloin."

"Will my twenty acres accommodate enough cattle to bring me the income I need to keep your daughter and your future grandchildren content?"

"Scarcity is the name of the game, son. My friend wants to control the market for this exclusive cut of meat. As the demand goes up, the prices will as well. It's a winner." Mr. Marchant walked to his desk and wrote a name on a piece of paper. "Now get to it." He slapped George on the back. "We want her married." He retracted his words. "What I mean is, we look forward to welcoming you to our family, George." He handed him the paper. "Contact my man."

—⁓—

The complaining started within weeks after the twenty cows and a bull arrived at George's ranch. "You're more attracted to your cows than me."

Sarah Marchant's sweet perfume and delightful demeanor wore off over the last months. George's greed, once suppressed by his lust for Sarah, resurfaced. "I can't propose marriage until I build you a suitable home. I need more land and cows to do that. Perhaps in two, maybe three years."

Sarah's moods turned more sullen and sour than sweet and endearing, revealing why she remained a single woman at twenty-seven. Sweet Sarah lashed out. She pressed her raging face close to George's. "You're keeping me waiting." She stomped her feet and shrieked. "No one keeps Sarah Marchant waiting for a marriage proposal."

Mr. Marchant entered the parlor to find George cornered and his daughter railing. "It's unfair. All I've suffered, enduring your distasteful clothes, greasy hair. The grammar, oh, Lord, the sacrifices I've made."

George, a veteran of the bloodiest battles of the Civil War, cowered. "Mr. Marchant, please."

Sarah, gasping for breath, fanning herself, near hysteria, turned to her father.

"Let him leave, Sarah."

Sarah stood tall and snuffled her running nose. She raised an arm and pointed to the front door, hurling words George never imagined she knew. "Get out, you whiffle-whaffling, manky oaf."

George looked at Mr. Marchant, who nodded toward the door. He no longer struggled to speak proper English but offered a bow. "I'm going back to sleep in my humble shack. That's where I'll be living for the next few years."

Sarah's hysterics calmed as a look of astonishment covered her blotchy, tear-streaked face.

"And I won't be speaking the King's English or fixin' my teeth. Goodbye, Sarah."

George walked away, as a demanding, shrill voice assaulted his ears. "George Smythe, you come back here."

But he didn't. A look of relief possessed his face as he pulled the reins on his horse, and his carriage carried him back to his shack.

George slept well that night, having escaped a future with Sarah Marchant. He dreamed of acres of land, grazing cows, and money. He dreamed of the challenge ahead, manipulating Abigale Birch into marriage.

X

The Manipulation

Seahaven, Massachusetts
May 1869

Abigale read and re-read the instructions to the new stove, determined to make full use of it. Lack of a man would not stand in the way of trying new recipes. She spent hours studying the diagram, turning it upright, upside down, and sideways, but could not, for the life of her, get that stove to heat. Exhausted from lugging wood and frustrated at her own helplessness, Abigale followed her now routine ritual of pouring an inch of her dead brother's whiskey and sipping it to the last drop before an early bedtime. She wanted to be fresh for her rare visit to town in the morning.

—⁓—

Abigale prepared, choosing her brightest dress, a beige linen with dark red stripes, embellished with a handsewn jacket with pleated trim to match. She chose one of her original hats, ruby red with a French lace tie, for the occasion. A lifelong loner, never prone to socialize, on this day, overwhelmed with pride, she greeted each person she encountered as she walked to the shipping office.

"Did you know my hats are in high demand in Boston?" Most didn't respond to her, but to the few who expressed interest, she exclaimed, "A famous milliner, a summer resident, fancied my creations and ordered two dozen." She moved her head, showing off her red hat. "They'll be in her shop window on Newbury Street."

Puffing and smiling all the way to the Cape Cod Railroad office, she gave strict instructions. "Ship these goods to this address in Boston." Tapping the packages, "I wrapped them in cotton and linen scraps with my own hands." She walked away, a smug look on her face. "They're my best work."

Abigale's joyful mood abandoned her when she arrived home to find wounded and slain chickens scattered across the yard. The farmhands were gone for the day, leaving it to her to gather up the dead, and chase and capture the other traumatized hens. She fretted, "Why is it left to me, today of all days, to gather these repulsive, bloodied, dead birds?"

A cranky Abigale, her dress stained with hens' blood, and dirt, prepared water for tea. She scowled at the sound of a voice at the door.

"Miss Abigale. Miss Abigale."

Wearing his church clothes and freshly shaved, George Smythe stood on the front porch, flowers in one hand and a burlap sack in the other.

A disheveled Abigale opened the door an inch. "Mr. Smythe, I believe I've made it clear we have no business."

He spoke through the crack. "Miss Abigale," he bowed from the waist. "I'd remove my hat, but..." he held flowers in the tiny opening. "For you."

She eyed the bouquet of red and purple tulips.

"I thought of you and picked them."

Abigale opened the door two more inches and with one hand, received flowers for the first time in her life. Her face flushed, as her heart fluttered. The day had been one of extreme moods, from elation to revulsion, and now confusion. She handed the flowers back. "No need."

George continued, "They're the first flowers of spring."

Abigale reached her hand out the door and snatched the flowers back. "You're welcome to them."

"Mr. Smythe." She straightened her back and lifted her chin, remembering the chicken carcasses. "Why would you think of me, of all people?"

At seventeen, George Smythe used his natural wits to survive the Civil War. Now, he used his shrewdness for another challenge. Without replying, he thrust a burlap bag through the door. "I thought you'd like one of these, too."

Abigale pulled a tiny kitten from the bag.

"Cat had a litter. This one's the prettiest. Made me think of you." He held his breath. As distasteful as the thought of courting this homely spinster was, the acquisition of forty acres to breed cows held great attraction.

She held it to her bosom. A rare smile lit her mud-stained face. She opened the door. "Look at me. I'm so rude. Mr. Smythe, please come in." She pointed to the boot scraper on the porch and George ran his boots on its flat metal edge before entering the Birch home.

He removed his hat, revealing hair matted down with his own spit. He looked around. "Never been in here before. Puts my place to shame."

Abigale stroked the kitten and poured some milk. "I'll warm it over the fire. Wish I could get the dang new stove to work. The house gets too hot in summer with a fire in the hearth."

If his clean-shaven face, flowers, and a kitten didn't win her over, fixing the stove just might. "I could look at it for you, ma'am."

Abigale declined. It didn't seem proper, alone in her house with a man. But then she remembered the cookbook and those recipes for chicken and biscuits with gravy.

"Thank you. I'd be obliged."

George wiggled the handle on the flue, then spent another ten minutes adjusting the wood and looking at the stove from left to right. He put his hand back on the handle. "Which way you been turning this?"

Abigale gestured left. "Sometimes right, as well. Just can't get the darn thing to catch."

George Smythe turned the handle to the right, opening the damper all the way. The wood caught, and the stove heated up. "Gotta open the damper." He adjusted it enough to keep the stove heating. "You'll be fine now."

Abigale conjured images of baked blueberry pie and cherry tarts. "Mr. Smythe, I am so grateful." She gestured to the mason jar. "The flowers…" She hadn't put down the kitten. "This sweet creature…" Her voice caught. "I've had such a hard day." She petted the kitten. "My chickens got mauled. I'd say a fox got to them."

George excused himself, returning two minutes later. "You won't be seeing any fox for a while. I fixed the latch on your chicken coop gate."

"In my distress, I didn't notice. Mr. Smythe, I'm so grateful."

George swallowed hard. He won the favor of the spinster, perhaps securing a life of misery for himself. "I'll be goin' now, Miss Abigale."

Abigale pressed the kitten to her cheek. "And the stove. Mr. Smythe, you do not know what a joy it is for me to have that monstrosity working." She smiled at her own enthusiasm.

George backed out of the house, hat in hand. He bowed. "And I'm sure you'll do some real cookin' now that it's working for you."

That's when Abigale thought of it. "Mr. Smythe. I've got stored apples. You'll have the first pie I make."

Abigale sat in her chair after George left. She stroked her purring kitten and kissed it on the head. "Such a nice man, isn't he, silly kitty?"

XI

Easy As Apple Pie

Abigale worked in earnest for hours to perfect the pastry for the apple pie she promised Mr. Smythe. She tossed the singed crusts of her first two failed attempts into the woods, blaming the stove and its inability to maintain a steady temperature, but the cause for the failure had more to do with her book. Steeped in the pages of Jane Austen's, *Sense and Sensibility,* she absorbed every detail of the love affairs of Elinor and Marianne Dashwood.

She thought herself more like the sensible and discreet Elinor for thanking Mr. Smythe for solving the mystery of her stove and fixing the chicken coop gate. But now she acted more like impulsive, emotional Marianne, following her heart, planning to endear herself to Mr. Smythe by pleasing his stomach.

Abigale's impulsivity convinced her the third attempt at a pie would do. She made her way through the gray fog, dressed in her church clothes, even wearing one of her favorite handsewn hats. Abigale used a square of green brocade material to cover the pie during its trip. She decided today, like impetuous Marianne Dashwood, to disregard the impropriety of an unannounced visit to a man.

With no other buildings, save the barn, on the property, she knocked on the door of a dilapidated shed, pie in hand.

"Mr. Smythe, Mr. Smythe." Receiving no response to her second and third harder knocks, Abigale looked at the rather overcooked apple pie in her hands and left it on the step.

Ten minutes passed before George Smythe opened his door and grabbed the pie. Abigale's unexpected visit caught him in his nightshirt and boots. Accustomed to a diet of ale and turnip, he used his one eating utensil and attacked the pie. After three attempts at cracking the crust, George stabbed a slice of hard apple. He filled his mouth, but with many broken and missing teeth, could not pierce either the crust or apple into portions small enough to swallow. The unpalatable pastry raised the question in George Smythe's mind. *Are forty acres worth being attached for life to a homely spinster who can't cook?*

An unkempt George returned the pie pan the following day. The orphan from London delivered high praise. "Your pie rivaled even my blessed mother's best."

Abigale suppressed the flutter in her stomach and served Mr. Smythe a cup of tea. "And a big slice of pie to go with it."

"Obliged, Miss Abigale. Very obliged." He wrestled the slice on the plate, capturing a bit of brittle crust, gulping it down whole, muttering a muffled, "Wonderful."

After a respectable amount of time, George prepared to leave. He teased his target. "I thank you for the visit and the tea and pie."

Abigale asserted herself like the impulsive Marianne Dashwood. "I'm cooking a chicken stew with biscuits tomorrow."

George hesitated, bowing his head. "Are you invitin' me, Miss Abigale?"

"Yes. Please join me."

He dropped his eyes as he exited. "My pleasure."

George's shoulders stiffened when Abigale shouted out. "It's my first time trying out the recipe."

XII

The Truth

Boston, Massachusetts
March 2018

Andrea returned to her condo in Boston's North End and waited for word from Tom Whelan. If she had any warm feelings left for Will, they turned cold after her first evening home. Still in her sweatshirt and jeans, she began the conversation. "We haven't talked about the news from Dr. Sherman."

Will snapped. "Not much to talk about. I see it as good news and bad news."

Andrea poured a glass of Cabernet for herself and one for her husband. "I can't wait to hear this." She sat on their navy-blue Pottery Barn sofa.

He took his name pin off his white pharmacist's jacket and threw it on the coffee table. "Good news first. I don't have to whack off in a jar anymore."

Andrea stiffened as if a bullet pierced her back. "Yeah, Will, you went through a lot."

Will stood facing the window, his back to his wife. "I suppose you're going to bitch you were the one who had to stick herself with needles and feel crazy from the hormones. Guess what, Andrea? I lived with a hormone-crazed person for the last six months."

Andrea moved toward the kitchen. She rested her glass of wine on the granite top kitchen island, her jaw too clenched to drink. "You didn't seem to mind it a year ago when this crazed person bailed you out of thirty thousand dollars of gambling debt you hid until after we got married. Did you?"

"Here we go. I make one mistake and you hold it over my head forever. Besides, you have that big pot of gold your daddy left you. I have a little pharmacy I pour blood and sweat into just to make a living."

Andrea tried to defuse the argument. She approached him. "Look at us. At each other's throats when the truth is, we are both hurting. I know all this is coming from your disappointment. I'm sad too."

Will wasn't having it. He faced her. "Truth is, Andrea, I'm not sad. I walked out of that doctor's office feeling a hundred-pound weight lifted off my shoulders. A baby is your dream, not mine. I don't want the responsibility. I went through the motions all these months to keep you happy."

The arguing stopped there. The elephant in the room appeared. Will never wanted a baby.

The anger left Will's voice. "Look, I have my sisters' kids in my life. That's enough for me. I love them, but I don't have to raise them. That's how I want it. Family at a distance."

She nodded, pushing back tears. "Family at a distance? You want family at a distance, huh? Well, you're gonna get your wish."

"What's that supposed to mean?"

"It means I'm keeping you at a distance, Will. This crazed woman is gonna quit her job and go live in the Birch family homestead, and it won't have parquet floors or a soaking tub. But you can bet I'll be happy."

—⁂—

Andrea checked in at the ad agency. "I'm changing my life, Liz."

Her boss didn't accept her resignation. "You're being a bit rash. All married couples fight. Exactly how do you propose to support yourself?"

"I have my inheritance, what's left of it. Will insisted we hit it for the down payment on the condo." She didn't mention the thirty thousand she spent paying off her husband's gambling debts.

"And?"

"I'll get the house in good enough shape so I can live there." She flushed pink. "I'll sell my paintings, give children art lessons."

Her good friend and boss smiled. "And then what?"

"I'll figure it out, Liz. I haven't gotten that far. Most of my thinking time is spent fantasizing how I'll refurbish the house. There's a magnificent fieldstone fireplace, the windows are original." She pointed up, and raised her eyebrows, "wood beams on the ceiling."

"Okay, go off, spread your creative wings. I'll send you projects. Is there Wi-Fi out there in them there woods?"

Andrea smiled as tears flooded her eyes. "You'll do that for me? It never occurred to me I could work remotely." She hugged Liz. "I won't disappoint." She paused. "This is a lot. Leaving Will, my job." She wiped tears from her cheeks. "I'm scared."

—⁂—

The accountant delivered the news to Will. "You've got problems. The pharmacy isn't making enough money to cover expenses. I'm looking at the past six months, and you haven't broken even once."

Will scanned the statements from the assets to the liability columns. He came up short by several thousand dollars every month. "Shit."

"Shit is right. You can't keep dipping into your equity loan to make up for these losses." The accountant resembled a rooster with wisps of red hair just above his forehead and a wattle under his chin. He took off his glasses and addressed Will. "There are two big chain drugstores within a half mile. The sad truth is mom and pop stores like yours can't compete."

"I get it. My wife keeps nagging me to close up and get a job as a pharmacist at CVS making seventy thousand. Have you seen the pace those guys work at? No thanks. Not for me."

Will walked the accountant out of his back office. "I'll be in touch. Maybe next month will get me out of the woods."

He didn't mention he forged his wife's signature on the equity loan application, or that she left him and without her income didn't have a chance in hell of keeping his pharmacy open. He didn't tell his accountant about his gambling addiction and the cash he took from the register every week.

XIII

Moving Forward

Tom Whelan and Andrea sat in a booth at the True Brew.

"It's so refreshing to walk through this center and not find one big box store or fast-food restaurant."

"I'm not sure the teenagers around here agree, although, in such a small town, there's not too many of 'em." He pulled a folder from his backpack. "You can get to the mall in six exits."

Andrea didn't follow Tom's stream of consciousness rambling. "Who's heading to what mall?"

He ignored her and spread what appeared to be a floorplan on their table. Tom's face contradicted his words. "Good news. Move your coffee." He patted the seat next to him. "Sit here." His cryptic speech pattern amused Andrea. She moved to get a view of his blueprint.

"This is your house." He waved his hand over the drawn structure. "I got the engineer's report. Aside from a few supports we need to add to your roof, the place is sound."

A wide smile crossed Andrea's face. "That is great news. Right, Tom?"

"Yup. Now, before you go gettin' too excited, pay attention."

Andrea wanted to giggle at the scene. She'd gone from an advertising executive in Boston to sitting with the likes of this old salt telling her to pay attention. "Yes, sir, I'm all ears."

He rolled the plans out another twelve inches. "Now, you got them low ceilings with those wide support beams."

She moved closer.

"What I'm suggestin' is, since the roof is gonna need extensive work, we take them low ceilings down and open the rooms right up to the roof." He looked at her through glasses perched on the end of his nose. "It'll make the place feel a hell of a lot bigger."

Andrea's eyes widened. "A vaulted ceiling."

"It's tricky, with that half floor you got, but I can make it work. You might be gonna say it's too much to heat, but once we get it going, that fireplace of yours can put out plenty. We'll drop a ceiling fan. Shouldn't be a problem."

"So far, I'm impressed. What other ideas have you come up with?"

"We can restore the wide pine floors throughout the house, including the bedrooms. You got the second-floor open attic for storage. There's got to be a ladder buried up there. And then there's closets. This house has no closets worthy of a modern woman's wardrobe."

"I also need an office… oh, and a place to paint." She stopped. "This is getting complicated isn't it?"

"Only if you make it." He pointed to the bedroom in the front of the house. "Both bedrooms are about twelve by twelve. I thought we could carve out a closet in the back of this room, taking a few feet from the adjacent bedroom. We'll make doors in your bedroom to access the closet. The smaller bedroom can be office space for you."

"I'll have to downsize big time to make that an office. I'll figure it out."

"Yup." He pointed to what appeared to be an opening on the outside wall.

"Patio doors? Are you suggesting a patio right off my office? Fabulous." She gasped. "That side of the house gets lots of sun, I could paint there, too."

Tom's lips curved in an almost grin. "You'll get plenty of light through them big doors." He nodded as if satisfied with his own presentation. "Now, you need a kitchen, and of course, that bathroom won't do." He moved his hand to the drawing. "Right here, we're gonna extend the back of the house out ten feet."

"Did I already say fabulous?" She traced a line on the floorplan. "What's this?"

Tom uttered two words. "Screen porch."

"Screen porch?" Andrea's loud voice caught the attention of other patrons. "This is overwhelming, Tom. I have so many questions. You know, what about the wiring and plumbing? And patio doors that aren't original to the house?"

Tom folded the plans. "No worries there. Got plenty of salvage from teardowns, glass doorknobs, a clawfoot bathtub, you name it." He paused. "I'll fix you up with doors that look like they been there all along. You like four-poster beds?"

She rested her hand on his. "You're my hero."

Tom's straight-faced expression didn't change. He slid his hand out from under hers. "Gonna be tricky runnin' wires and pipes with the lath and plaster walls, and all. But I've done it before." He winked. "Just takes patience and time, and I got plenty of that."

Andrea slid from the booth and left ten dollars for the two coffees. "How soon can we get started?"

"After you sign." He pulled a paper from his shirt pocket. "First phase's gonna cost ya fifty grand."

XIV

Living the Dream

By early spring, Tom had the roof repaired and ceilings torn out. Andrea moved in, willing to tolerate the dust, tools, and workmen, rather than the dank, smelly room at the Seahaven Inn. She reserved showering outdoors for only the best days and perfected her dash from the shower back into the house without being detected.

"Now that we have new wiring, I can make you a cup of coffee."

Tom accepted the brew. "You can hook up your modem, too."

"Good, I need to contact my boss and get some work going."

Andrea's days were full. She used mornings to work, and helped with the renovation afternoons, washing off years of soot and dirt from the shiplap walls. She bruised her knees scrubbing the wide pine floors. "Tom, oh my God."

"What's up?"

"This floor. It's painted in a green and red plaid pattern all around the hearth. Can I keep it?"

"Sure. Just hit it with a coat of clear shellac. Do the walls, too. You'll keep the original color and all the dents and holes."

—∞—

Andrea developed a routine. After Tom left, she prepared a light dinner. In the early evening hours, she searched the Internet for ways to modernize her home while maintaining its character and historical significance. She didn't find time to paint landscapes.

She called Liz several nights a week. "Got a lot going on here. Busy, busy."

Liz knew her friend well. "Livin' the dream, are you?"

Andrea lifted her glass. "Livin' the dream."

"Okay, now tell Liz how you're really feeling. I can hear it in your voice."

"Of course you can." Andrea took a deep breath. "I guess I'm just processing. It seems like in the blink of an eye, I left everything familiar and moved away. And I can't remember why."

"You were a bit impulsive, darling."

"I know. Blame it on the hormones, or more likely, being married to Will. We weren't a good fit. I always felt like my shoes were on the wrong feet."

"Ouch. Hard to walk."

"Yeah. It was like I wanted to go one way, but my feet kept taking me somewhere else."

"What about now?"

"Hmm. Now I'm less angry at Will and looking at my own culpability for the failure of our marriage. It wasn't fair to him that I was settling, knowing I couldn't have Paul."

"Well, darling, my diagnosis is you are spending too much time staring at your belly button. The trip to Boston next week is right on time."

"I have to admit, I'm excited. Haven't been to the big city in a few months."

Liz chided her. "You sound like a country bumpkin. Can't wait to see you."

—⁓—

The city felt dirty, the noise of cars and trucks invaded Andrea's head. She sat at a high-top table in a downtown hotel bar. Liz, as expected, arrived late. Andrea grinned when she spotted her, a woman past sixty, wearing three-inch heels, her white hair styled in an edgy short cut. Her exuberant self, she leaned in for a double cheek kiss. The three thousand dollar an ounce Amorem Rose surrounded her like a cloud.

"You look marvelous." She raised her voice. "Marvelous. Stand up, twirl. My God. You're blonde and tanned." She flipped the ruffle on Andrea's dress, "and dressed in sexy pink flowers."

"No more black linen pants and white blouses for this girl."

Liz put her hands on her hips and swayed. "And the body."

"Yup. Reclaiming my old self. Running on the beach five miles almost every day. Back into my size six. Bought this cute number to celebrate." Andrea adjusted the off-the-shoulder pink print dress. "Sexy, huh?"

"Truly, darling. You look wonderful. Restored is the word I'm looking for. Restored to your former self and beyond."

"Geeze, Liz, you sound like you're writing copy for an ad."

"I did write it, last year. A very successful magazine ad for an anti-aging face cream. I'm recycling it for you."

The women enjoyed two glasses of wine and requested more peanuts and popcorn. Andrea didn't notice when Liz's eyes glazed over as she described her handiwork. "Washing years of dirt off walls and floors isn't easy. I scraped, on my knees, I'll have you know. Then there's the shellac." She stopped. "Wait, what?"

Liz held her napkin to her eyes. "This is too funny. Picturing you, an old washer woman, hair wrapped in a bandana, knees bleeding raw, scrubbing the floor."

"I'm glad you're having a chuckle over my bloody knees. And, for your information, I wore a baseball cap, not a stupid looking bandana."

Andrea took a breath. "You want funny? Try timing your outdoor shower between workmen coming and going in the house and backyard. One day I spent two hours, just me and a towel, shivering out there until they finished sawing down trees in my backyard."

Liz snorted and wiped her nose. "Wine up my nose. Oh my God. You're such an outdoors kind of gal."

"You don't know the half of it. I almost burned the house down, trying to cook a hamburger on a hot plate. I mean right on the hotplate." Andrea slapped the table. "Thank God for wine."

They never got to discussing the new project for Andrea. As they were winding down, Liz lowered her voice. "You haven't mentioned Will."

Melancholy from the effects of the wine, she adjusted her dress to expose her shoulders. "Will. What can I say about Will? I'm stopping by the condo tomorrow to take my paintings off the walls. I'm shipping them to Seahaven."

"So, you'll see him?"

"Don't know. I left a message on his cell. It's anyone's guess if he'll be there waiting for me."

"Let me put it this way. Do you want to see him?"

Andrea shrugged. "Don't know that, either."

They got up to leave. "You need a ride?"

"Nope, thanks, Liz. I'm staying right here at this hotel. Night."

"Not so fast, missy." She pulled Andrea in. "Don't let it be too long before we see each other again. I miss you, my friend."

Andrea looked at Liz's face, always dressed with red lipstick and framed with black diamond drop earrings. Today, it was an advertisement itself for long workdays and lonely nights in the company of too many dry martinis. "You'll come visit. Promise?"

—⁓—

Andrea took extra time getting ready the next morning. Never a classic beauty, she was more the cute, wholesome girl with the big smile. She'd asked the hairstylist in the Seahaven salon to glam her up.

"Let's lighten up the color a couple of shades. You've got the right skin tone, and a brighter blonde will bring out your hazel eyes." She also suggested a chin length bob and bangs. "That middle part and shoulder length hair is so yesterday."

Andrea studied her reflection, applied a last touch of blush and a coat of lip gloss, and packed her overnight bag. She headed to the condo, wondering what side of Will she would see. In spite of his shortcomings, he had a certain charm. When they were dating, he often planned evenings watching old classic movies, and cooked gourmet meals for her. "And tonight, my sweet, I am pairing our Veal Scallopini with a delicious Chianti from my family's home region of Tuscany."

She loved hearing him expound on politics, sports, and the economy. When his mood was right, he could be funny and endearing. Those qualities drew her to marry him, and she admitted to herself, alone in the car, at thirty-two, her biological clock was alarming, and she wanted a family.

She stood in the building's lobby and debated ringing the doorbell or letting herself in. She used her key.

Will greeted her, dressed in pajama bottoms and a T-shirt. "I made coffee."

She stayed close to the front door. "No thanks. I left you a voice message. The packers are coming in twenty minutes." It looked to Andrea that Will hadn't shaved in a week, perhaps not even bathed.

"Not working today?"

"Taking a couple days off. Just a cold. I need a break."

Will had always played the sick little boy who needed a hug. *Not today,* she thought. She moved toward her favorite seascape. "Okay then, I'll take my paintings off the wall. The packers will wrap and ship them to the Cape."

Will didn't comment on her new hairstyle, or the yellow polka-dotted shift she wore. He didn't seem to notice she earned back her slim body.

Andrea finished removing the ten watercolors. She wandered into the bedroom and opened her closet, releasing a deep sigh at the dozens of black and navy pants and cotton blouses. "I'll arrange for a charity to pick up these clothes."

"So, you're not coming back?"

Andrea turned to face her husband; anger rushed forward. "What would I come back to?"

She'd vowed not to get into a debate or argument, but the words she rehearsed to herself over and over tumbled out. She swept her arm around the bedroom. "A sham? While I did everything I could to start a family for us, you were faking it. I suspect breathing a giant sigh of relief each time I cried when my period came."

Will shook his head. "No, hon, it wasn't like that. I didn't sort my words very well about all this. I didn't have it so good, you know, with my father." He looked at her. "It's hard to explain."

Andrea regained her composure, remembering her vow not to engage in an exchange with Will. She fought the flush on her face. "There's nothing here I want. It's all yours."

Will rubbed his three-day growth. He lured her into a fight. "Truth is, Andrea," he paused. "And we both know this, you were only after me for my sperm."

She took the bait, and screamed, "What?"

"Face it. You married me so you could have a baby."

"You bastard."

She rushed from the bedroom.

He followed, lobbing one more. "Yeah, I'm no use to you now, so, just throw old Will aside and move on."

Andrea composed herself when the movers arrived, giving them instructions to wrap and ship her paintings. She released her fury weaving in and out of the narrow, winding streets of Boston and headed south on the highway. Pressing the accelerator to sixty-five, then seventy, she grunted, "After his sperm. What a jerk."

XV

A Lofty Wish

The stiffness in her neck eased as she drove down the bumpy driveway. Andrea smiled when she spotted Tom's truck. This strange man who wore a ball cap, overalls, and old boots, had become more than a contractor. Andrea considered Tom Whelan a friend.

Andrea walked through the front door. "What a transformation." She looked around the once dark main room, now bright, as if painted with sunlight. She turned to Tom. "You did all this in two days?"

The man of few words pointed to the wall where the narrow wooden door leading to Andrea's office had been.

"French doors? You put in another set of French doors."

Tom took an unlit pipe from his mouth. "Figured you had all that sunshine coming into your office from the patio doors, why not bring it on into the main room?"

"Tom, you're a genius. How can I ever thank you?"

He shrugged. "Had the matching set in my garage. Put it to good use." He looked up. "What do ya think?"

"Skylights? Oh my God. You gave me two giant skylights."

Now Tom allowed himself a grin. "Thought I'd surprise you."

Andrea walked about the room. She peered through the new French doors into her office and straight out to her new patio. "I needed this today, Tom. You can't imagine."

Tom busied himself poking the fieldstones in the floor-to ceiling-hearth. "Gonna get someone in here to fix this up. Loose stones here and there."

"Let me change out of this dress and I'll make us coffee."

"Not for me, had my three cups."

"Oh, well, maybe we could talk. I've been thinking."

"Let me guess. Two days in the city, and you have a new idea. Is that it?"

"You're right."

He walked to the front door and held up his pipe. "Let's sit outside while I listen to this."

"I'll just grab myself a glass of wine. Beer?"

"Never touch the stuff."

Once they settled in the wicker rockers, Tom smoking, Andrea sipping a light red from Napa Valley, she blurted it out. "A loft. I need a loft."

Tom continued to rock and draw on his pipe. "You havin' company?"

"I could." Andrea thought about Liz. "My boss, a friend from Boston. I invited her to visit, but where would I put her? A loft, right? Make sense?"

"Where you supposin' to put this loft?"

"I thought, if anyone could make that second story open attic a loft, it's you."

Tom looked around. "Gettin' dark. I'll be packin' up for the day."

"What about my loft?"

"Talk tomorrow." He loaded the last of his tools and drove off.

Andrea went into the house and poured herself another glass of Pinot Noir. She walked about, staring at the vaulted ceiling. She faced the front of the house, the half story overhead. "That'll do."

—ᴡ—

Andrea prepared a plate of scrambled eggs and bacon for Tom the next morning. She set it down in front of him. "Nothing fancy."

"You talkin' about the eggs?"

Andrea saw Tom wasn't smiling. "Did you forget about our talk yesterday?"

"You mean your talk. I don't believe I said much of anything."

"The loft."

Now he smiled. "Had ya there, didn't I?"

Andrea sat at the temporary kitchen table, a piece of plywood on two sawhorses. She hadn't bought any real furniture yet. She checked out local antique shops and several warehouses full of consignment furniture and carpets but planned to wait for the house to be complete.

"So, you did think about it."

"Did."

"And?"

Tom finished his eggs and saved the bacon for last. He put it between two pieces of buttered toast. "More coffee, please."

She put the steaming mug in front of him. "So?"

He looked at her, flecks of egg caught in his beard. As if in slow motion, he lifted his mug and sipped the coffee.

"You're making me crazy here, Tom."

"We'll make use of that half story in the front of the house. It's just storage now, but I can build it out six more feet. The ladder won't do. I'll tuck a staircase next to your office."

"So, you agree, we'll expand the open attic?"

Tom nodded. "It's your only option. You'll have a loft going across the front of the house with a depth of about sixteen feet."

"That's more than I hoped for. Thank you, Tom."

He didn't acknowledge her enthusiasm but kept on with his plans. "The windows will give it plenty of light. Maybe use one wall to make built-ins with drawers. You take care of the rest."

"Oh, no worries there. I spent hours awake last night, decorating and redecorating. I got that part covered."

Focusing on new beginnings eased the sting of Will's words. And within a few days, her paintings would arrive.

XVI

Dealing With the Devil

Will didn't have a cold. He closed the pharmacy for a week, obsessing over winning enough money to bail out his business. Incurring gambling debt and then gambling to make money to pay it off wasn't working. The loan shark who visited his pharmacy made it clear. "You pay up, or we burn down your store. Got it?"

Fear sent him to the hidden smokey back rooms, playing cards all night, and spending the days under the glaring lights of casinos, the clicking of the roulette wheel reclaiming his meager winnings.

It came time to make a deal with the devil. "By my calculations, with interest, it should take about three years to pay off the debt, provided you're not stupid enough to keep gambling."

"Listen, I've hit bottom. My wife left me, I'm months behind on my mortgage. I don't have any money. If I did…"

"Maybe you got no money, I know for sure you got no brains. So, here's what you're gonna do." The devil, dressed in a designer Polo shirt and khaki shorts, looked around. "This is how we work it. You supply us with a minimum of sixty pills a month. Brand names, no generics."

"I'll lose my license, go to jail."

"How does losing your fingers sound? You can't count pills with no fingers."

"I gotta think about all this. There're rules to handling narcotics, you know. The DEA will be all over me if they smell a problem."

"Figure it out. My man will be here Tuesday. Fifteen pills for starters."

Unlike large chain pharmacies with higher volume, Will still hand-counted each prescription. His pharmacy technician worked three days a week, so Will had him backdate the documentation indicating he performed a second count. In six years of operation, he never had an issue with the DEA, and on occasion, socialized with several members of the pharmacy board. He was well regarded for his meticulous record keeping, secure medication storage, and proper dispensation of controlled substances.

"I have to pay for those pills."

The devil grabbed Will by the lapels of his white jacket. "My guy will be here every Tuesday. Fifteen pills or better."

Will knew how to do it. He'd read enough articles about pharmacists being prosecuted for narcotics diversion. He devised a plan, using several techniques to syphon the pills. If the prescription was for an elderly customer, he shorted them two pills, assuming they'd lose track of the count, anyway. He didn't alter the count on regular customers with chronic pain. They depended on every dose and would notice if pills were missing. When a customer came in with a prescription for fifteen ten milligram Vicodin for pain after a dental procedure, he gave them fifteen five milligram pills and kept fifteen five milligram pills for himself.

After the first month of skimming medications, Will called the loan shark. "There's gotta be another way, I'm living in fear of getting caught. There are pharmacists in prison for doing this. I can't eat, can't sleep, I'm dying here."

The loan shark responded, "You're dying either way, pal. See you Tuesday."

—∽—

The phone call intruded on Andrea's quiet evening of reading. Will used his most contrite tone. "Don't hang up. You have every reason to hate me, and you can, but I have to apologize, or I can't live with myself."

A sense of relief passed through Andrea's body, but she didn't let it show in her voice. "You're right. I have reason to hate you." She took the high road. "But hate is a strong word. I don't subscribe to it."

"I've been thinking. You've been right about a lot of things. Maybe I should give up the store and go work for a chain. I think the stress is turning me into a monster."

"That's your decision, Will." She sat in a second-hand stuffed armchair, a recent yard sale find, book in hand. "I've moved on." She considered her next words. "You should, too."

"Some of this is your fault, you know. It wasn't all me."

Andrea sat upright. She put the phone on speaker. "I don't think so, Will. You said those awful things, not me."

Dressed in only boxer shorts and socks, Will paced the condo's living room. He hadn't picked up his coffee cups or the newspapers in days. "Don't you think it hurt me, watching you land contract after contract, becoming a big shot in Liz's firm, going out with clients to bars and restaurants?" He caught his breath. "I bet you never considered how it felt to me."

"What?"

"Every time you got a raise or a promotion or spent an evening out with clients, I waited, sure you were going to dump me, just leave me in the dust as you soared to success."

Andrea wanted to tell him he was talking crazy except he wasn't wrong. She often fantasized being married to one of the successful clients she worked for. Their motivation and confidence attracted her. She thought of reassuring him but caught herself. It was another Will move to make her feel guilty.

"Why are you calling? If it's to apologize, you did, so goodbye."

"Wait. I want to see you. I'll come to the Cape."

"To the dump?"

"Seriously, I'd love to see the house and all you've done to it. I'll be there Sunday. Pick a restaurant for dinner."

A part of Andrea wanted to show Will her new life, the home with real wood, a roof that welcomed sunshine, land where she could walk and breathe. Her home had character and history, not like Will's anonymous glass and concrete building squeezed between others that looked the same.

—⁂—

Will searched the banking paperwork Andrea left behind and confirmed the balance in her trust account was more than enough to pay off his debt. In addition to owing the loan shark, he was behind on his equity loan payments and the mortgage for the condo. The land in Seahaven was his ticket out of this mess.

He arrived as promised at five o'clock on Sunday.

Andrea commented, "You've lost weight."

He wore his best Banana Republic cotton shirt, laundered and pressed for the occasion, and used a credit card to charge a rental car and a pair of Dockers straight leg khaki pants, the style Boston hipsters wore. He smoothed the shirt. "Stress. Been working long hours. Cut out the subs and fast foods."

She nodded. "And the hair and 'stache.'"

Will's close-cut hair had grown out to a full head of dark curls. He touched his mustache. "Just trying it out."

Andrea selected the off the shoulder pink and white floral dress she wore to Boston a week before. Her hair was freshly colored and styled.

"Wow. You look amazing." He paused. "I guess I didn't tell you that often enough, you know, before."

Will's compliment caught her off guard. She smoothed her hair. "What's that you got?"

He held out a bouquet of red roses and baby's breath. "Oh, of course. For you."

"How sweet."

"And I brought a bottle of your favorite red." He hesitated. "Barolo, for later."

The scene made Andrea uncomfortable. She didn't expect to like him, or notice his new hairstyle, or sweet-smelling cologne. He disarmed her with the flowers and wine.

"I picked a local place. You'll like it. I'll drive."

They lucked out. Two patrons finished their beers, and Andrea and Will scored their seats at the crowded bar. They ordered their usual, bacon, mushroom cheeseburgers, no mushrooms for him. He fed her an onion ring, teasing first before landing it in her mouth. She remembered how sweet he could be, how engaging, even cute. They washed down their burgers with two Cape Cod craft beers.

It was country music karaoke night, and talented locals belted out Merle Haggard and Willie Nelson classics. Will led Andrea around the dance floor when the bartender took the mic. "This is a request from Will Rossi." She sang Patsy Cline's *I Fall to Pieces*.

"One more for the road," he proposed.

"You're driving back to Boston. Take it easy."

"You are correct. Let's head back to your house and get my car."

The remark, 'your house' hurt. It was her house, and he didn't live in it with her. As she drove from the center back home, Andrea tried to recount in her mind how all this happened in a matter of a few months. She wondered if the fertility hormones played with her mind.

"Invite me in."

"Will, it's a long drive to Boston."

"One glass of wine, and then I'll go. Promise." He made the Boy Scout sign.

Andrea relented. She liked his company, their familiar banter, the flirting. She also wanted to show off the progress of the renovation. After the tour and tutorial on restoring shiplap, they sat on a second-hand Victorian style loveseat. They sipped the Barolo, one glass leading to two, and a second bottle. The conversation went from mutual apologies for their own shortcomings to tears, hugs, and forgiveness. Then the teasing began, as they recounted their first date.

Will started. "I couldn't believe it when my sister fixed us up. You were so cute, so smart. Way out of my league."

Andrea held her wine glass to her lips, her eyes smiling. "How so?"

He twirled her bangs between his fingers. "Great body, funny, tall. I just wanted our first date to be over so you could crush me, and I could slither home."

Andrea slapped Will's hands. "No way. I thought you were adorable." She lied. She found him morose that first date but didn't want to hurt him.

Andrea topped off Will's glass with the last of the second bottle. "We have a dilemma. I'm going to bed after this," she poked his chest, "and you can't drive home."

He grabbed her hand and kissed it. "You don't know how much I've missed you."

She rested her head on his shoulder. "Too much wine."

He kissed the top of her head.

"You coming?"

He pulled her close and whispered. "Don't expect to get much sleep."

—⚊—

Will served up mimosas the next morning. "A hair of the dog that bit you."

The memory of the lovemaking the night before blurred. Andrea's temples pulsed as she sat on the front porch soaking up the morning sun. She bit into a raspberry scone from the True Brew, wondering what price she'd pay for her vulnerability the night before. It wasn't long before a Mercedes-Benz rolled into the driveway and she got her answer. It was Rick, Will's realtor friend.

"What's he doing here?"

"Now stay calm. I think you'll see that Rick has good news."

Andrea braced herself, placing her drink on the porch floor.

Rick leaned against the banister and flipped through a pile of papers. He handed both Andrea and Will a glossy folder.

"Will tells me you two are eager to sell, and I have to tell you, it's the right time. The market is hot for Cape property."

"Is it?"

"Oh yeah. I did some comps. But for you, it's not a simple case of selling a house." He paused. "You're sitting on a gold mine. Not real gold, of course, but sixty acres in this market is a gold mine."

Will interjected. "What's the bottom line, Rick? How much can we get?"

The 'we' infuriated Andrea.

"I've queried a couple of developers." He turned to Andrea. "You may have seen them surveying the property. They made inquiries with the town officials, you know, asking if the land is conservation and finding out any environmental concerns about the wetlands that would prohibit building homes or whatnot."

"Whatnot? What the hell kind of word is whatnot? And who are you to talk to the town about my property?"

Will stood from his wicker rocker and paused next to Andrea. He put his hand on her arm. "Let's just listen to what Rick has to say, hon."

Rick announced he found a builder, known to the town, who felt confident he could develop the sixty acres into a condominium community for folks over fifty-five. "The Cape is a haven for retirees. There's a housing shortage, so sixty acres in this town is a godsend. There're no kids to worry about, so Seahaven won't have to build new schools. The town welcomes a proposal."

Andrea rose from her rocker and spoke through clenched teeth. "I'm the owner of this house and land. Will had no business engaging you." She gestured from the porch to his car. Once he cleared the driveway, she turned to her husband. "You son of a bitch. Get out."

Will held out both arms. "Now wait, hon." He paced his words. "You may be mad, but just look over the assessment."

"Don't 'hon' me. You're disgusting. Last night was all about money. You don't give a crap about me. I can't believe I married you." She wound up. "And, by the way, I'm glad you're stinkin' sperm didn't take. I wouldn't want to bear a kid with your pitiful genes."

"Grow up, Andrea. You think your ancestors roamed this land and left it for you so you could sing camp songs? That's bullshit. A fantasy. The truth is, some lonely old maid, your father's distant cousin, died, and you're the last of her line. How can you feel sentimental about relatives you didn't know you had?"

She held her firm tone. "Well, Will, my dead relatives were more loyal to me than my husband. Get out."

Will filed for divorce two weeks later. The papers stated he wanted the pharmacy, condo, half of the value of both the homestead and Andrea's trust fund.

XVII

Cutting Ties

Seahaven, Massachusetts

Andrea set up her easel and paints on the new patio. *Good therapy*, she thought, which she needed after reading and re-reading the divorce papers.

She stared at the blank canvas and twirled the tip of her brush in green paint. No ideas came. She stroked a few blades of grass, then washed the upper part of the canvas in a deep blue. Her mind wandered back to the demands of the divorce papers threatening to take away her home and trust fund.

The afternoon sun slipped behind swirling clouds, drawing her attention. She dipped her brush in gray paint, splashed a cloud, and then another, overlapping the first. Their outline in black paint warned of the danger of the storm approaching.

A clap of thunder startled Andrea. She'd been painting for an hour. Another roll of thunder, and a jagged charge of lightning burst from the sky. The clouds unleashed their fury, and Andrea gathered her supplies and retreated inside. She set her wet painting, absent her usual soft blues and greens of oceans, rivers, and mountains, on its easel, and saw instead cautionary thunderclouds sweeping over a foreboding gray sky. *You're an angry woman,* she thought. *This has to stop.*

The phone rang. She hesitated to answer in a lightning storm but saw the caller I.D. Her greeting, a flat, "Hello, Will."

"Don't hang up."

"Seems you start all your calls to me like that."

"I'm in trouble. Can you just listen for a minute?"

This was a line Andrea heard before. "Do you have more lies to tell me?"

"Andrea, if you don't help, I'll lose everything, the condo, the store. You know I don't profit enough in a month to make the payments there and on the condo."

"You should have thought of that before you turned into an asshole."

There was no comeback from the man on the other end of the phone. Andrea filled the silence. "Listen, you have a lot of nerve calling me when you're trying to take everything I have. My trust fund is from my father. He saved every nickel, knowing I didn't have anyone else in the world."

Will used his sad little boy voice. "I get it. I'm sorry about that. A lawyer friend told me to do it."

She fought the tremble in her voice. "And to add insult to injury, you also want to take away this house, my only connection to family. You really piss me off, Will."

"I have a proposal."

Andrea let the silence sit.

"You there?"

"What's the proposal? You want the car, too? You came into this marriage with nothing but debt, which I paid off. My salary supported us while I patiently waited for you to wake up and realize a corner store pharmacy is a dinosaur."

"Let me know when you're finished flogging me so I can speak."

"I'll prolong this divorce for months. You can't afford to support yourself that long. So good luck." She let out a final huff. "Okay, speak."

Will stood behind the pharmacy counter in his empty store. "I want to call a truce."

"It must be in your interest."

"Yes. You are right, Andrea, as always. Now can I get on with my proposal?"

She watched as the torrential rains battered the front windows. "Sure, why not?"

"I'll settle for the condo and the store. That's it. I'll walk away."

She jumped from her chair. "Settle? You'll be walking away with at least two hundred and fifty thousand in equity. And may I remind you, it was my trust fund that provided the two hundred thousand dollar down payment."

"Yes, Andrea. I know, Andrea. You remind me every chance you get. And thank you for the tongue lashing."

Andrea mumbled, "tough shit."

"You're all tough and mean now, but in the end, lawyers or not, I'll get half of everything. So, actually, I'm offering you a deal."

Andrea was standing and pacing. "I'll think about it."

She hung up and dialed Liz. "God, do I hate him."

"Hello to you, too. You're referring to Will, I assume."

Andrea and Liz sipped during their evening chats. "Is there a martini in your hand?"

"Is it four o'clock? Of course, there is. What's up?"

Andrea unloaded her frustrations, finishing up her tirade with, "And to think less than a year ago I was trying to have a baby with that jerk."

"You have had a tough year, hon. And you didn't deserve it after losing your dad."

The affirmation brought Andrea to tears, and then sobs. She looked at her painting of a dark sky and menacing storm clouds. "I'm so angry. I want to be married, pregnant, working in the office next to you. But I'm none of that. I don't even know how this all happened."

Liz, a no-nonsense New Yorker, didn't mince words. "Well, what are you gonna do about it? Pour another glass of wine, turn on cable TV and watch *The Titanic* so you can cry some more?"

Andrea sputtered. "I am pouring myself another glass of wine. How did you know?"

"Seriously, darling, you know what you need, don't you?"

"Liz, don't say I need to get laid. I know how you think."

"Okay, but that's what you need. Go out, girl. Have fun. An orgasm will do you a lot of good. Change your outlook on the world."

"One orgasm will do all that, huh?"

"Possibly bring about world peace."

Andrea heard the clink as Liz stirred the martini decanter. She exhaled a deep sigh. "Yeah, maybe. I can't remember the last time I was out, except to buy building supplies and food. How come you're always right?"

"Not always, darling. Just when it comes to you. Love you. Goodnight."

XVIII

Andrea Steps Out

Seahaven, Massachusetts
July 2018

Andrea had never gone to a bar alone. She bolstered her courage by wearing a red sleeveless shift and perfecting her hair and make-up. She headed to Whalers' Tavern in town. The night she and Will had burgers, locals unwinding after a long day hauling lobsters or dogfish, or landscaping rich people's estates, packed the bar. Most of the other places in Seahaven were fine dining seafood restaurants for tourists, or take-out for beachgoers.

Andrea approached the front entrance expecting to push through hordes of people hollering over each other and swigging draft beers. Instead, after her eyes adjusted to the dark, she found a quiet, empty bar. She took a seat and ordered a Corona.

"Where's the crowd? I was here a while back and had to fight for two seats at the bar."

The young bartender flashed a smile. "Tuesday night. The empty parking lot didn't tip you off?"

"Is there something special about Tuesdays in Seahaven?"

He put the beer in front of his only customer. "Nice dress, by the way. I'm Michael."

Self-conscious about being overdressed, Andrea punted. "Oh, just came from a work thing." She extended her hand, "Andrea."

"Tuesday nights, no one has any money. They're tapped out until Thursday when they get paid." Michael put a bowl of popcorn on the bar and chatted for the next hour. As Andrea explained she was restoring her old house, and Tom Whelan was her contractor, Michael nodded as if he recognized Tom's name.

"You know Tom?"

"Oh, yeah." An older man took a seat at the opposite end of the bar. Michael poured him a draft beer and took his dinner order. He resumed talking to Andrea. "Where were we?"

It occurred to Andrea this was her first conversation with a live person, except for Tom and his crew, in weeks. She didn't count the disastrous date with Will. "So, you know Tom?"

"His son graduated high school a year before me."

"He never talks about his family. Is he married?"

"Can I get you a burger? C'mon. Let me order you one. There's a cook back there checking his Facebook page."

"Your cheeseburgers are great. I'll take one, well done with mushrooms." Talking to Michael was easy and fun. "So anyway, Tom?"

"Yeah, Tom. I'll give you his vital statistics. He's about sixty, not married anymore, far as I know."

Andrea finished the last of her second Corona. "More, please."

"More beer, or more about Tom?"

"Both."

"It's a quiet night. I'm gonna join you." Michael poured two beers. "Is this gossip?"

"Hey, what else do you do in a bar on a Tuesday night?"

"Okay. Tom's a good guy. Just had his problems." He held up his glass. "I haven't seen him in months. Probably back on the wagon."

"Wow. Interesting."

"Enough gossip. And what about you, Miss Andrea? What's interesting about you?"

After two-and-a-half beers, Andrea considered telling him her friend Liz suggested she get herself laid but fought the impulse. "I paint. Watercolors."

"Excellent. Could you paint me?"

"I could, but I'd have to dress you in a grass skirt and float you out with the tide. My paintings are mostly landscapes and seascapes."

"Dress me up? Isn't that called abstract?"

The two flirted and bantered through Andrea's mushroom cheeseburger and third beer.

She patted her stomach. "Wow. Best meal I've had in a long time, and I didn't have to cook it."

"Glad you enjoyed. Another beer? On me."

Andrea put a twenty and a ten on the bar. "It's tempting, because I like your company."

"Okay, no pressure." He checked the bills. "Did you write your number on that twenty? Rejection kills me, so I won't ask you out."

She gave him her cute look and an "Aw."

"I'll be taking my boat out Sunday from the town pier."

The beer made Andrea's brain rush. "I might be there."

Michael slapped her change on the bar. "Tide's in at ten a.m."

—⁓—

Andrea hadn't worn a bathing suit in years. After trying on a two-piece from her college days, she settled on a black tank under a pair of white shorts and a black T-shirt. She downplayed the date to Liz during their chat the night before.

"I think he's in his mid-twenties. I'm robbing the cradle, but what the hell, it's a ride in a boat."

"Age is a number, dear. I should know, cougar that I am."

They both laughed at the comment since Liz hadn't dated in years, although she played mistress for the owner of a New York ad agency for ten years. A bout with breast cancer motivated her to leave New York and strike out on her own in Boston.

"Anyway, I'm not getting tied up with a bartender. Remember, I married a guy with no ambition. One of those in a lifetime is enough for me."

"A day at a time, dear. Sex is food for the soul. You don't have to marry him. Just have fun."

—⁓—

With all the confidence she could muster, Andrea walked along the pier, checking the name on each boat. Michael stood midway, waving his arms.

"You came."

"I did." She hoped he couldn't see her heart pounding. "Your boat's named Grady White?"

"No, silly. That's the brand, you know, like a Ford or a Chevy."

"Ready?" Michael helped her board The Whaler and brought her to the helm. He put her next to him.

"You've probably guessed I'm not much of a boat expert."

"Let me give you the tour." He pointed to the console. "Fish finder, fish washer, shower for the fisherman, and head, which you are welcome to use."

"Wow. You could almost live here."

"Almost, hang on." He pushed the throttle, and they took off. "We're going about two miles out to a cool sandbar."

Andrea snuck a long look at him now that they were in daylight. He was young and muscular, probably six feet tall. He had a cap on, but she noticed in the bar that his hair was thinning on top. She thought how she'd describe him to Liz. "Strong bones, good teeth, thinning hair, big boat."

They moved along, bumping gentle waves. Andrea held on to her wide brim straw hat while the sea sprayed a salty mist on her face. They passed sandbars freckled with black specks. As they got closer, Michael pointed out. "They're seals. Thousands of them."

"What are they doing there?"

"Catching the rays, like us."

Michael eased off on the throttle and steered the boat to the right. They floated into shallow water on the edge of a sandbar. "Our own private island in the middle of the ocean." He dropped a cooler on the sand and laid out a blanket. "Always be prepared."

"You've done this before, I'm guessing."

"Once or twice. I'm still perfecting it. Beer?"

The cold beer tasted delicious. Andrea slipped off her shorts and T-shirt and relaxed. Michael stretched out next to her. She could smell his cologne and hoped hers was holding up against the sea spray. "I have to ask. You named your boat after the bar you work in?"

"Close. I named the bar after the boat I work on."

She scrunched her face. "Huh?"

"Whalers' is my bar. Get it? My boat, my bar."

She tapped her temple. "Ahh. I'm a little slow. Must be the hot sun."

He stood and took her hand. "C'mere. I want to show you something." He brought her to a pool on the sandbar. "The tide comes in and fills the hole. Then, when the tide goes out, we have our own private seawater pool."

Maybe it was the salt air, sun, and beer, Andrea slid into the natural pool. Michael followed. He hummed the theme song from *Jaws* and chased her around. Andrea played along.

"Help, help. Shark in the water."

Michael jumped up and pulled her under. They spent the next hour splashing each other and playing like children. When they got out, he wrapped her in a towel and hugged her. "There, that should dry you off."

She pressed herself into his wet body and his arms tightened around her.

Later, he lit a charcoal grill and cooked burgers. Alone on a sandbar off the shores of Cape Cod with a handsome man, Andrea hadn't had so much fun in years.

They talked more. She learned Michael came back to the Cape after college. "It's my home. I'm not the big city type. But I'm not a fisherman, either. The only way I could stay was to run my own business."

He talked about his family. "We're original Cape Codders from back in the sixteen hundreds."

"Amazing." She didn't mention she knew nothing about her family roots.

"Yup. We're a long line of fishermen. My grandfather used to tell us his grandfather swore our ancestors were released from jail in England and sent across to Cape Cod."

"Did they come over on the Mayflower?"

"Not quite. But if you look around the bar, you'll find original lances and harpoons they used to spear Right Whales in the seventeen hundreds."

Michael was nothing like Will. He had ambition, empathy for others, he asked about her. He was funny. This was a new experience.

Michael let her take the wheel on the way back. He stood behind her, his hands around her waist. She hugged him when they docked. "Best day in a long time."

He hugged her back, then took off his sunglasses and stared into her face.

She touched the tip of his nose. "You got a sunburn."

He touched hers. "You, too."

It was an impulsive gesture. "Listen, this day's been too great to end. Come back for a glass of wine. See what we've done so far with the house."

She drove toward home wondering if he would think her invitation was code for 'let's have sex.'

Once home, Andrea headed for the shower. "I have to wash off this salt and sand." She tossed him a towel. "There's an outside shower. Hot and cold."

Both refreshed, Andrea offered Michael a glass of wine. "Nice choice. Sangiovese. Love their regional wines."

"You've been there? To Italy?"

"A few times. I thought the owner of a bar should have a good first-hand knowledge of wines." He shrugged. "Turns out, my clientele prefers a good cold beer over an aged wine."

Michael looked around.

Andrea raised her hands. "Don't say it. I know. It's a work in process. I'll give you the ten-cent tour."

Michael had only one comment, "Yup, you have your hands full."

"Be quiet. The next time you come, well, wait and see."

"I like that, 'next time.'" Michael leaned in for a kiss.

They settled on the sofa and passed the evening kissing like teenagers, between conversations about the house, the bar, boating, and fishing.

Halfway through a second bottle of red, she took Liz's advice and invited Michael to stay.

—∽—

Andrea called Will the next day. "I'll have my lawyer draw up the papers. Sign them within twenty-four hours or the deal is off."

"No problem, Andrea. This is in both of our best interests."

"Don't bullshit me, Will. I know you're up to your eyeballs in gambling debt and God only knows what else."

She hung up and whitewashed over the painting of the dark clouds. *Gotta give up the anger. Be positive. The house is gonna have a new life, and I am, too. In one hundred and twenty days, when the divorce is final, I'll be Andrea Birch again.*

XIX

Meeting Abigale

"Now that the humidity and heat are passed, you can get to emptying that attic."

Andrea played all summer, hanging out nights with Michael at Whalers' and spending weekends on the boat. "Okay, okay, Boss Tom. I'll get to it. I guess I'll haul it all into the barn for now."

"Fair warning. You got about three weeks. What's left goes in the dumpster. I gotta get started on your fancy loft."

Andrea was used to Tom's digs. She knew it was his way of being affectionate. She came right back at him. "A loft is not fancy, Mr. Whelan. It's a simple solution for a guest's sleeping quarters. So there."

She climbed the ladder to the loft and called down. "Tom, did you know this place is covered in cobwebs?"

"Spiders won't hurt ya. It's the furry critters you got to watch out for."

Andrea scrambled back down the ladder. Tom stood at the bottom, his unlit pipe in his mouth. "Gotcha."

"Seriously, I don't do critters."

He held the ladder and gestured. "Go ahead up." As she reached the top, he added. "They're all dead, most likely, anyway."

"Very funny." Andrea scanned the piles of magazines, books, hat boxes, trunks, and what looked like discarded kitchen tools and pots. There were rolled up carpets, and a couple of old Singer sewing machines. She spotted old dress forms and two shelves stacked with ladies' hats. She whispered to herself. "I don't know where to begin." And yelled down to Tom. "Okay, I'm done…Just kidding."

It was dusk before she finished lugging stacks of fashion magazines from the loft and out to the barn. She thumbed through a few, dated as far back as 1868. "Hmmm," she said aloud. "My relatives were into fashion. Who knew?"

Andrea called Michael around six. "Help. You should see the stuff I have to empty out of the attic. Any chance you could give me a hand tonight?"

They had been together since July, seeing each other two or three times a week.

"Sorry, babe. I promised the guys."

"Okay. Have fun."

"Coming out tomorrow night?"

After their first month of dating, Andrea did not expect too much from Michael, except fun in bed. He either worked at Whalers', or on his nights off, hung out there. In the beginning, she joined him, but learned she preferred quiet dinners at her house.

"Probably not."

Andrea liked her alone time, painting, reading, and thumbing through decorating magazines. Michael hung with the guys, a group of high school buddies who drank, played softball, and fished for fun every week. She knew their time together was limited.

—ɯ—

Three days into her excavation of the attic, Andrea moved out enough musty books and rolls of old textiles to reach a trunk. The dust made her sneeze as she used a brush to clear it. She opened the lid to find a few yellowed bonnets and hats and a pile of diaries. Andrea sorted the small notebooks by the dates recorded on their first pages. The covers were tattered at the corners and separating from the binding. She feared the pages would disintegrate if she was not gentle.

After dinner, she settled in her chair with a glass of Cabernet and picked one of the journals at random. The faded script made it difficult to read. She made out the name of the author, Abigale Birch, 1869. It was past midnight when Andrea put it down.

May 5, 1869

George Smythe came calling today. He returned my pie tin after devouring my apple pie. He testified it was more delicious than pies baked by his own mother.

I can see Mr. Smythe is a hardworking man, like my late brother, Caleb. Men dedicated to making a living off the land are less concerned with their appearances than men, for instance, of the cloth, or teachers, or doctors.

I've spent my life alone, with my sewing and books for company. I do love romance themed books, and, except in rare moments, accepted they were the only love stories I would personally know.

Although I rejected the plan Caleb made to marry me off to Mr. Smythe, today I understand the wisdom of my brother's foresight. A woman shouldn't have to bear the frustration of a stubborn stove or collect the carcasses of slain hens. It's a woman's place to clean and cook and prepare a proper home for her husband and raise the children.

May 6

Mr. Smythe attended the supper of chicken stew and biscuits I prepared tonight. He was quite generous in his praise for the meal, although due to a fussy stomach, limited the amount he ate. I suspect his sparse teeth cause him difficulty when chewing.

I can't help but notice his lack of proper English and poor table manners, but, again, like my own late brother, he is a hardworking man and that is a strong characteristic deserving of admiration.

Mr. Smythe reported to me tonight, with some hesitation, he observed one of my farmhands asleep in the fields. This dismays me as I depend on their work for income. Sales of my custom hats will surely at some point in the future support me, but for now, I depend on the income from the turnip and asparagus crops.

May 7

Mr. Smythe appeared this evening, unannounced. In my work dress, and covered with soot from cleaning the hearth, I was unprepared to host him. I asked he return tomorrow and offered to cook him a dinner of turnip soup and biscuits. He declined the meal but agreed to return tomorrow evening.

May 8

George brought me carrots from his root cellar. I am obliged and impressed with his generosity. We sat on the porch for an hour, without much conversation. I resisted reading my book, although it seemed more interesting than sitting in silence. Mr. Smythe is a quiet man, and I myself am used to solitude, although I appreciate his company.

May 10

We sat on the porch again this evening. I felt it honest to inform Mr. Smythe I am nearly the age of twenty-seven. He didn't seem affected by the news, or even surprised. I thought he might doubt my ability to produce children should we marry.

May 18

Mr. Smythe has been absent for one week, which causes me to conclude what appeared to be a courtship was not. Perhaps it was less my personality and more my age. My house seems cold and quiet except for the purring of my kitty. I have no interest in reading about the love struggles of the women in my books, I now have my own affairs of the heart to brood upon. I'm reminded of Alfred Tennyson's quote from his poem, "In Memoriam A.H.H."

> "Tis better to have loved and lost,
> Than never to have loved at all."

I question his wisdom.

June 1

I've never felt such heartache, dealing with the absence of George. He stole my heart and now what was a life alone is a lonely life. I don't even sew my hats, despite the pressure of an order for twenty-four from the Boston milliner. My nights are filled with terror. If I manage to sleep, disturbing sounds awake me. Rattling windows, and thuds at my front door have put me in fear for my life. My sense of security is shattered.

July 1

I'm alive with joy. George appeared at my door today. I now know the heights of ecstasy. He confessed he, too, had been sad, but forced himself to stay away, sure I would find him not worthy as a husband. Such a fool. So humble.

Fearing George again would doubt his worthiness, I hastily arranged with the pastor for a quiet commitment of marriage.

The entries in the diary fascinated Andrea. It was her first acquaintance with a Birch relative, except for her father. When Michael arrived the next evening, she introduced him to Abigale.

"What the heck?"

"It's a dress form I found in the attic." The form stood wearing a floor length green taffeta dress with a high neckline. "She's a relative."

Michael walked around the model. He picked up a pair of worn black laced boots Andrea placed at its feet. "She was tiny."

Andrea spoke as if making a presentation for an ad campaign. She drew her hand down the dress's arm. "Note the sleeves, trimmed in white French lace, closing at the wrist. The satin jacket, cut away to accent the lady's wee waist."

"Cute. What's with all the hats? This is getting creepy."

The loveseat was piled with hats and bonnets. "I think she was a seamstress. These hats are handsewn, but there's a couple of sewing machines up there, so I bet she made the dress herself."

Michael stared with his hands on hips.

Andrea jumped in. "Hey, I'd love to find the dry goods store where she sold her hats. Any original buildings left in town? I stayed at the Seahaven Inn for a week."

"Seahaven Inn. Eww. Musty as hell in there. Cape ambience, I guess. Original buildings? Have you had dinner at Sea Shells yet?"

"Don't know of it."

"It's the last building on Main before your cross Ocean Avenue. Pricey place, only serve shellfish, you know, oysters on the half shell, mussels diablo. They have a killer warm clam dip in a bread bowl."

"You're making me hungry. So, it's an old building?"

"Yeah. I got off the track there, thinking about their food. Check it out. They kept it as original as they could. Used to be the General Store when I was a kid. They had penny candy in a wooden barrel." He clapped his hands. "You ready to go?"

"I thought we'd stay in tonight. I'm grilling fish."

Michael slapped his forehead. "Didn't I tell you? Oh, sorry, babe. A bunch of us are taking our boats out to the sandbar tonight. Low tide.

Great night for a bonfire, brews, tunes. Winter's coming, gotta do it now, you know."

Andrea did know. He'd probably have a few beers and try to talk her into a quickie on the other side of the sandbar. "I'll pass. Too much going on here." She waved toward the attic and then the kitchen. "Lots of construction happening."

Michael headed for the door. "Catch you later."

"Wait, I need you to haul down those big sewing machines."

He tapped his wristwatch. "Gotta catch the tide, babe." And he was gone.

Andrea ran her fingers down the straight row of gold-colored buttons on the green dress. She spoke out loud. "So, Abigale, did you make this lovely frock for a special occasion?"

She settled back down in her favorite reading chair and picked up where she left off.

July 12, 1869

It's been several years since I sewed the dress. I thought it was an appropriate color and style for my interment, or if one should arise before my death, a special occasion. I took it from the trunk, it was well preserved having been carefully folded and wrapped in paper.

It was only me, George, and the preacher, but it was my personal pleasure to wear the green taffeta. The wedding was hastily planned, I admit. George commented, "Sunday or not, pigs can't go hungry," when he appeared in his work clothes.

I bathed, anticipating we would consummate the marriage on the day of our wedding. George, however, spent the night at his home, humble as it is, claiming a responsibility to his pigs and cows. I slept alone, grateful, at least, the mysterious night sounds stopped.

Exhausted from the day of working in the attic, Andrea fell asleep in the chair.

XX

Sixty Forty

"It's time to talk kitchen, missy." Tom held a stack of kitchen design magazines, each with pink, yellow, and blue sticky notes waving from the top of the pages. "I can see you have your own ideas." They sat together on the loveseat, now cleared of hats. "You want to be true to the house, do I get that?"

She nodded.

"Here's what I've come up with." Tom produced a floorplan of his proposed kitchen. "We pushed out the back an extra ten feet, so you got room for a good size kitchen." He outlined the walls of the design. "The west side of the house gets all the afternoon sun. I'm thinkin' we'll put the sink there. I'll getcha a nice soapstone one with a high backsplash. Very reminiscent of the period of the house. Dishwasher can go next to it."

Andrea nodded.

"We'll give you a window extending from the top of the backsplash to the ceiling. Give ya lots of light. Nice white subway tile, so not to take away..."

"Tom, wait..."

He didn't. "We'll keep it bright with nice Red Oak panel inset cabinets, custom, on either side of the window." He pointed toward the far wall of the house.

She tried to interrupt again. "Tom?"

He didn't stop. "Now I know you're thinkin' how do we have a dishwasher and keep the character of the kitchen."

"That's not what I'm thinking, Tom. I'm thinking about money."

"Don't think about the money. Just listen." He pointed from where they sat on the loveseat to the back wall of the house. "That wall's the sightline from where we sit, and you got the screen porch on the other side of it."

"What's your idea?"

Tom produced a sketch of his proposal, detailed with colored pencil, including period hardware, and braided rugs. "I'm gonna take a bit from the screen porch and recess a custom pantry, Craftsman style." His finger touched the drawing. "Floor to ceiling, with quarter-sawn Red Oak, like the cabinets." Tom closed his eyes for a moment. "The top doors will have leaded glass inserts to match the ones on your kitchen cabinets."

Without looking at Andrea, he moved his finger along the drawing. "We got Red Oak corbels in the corners…You won't know there's a dishwasher, I'll put a cabinet door on it. Look at this. I got you a faucet, looks like a well pump."

Andrea put her hand on Tom's knee. "This all sounds so beautiful. More than I imagined." She patted the decorating magazines, now piled on the floor. "But Tom, you said it yourself, the money. I mean, a custom-built pantry, leaded glass windows. Red Oak."

This man, who had become a constant, dependable presence in Andrea's life put his hand on hers. "It's my house gift to you."

"No, I couldn't."

He popped up from his seat. "Too late. Did the measurements, started cuttin' the pieces. Making the insets for the cabinet doors."

Andrea stood as well, took a chance, and hugged her friend. Tom lifted one arm and patted her back. He whispered, "I'm comin' back to life right along with this old house."

They both swallowed hard.

—m—

Andrea filled her days sorting through the trunks and boxes, and piles of books and magazines she'd moved into the barn. She finished a project for Liz, refreshing a magazine ad for a client's high-end men's cologne.

"I'm happy to come up to Boston for the presentation."

"No, no, darling. It's not worth your time. I'll have my adorable intern cut her teeth on this one. It's just a quick update of the same old ad."

"Okay, but I'm disappointed. I was looking forward to seeing you."

"In time, my sweet." Liz ended the conversation. "Watch your email for your next project. Kisses."

With time on her hands, Andrea faced the fear that burdened her for months. She made an appointment with the owner of Seahaven Gallery in town.

She arrived as requested by the owner at forty-thirty. "My car's a Prius, so I only brought these two." Andrea unwrapped a watercolor of a beach scene in soft blues, whites, and beiges. "I thought tourists would be most interested in ocean and beach scenes."

The owner of Seahaven Gallery dressed in Cape Cod casual, as locals called it. He wore a crisp blue cotton shirt, khaki pants, and brown loafers, no socks. Despite his casual look, he was all business, staring at the painting and shaking his head. Andrea looked around to see walls filled with paintings of calm ocean waves and sandbars. She congratulated herself for her second choice. "This is a little different." Steadying her hands, she tore the last of the paper from a two-foot square canvas painting of a tree of life.

The gallery owner's expression didn't change. "How clever, a Japanese Cherry Blossom tree. You've blended the pinks, blues, and greens beautifully."

Unsure of her next move, Andrea waited.

"To be perfectly honest, Miss Birch, as you can see, you have a lot of competition for your seascapes." He looked at the tree of life painting, his hand on his chin. "This, I think would sell."

Having never negotiated the sale of a painting, Andrea let the owner do the talking. "Anything I accept is on a consignment basis. Sixty, forty."

"Sixty for you?"

"No, dear, forty for me, sixty for you, provided it sells in thirty days. After that, I'll keep it for another sixty days at fifty, fifty."

"And after ninety days?"

"It's yours again." He pointed at the tree of life painting. "It's quiet on the Cape in winter. But we get a fair amount of traffic until Thanksgiving. I'll take this one, only, on consignment and see how it goes. I close after New Year's."

"Thank you, can you suggest a price?"

He picked up the canvas. "Matted and framed, it will be a good size. I'd go with thirteen hundred dollars to start."

Andrea fought the urge to cheer and began wrapping her watercolor seascape.

"Oh, well, Ms. Birch. Leave the seascape. You never know."

—⚁—

Andrea left the gallery and walked down Main Street to the corner of Ocean Avenue. The restaurant, Sea Shells, sat on the corner. Its sign read, OPEN AT 5:00 PM. She checked her watch and wandered into what felt like another century. "It's just as I pictured."

A handsome young man dressed in a crisp white cotton shirt and navy-blue Bermuda shorts greeted her. "Yes, this is a historic building. One of the only structures original to the town."

"That's why I stopped in. Can I just look around?"

He offered a rehearsed response. "We suggest guests order first, and wander while we prepare their choice of food and drink."

"Of course." Andrea sat on a wooden stool with a brown leather top at a bar that looked to be made of reclaimed wood.

"Deck planking."

"Excuse me?"

"The bar is made from deck planking from a ship that broke up in a storm a few miles out. Pieces washed ashore."

She ordered a glass of Chardonnay and a shrimp cocktail. "I guess part of the job is knowing the history of this building."

The bartender offered to walk her around. "Follow me."

He pointed out the ceiling, "Original tin. We got the building almost fifteen years ago. Before that it was the General Store."

"That's what I heard from a friend." Andrea looked up to see old pots and pans hanging from low set ceiling beams. "Was it a dry goods store at any time in its life?"

"Was. The General Store owners didn't change much, so when we took it over, we obviously had to add the kitchen, upgrade the electric, that sort of thing."

"What's original?"

"The walls. Dark walnut. We kept the beams. Check us out in the winter, we've got three fireplaces roaring."

"We found two dozen or more of those wooden barrels in the barn behind this building."

"Cool. Now they're seats at high top tables. I love it. I can definitely feel the effects of the years on the floor."

"Wide white pine planks. We cleaned them up, but as far as we can tell, they are original, too. It was like an archeological dig, getting through the stuff in the barn. If we could clean it up and use it, or display it, we did, you know, glass decanters, hardware, pictures, even pewter plates."

The bartender ushered Andrea back to the bar. "Food's up." He placed a glass of chilled Chardonnay and five gigantic cold shrimp in front of her.

"Oh my, this will be dinner. Tell me, did you find any hats, ladies' hats?"

He contemplated, and then shook his head. "I'm the cousin of the owner so I wasn't here from the first days, but I don't recall hats. Hat boxes, yes." He nodded to the right. An old hutch stood against the wall; several hat boxes were stacked on its two shelves.

Andrea walked over to the hutch with an assortment of patterned ceramic plates behind its glass doors. "Hmm, I wonder."

More customers had taken seats at the bar and chatted among themselves. "Five o'clock regulars," the bartender whispered.

Andrea finished her wine and a few of the shrimp. "Well, this has been fun. There's so much more to see, I'll have to come back soon."

Feeling closer to Abigale, she was anxious to get home and read more of her life.

XXI

Duped

Seahaven, Massachusetts
September 1869

George Smythe didn't like Abigale Birch. He found her homely, bird-like, dull. She smelled musty, with a mix of garlic and fireplace smoke. He continued to sleep in his own shack after the marriage, spending his days exploring the forty acres he acquired at great personal cost. George comforted himself knowing he'd be rich once he contracted for another thirty cows. A day after the wedding, he informed the cattle entrepreneur he'd be taking more cows within weeks.

George's humble demeanor changed. Resentful of the farmhands' loyalty to Abigale, he fired them and brought his own men to manage the crops. When Abigale objected, he shut her down. "Woman, you have no say."

She argued against clearing the land to raise cattle. "This land has been preserved for over sixty years, since my grandfather claimed it."

Once again, George let her know he was in charge of the Birch homestead. "You can't let land stay idle. The trees ain't worth nothin'. Let the business to me."

Blinded by his own greed, and in his haste to lure Abigale Birch into marriage, George Smythe didn't fully explore the forty acres of land he lusted after. He hadn't gone further than the chicken coop when he released Abigale's chickens, or the dark perimeter of the house, when he skulked around at midnight rattling the windows and banging on the door.

Now, riding through the land in the daylight, he discovered most of the Birch forty acres was marshland, not suitable for cattle grazing. His plan to breed more cattle, dashed. He was saddled with worthless swampland and a woman whose odor repulsed him.

An angry George punished his wife for his own avarice.

XXII

Abigale's Remorse

Seahaven, Massachusetts
October 2018

Andrea followed her evening routine. The fall chill was reason enough to light the now working fireplace. Glass of wine in hand, she picked up a diary and continued.

September 1869

It's been only weeks since my marriage to George Smythe, and already I regret it. I don't know what possessed me to accept a man so young, who mangles the English language. I question why I overlooked his poor hygiene, jagged teeth, and disinclination for romantic gestures. I can't liken my foolishness to any character in literature I have ever known.

As I examine my own poor decision, I can only attribute it to the anxiety I suffered when unable to light my stove, the trauma of finding my chickens mauled, and the terror I suffered from the strange noises that came in the dead of night. It seemed when he appeared, my struggles disappeared.

I suppose that was the attraction. I don't crave company, I'm quite content to sew and read, although my thoughts have wandered from time to time, imagining being loved with desire and passion. Now, after weeks, I'm in a marriage that has yet to be consummated, and I have no wishes for it to be.

October 1869

George Smythe is an angry man. In spite of my objections, he fired my farmhands, men I've trusted for years. He wants to ruin the purity of the Birch land by stripping the forests and breeding cattle. The disappointment in finding the land is too wet for his purposes has set his fury free.

He came to my bed last night for the first time. No longer imagining a wedding night replete with seduction, passion, and intimacy, I laid still on my back, feigning sleep. I could hear heavy breathing and opened one eye. In the light from the moon, I saw his chest heaving.

In one violent move, he covered me with his body. I stiffened, and squeezed my eyes shut, as if that would make the next minutes less painful. He moved about quickly, arranging his nightshirt, pulling up my nightdress. I clenched my whole body in defense, but he persisted. Pain shot through me as with hostile vehemence he shoved and pushed in a rhythm that seemed to say, 'I hate you...I hate you...I hate you.'

When he stopped, he left me, nightdress askew.

Andrea rested the diary on her lap and turned to the dress form standing in the back of the living room, still wearing Abigale's green taffeta dress. "I guess I'm not the only Birch woman who picked the wrong husband." She looked at the clock. "I'll read for another hour. She searched through the pile of diaries and found one dated 1854. "Let's see what Abigale was up to back when."

The diaries were filling in the past for Andrea. She wanted to know more.

Andrea's deceased father, Mason, knew little about the Birch family, except his father's name was John. She remembered him telling her about his childhood.

"My mother, God bless her soul, raised me until I was ten. She told me the same bedtime story every night, how she and my dad loved each other very much. 'He went off to war,' she'd say. 'World War II. I sent him a letter, but...' Then she'd perk up, 'he'll be back for us. You'll see.'"

"I'd ask her to tell me about him. 'Your daddy, John, was a handsome, tall, kind man.' She'd touch the tip of my nose and say, 'You're gonna be tall, just like him.'"

And he was. Andrea's dad was six feet, two. He said his mother gave him the Birch name, "Because she knew my dad would be pleased."

Mason always became sad when he told Andrea the rest of the story. "Mom died when I was ten years old. That's why her sister raised me. I found out my father was killed in the battle of Normandy. It was the beginning of the end of the War, but many paid with their lives. Mom died not knowing why he never came back for us."

XXIII

Making Acquaintances

Andrea bundled up against the early November chill and walked toward the family cemetery. Gravestones and markers didn't seem to be ordered by date. She found one stone lying face down, partially covered with dirt. She stood it up and tried to make out the words. Years of weather and dirt coated the stone.

She returned the next day, this time prepared with a small stool and wire brush. She sat, wind whipping off the ocean, and scrubbed. She read the letters as she uncovered them one at a time, C A L. She knew from the diaries, this was Abigail's brother. She scrubbed more.

Caleb Birch

1826 – 1868

Andrea righted the stone, and having enough of the wind, retreated home. Later that evening, she settled in front of the fire with a cup of tea, looking through the diaries to see what Abigale had to say about her older brother.

April 1859

I turned sixteen today. I didn't mention it to my brother, Caleb. We never talk about my birth because my mother died the same day. Instead, he walks to the graveyard on the hill and puts flowers where she's buried. My father's buried there too, and Caleb's mother.

Caleb doesn't know, but I've gone to the cemetery alone. I know all my relatives' names, even though I never met one, except my father and Caleb. My father told me their stories, but never about his brother dying in the ocean during a storm. He spoke mostly about the past, probably because he spent so many years feeling sad after my mother died, that's all the memories he had.

He said his mother and father brought him and his brother to America to be free and wealthy. Grandfather, Edmund, hunted whales. He'd go to sea for weeks, and come home exhausted from the work, but with a pocketful of money. Father said he died when his blood got infected from living below deck with the rats and roaches and having no air to breathe.

It was Grandfather Edmund who built the house on the hill. According to Caleb, it was an imposing house with four bedrooms, built with the money Grandfather earned slaying whales and selling their oil. It was destroyed in the storm that caused my father to turn his back to the ocean.

It's Friday night. Caleb will go into town. He thinks I'm asleep when he brings women back to the house. But how can I sleep with all their noise? His room is next to mine. I never mention it in the morning.

Andrea thought, *well you can't really blame Caleb. He's a young guy raising an almost teenage girl.* She grabbed another journal.

April 1859

I hate Caleb. He expects me to clean the hearth of soot, collect the eggs, and cook for him like I am a servant. My friend from school invited me to walk to town, but Caleb forbid it. Says I can't be with a boy alone. Says he knows the boy, and he's up to no good. I fear I shall never marry.

I spend my days scrubbing and cleaning for him. I know he sneaks a gulp of whiskey whenever he is in the house and drinks from his tin at night.

My only pleasure and relief from maid's work are my diaries and reading The Scarlet Letter. Yes, Hester Prynne, I, too, know suffering.

Caleb will be sorry when I leave to go to Boston to live.

A petulant teenager rebelling against her guardian. Andrea closed the journal and picked another.

July 1859

A boy, new to town, asked me to pick blueberries with him on Saturday. I was especially pleased because the boy has a winning smile and bright eyes. Caleb forbid it, once again with no basis, judging the boy to be unworthy of me.

October 1859

    Caleb is courting the daughter of our neighbor to the west. She is unnaturally tall like my brother. Her face is as long as her feet are large. So large they cannot be entirely covered by her skirts. When she walks, each foot points outward. Her voice squeaks like a sad bird. I am the woman of this house, and no other shall intrude.

    I made the decision to visit her. As if I were writing my own fictional novel, the words poured from my mouth. I told her I'd come out of pure concern to warn her of my brother's temper. When she seemed unaffected by the news, I embellished, adding he had courted three other equally lovely women in the past two years, each of whom abandoned the relationship after suffering through his drunken rages. I added, save for my interference, the last woman may have been injured during one of his violent episodes. Sufficiently appalled, but grateful, the woman thanked me for saving her from a life of misery and possibly physical harm. The concerned woman hastily informed other women in town, protecting them from Caleb Birch's wickedness.

    Caleb, who so swiftly dismissed my suitors and at the same time, my future, suffered deeply from the wound of rejection.

It was closing in on midnight. Andrea shut the journal. *I guess there's no messing with Abigale.*

XXIV

The Cobbler's Widow

Seahaven, Massachusetts
December 1869

George Smythe was dejected after being bamboozled into marrying sour-faced Abigale Birch in exchange for useless land. At the end of his long days, he faced Abigale's unsavory meals and the sound of her incessant humming as her foot rode the treadle on the Singer. He groused to her deaf ears, "I work from morning till night, slopping pigs, feeding cows, and trying to grow damn turnips."

George was restless. There were no riches on the horizon. His ambition and greed ate away at him. He would not settle for a life without the love of a beautiful woman or the trappings of wealth. His thoughts wandered to the Widow Shoemaker, whose land abutted his, and who had the potential to give him both.

He visited her to convey his condolences. "I knew your husband well. A frugal man."

The widow concurred, "Yes." She looked around the sparsely furnished house. "My husband preferred investing in land, rather than a comfortable home, I'm afraid."

"And a good cigar, as I recall." The rotund cobbler could always be found with a wet cigar dangling from his lips.

The lovely young woman's marriage had been arranged by her father. She clucked her tongue. "I'm afraid my dear husband inhaled a good bit of dust and fumes over the years. He'd just finished stitching the leather on a pair of worn boots when his heart failed."

George visited the widow again, gracing her with a loaf of homemade cinnamon raisin bread. He lied. "Baked by my own mother's hands. I thought you'd enjoy."

"And wrapped in holiday cheer. Thank you, Mr. Smythe."

He won favor by helping her with household chores not meant for a fragile woman. "Your late husband would do it for me. Let me chop the wood."

It was unlikely the cobbler would have helped anyone, but the Widow Constance welcomed George's visits. "I'd be lost without you. My husband's sudden passing has left me..."

"Helpless? Yes, Constance. When my good father died, my mother was lost. I was there for her, too."

George edged his way. "Mrs. Shoemaker, Constance, I understand your husband's passing left you in a predicament."

The genteel woman, so different than Abigale, responded, "Yes, it is difficult for me to clean the soot from the hearth, and the ice melts far too quickly in my icebox."

"Minor concerns any hired hand can take care of. I'm talking about your future. You are a young woman."

She flushed. "I'm embarrassed to say, my husband did not make plans to provide for me if he should..." She paused, "pass."

"I may be able to help you. I've become a wealthy man since my relationship with an entrepreneur from New York. I don't share this information easily, but for you..."

"Let me make tea, George."

At last, the love of a beautiful woman and a lucrative business opportunity were right in front of him. "Together, he and I can manage your land and provide you with a dependable income."

Constance seemed more enthused about George than the business proposition. "Did you say you live alone, George?"

"Yes, I'm a lonely bachelor, eager to help a lady in distress."

Constance wasn't shy. "Come back another day. We can talk then."

George rode back to the Birch homestead with thoughts whirling through his mind. He arrived home to find his wife sitting in her chair, romance novel in hand, and her precious Kitty, now a full-grown cat in her lap. He went out to the barn to think.

XXV

Betrayal

Abigale adjusted to the marriage with George. He hadn't visited her bed in six months. It wasn't a disappointment to her, since his previous visit didn't live up to the expectations set by her extensive reading of romance novels.

She busied herself creating a more attractive and expensive collection of hats for the spring season. The work was a healthy distraction. She expanded her offerings, making dresses from Butterick's patterns, always adding her own touch of satin trim or lace at the hem.

During her last visit to Boston, the milliner introduced her to an English gentleman, an associate of the milliner. He paid her extraordinary attention, being particularly complimentary of her work. "Mrs. Smythe, I've been looking forward to meeting the artist who creates these impressive pieces."

Flustered at the praise, Abigale stuttered, "Wh, wh, why." She bowed and recovered, exuding charm. "Thank you, kind sir."

"My brother has a shop in London. May I be bold enough to offer him your creations? I believe your sense of fashion rivals European designers."

The stuttering returned. "I, I, it would be an honor, sir. A pleasure."

"Give me time to consult him."

The encounter provided fodder for Abigale's fantasies of genuine romance and she recounted it, sometimes embellishing the meeting, over and over in her mind.

Christmas was nearing, and Abigale was persistent in perfecting loaves of cinnamon raisin bread as holiday gifts for her neighbors. It was her first year as a married woman, and she thought, to keep up appearances, she would grace her neighbors with her homemaking skills. She used scraps of material to create unique wrappings, all with Christmas colors of red and green, for her loaves of bread. As she loaded the breads into the carriage, she counted only four. She was certain she had salvaged five from the dozens she baked.

"Merry Christmas to you." Abigale handed her wrapped cinnamon raisin bread to her nearest neighbor.

"And to you." The neighbor noticed the homespun wrapping. "How festive. Thank you, Abigale."

She went about to three more neighbors. The third, the widow of the town cobbler who Abigale had yet to meet, bordered George's farm.

"How lovely." She stood at her door and reached for the merrily wrapped bread. She invited Abigale in. "I'll just place this right along with the other gift I received this morning."

To Abigale's shock, the missing loaf, which she lovingly prepared and wrapped in red and green holly print fabric, sat on her neighbor's kitchen table. Lost for words, she pointed.

The widow delighted in telling her a young man had been calling on her. "Prepared by his mother, a sweet elderly lady who loves to bake."

Abigale's holiday spirit abandoned her as she listened to this betrayal. George Smythe posed as a single man, courting a widow whose land abutted his. She excused herself. "I wish you luck with your young suitor."

She rode the horses hard on the way back to the Birch homestead and wrote about the day in her diary.

XXVI

Happy New Year

Seahaven, Massachusetts
December 2018

Andrea called Liz to ring in the New Year. "You got your champagne in hand?"

"Well, it's a martini, but it's alcohol, so it counts. You've had a hell of a year, my darling. Let's raise our glasses to a wonderful twenty-nineteen."

Andrea sat alone in front of the burning fire. "Here, here. This would be a lot more fun if you were with me."

"You know how it goes, no rest for the wicked. Where's your handsome boy toy?"

"Michael? Things just faded off with us. I'm such an old lady compared to him. I think I'm learning to be happier alone." Andrea hadn't seen Liz for months. "Enough about me. Listen, Liz, the loft is the last part of the renovation. As soon as it's finished, you're coming for a visit, even if I have to drive to Boston and kidnap you."

"Send pictures. Kisses, darling." Liz hung up.

It wasn't quite midnight, Andrea opened one of the diaries.

December 1869

The slithering, poisonous snake who is my husband is wooing a widow neighbor. I'm injured enough at this humiliation without the added insult that he's winning her favor by pretending his mother baked my loaf of cinnamon raisin bread. I can't breathe as I sit, comforted only by the soft fur and purrs of my precious Kitty.

George will soon find he is betraying the wrong woman. I'll be a widow before I'm humiliated.

Yikes, Andrea thought. *Old George better watch his back.* The clock struck midnight.

New Year's Day 1870

    I kept it to myself that George stole one of my homemade breads, and that I knew of his dalliance with the Widow Shoemaker. If I learned anything from reading my books, it was that an act in the heat of the moment always goes wrong.

    I found it out of character when George offered to make me a cup of tea. I didn't know he could boil water; he never did to bathe. I accepted, rather than seem ungrateful for the gesture, and found the jar of raspberry tea leaves for him.

    He brought the tea as I sat in my chair with Kitty purring on my lap and went off to work in the barn. The tea was quite bitter. I set it down and went to the cupboard to search for honey and returned to my tea within minutes. It was by far the worst scene of my life, my teacup, turned over on the floor, was empty. Beside it lay my sweet Kitty, taking his last breaths.

    George Smythe committed the unforgiveable act of killing my precious Kitty. My untethered wrath, public flogging, or mutilation will not bring enough pain to render the proper punishment.

    I recovered from my shock and placed dead Kitty in a burlap bag on the front step. I posed at the kitchen sink and waited for George to return from the barn, knowing he expected to find my corpse sprawled on the floor. Instead, after he passed Kitty's bagged body, he found me wiping the teacup clean. My only words. "Heavenly tea, George."

Andrea found it hard to sleep after reading Abigale's last passage. She planned to visit the family cemetery the next day.

It was a bitter wintry morning. She bundled up and hiked to the graveyard, tools in hand. She walked among the stones and markers, some covered with frost, others too worn to read, until she discovered what she came for.

George Smythe
1846–1870

She put her gloved hand to her mouth. "Damn."

XXVII

Hit Me

Boston, Massachusetts
January 2019

Will Rossi sold the condominium in the North End. He paid off the balance of the mortgage and pocketed three hundred and sixty thousand dollars. Now adjusted to the anxiety of forging prescriptions and shorting patients of narcotics, Will reasoned he could double, maybe triple his three hundred and sixty thousand at the casino.

He warmed up at the Roulette Wheel, starting slow, placing a thousand dollars in chips on the odd section. The wheel spun and landed on the zero. "House wins," called out the croupier. Next Will tried a split bet. He placed a thousand-dollar chip between the sixteen and nineteen. "And the winning number is sixteen."

"Yeah, baby. Seventeen to one. Slide over those chips."

Now up sixteen thousand dollars, Will's confidence soared. "Okay, I'm putting sixteen thousand up." He placed the chips at the intersection of four numbers. The click, click, click of the wheel stopped. The croupier reached and slid Will's sixteen thousand to his side of the table.

Will eyed the Blackjack table. "I'm gonna move along after the next spin." He picked up one hundred thousand dollars in chips. "I got lucky with the split tonight. I'll stick with it."

Other gamblers moaned as the wheel stopped. Once again, the croupier collected Will's chips.

He took a seat at the five-hundred-dollar Blackjack table. Hand after hand, Will couldn't catch a break. After two hours, he was down a hundred thousand. He held the best hand of the night, a ten of clubs and ten of hearts. If he said, 'hit me,' and got an Ace, he'd rake in a cool fifty thousand. If he stood, there was a chance another player or the dealer would catch twenty-one. Will had a lucky feeling. With no hesitation he called out. "Hit me."

The dealer drew a two of hearts.

The casino comped Will a suite for the night. By seven a.m., he showered and finished a breakfast of bacon and eggs. Sitting at the same seat he had the night before, he called. "Hit me," and lost again.

Will started drinking complimentary Screwdrivers at ten a.m. The last of his money was in chips. He won with an eighteen and was up three thousand dollars. A ten of spades and two fives got him another three thousand. Bolstered by the winning streak, and sipping his third drink, Will bet it all, and drew sixteen.

—❧—

An anguished Will opened the pharmacy on Monday. He had debt, bills to pay, a mortgage on the store, inventory, and a loan shark appearing every Tuesday.

XXVIII

Revelations

Boston, Massachusetts
March 1870

Abigale rode the train, her spring collection packed by her own careful hands. This visit held more than the usual anticipation. She was to present her collection to the charming Englishman she'd met in the fall.

She imagined the meeting a dozen times, her manner genteel, perhaps coy. "Kind sir, I'm charmed to see you once again." He, whose name she'd forgotten, would be proper, but friendly, perhaps admiring or even flirtatious.

He'd bow and sweep his arm. "My dear, you look as fresh as spring flowers. A pleasure." Apprehension sent tingles up her neck to her head.

Her presentation was a triumph, beyond what she imagined. The English gentleman, whose name she learned was Mr. Ellis, was as solicitous as she expected, regaling her work as, "Jolly superior."

She, in her own estimation, was delightful and demure. Abigale imagined herself a character in her own novel when Mr. Ellis implored, "Mrs. Smythe, please, if I may be so bold, would you do me the honor of tea on your next visit? Perhaps I'll have a special request of you."

Abigale curtsied. "My pleasure," and thought to herself, *Such a contrast to crass George Smythe.*

Abigale rode the train back to Seahaven with illusions of a romantic rendezvous to ponder until her fall visit to Boston.

—◊◊◊—

A mid-March storm blasted the Cape the next morning. George grumbled to Abigale, "I'm off to my place to check the animals and secure the barn doors." Abigale didn't answer her husband. "We could be havin' a hurricane with these winds and freezing rains."

Icy snow and hailstones blew sideways as dark clouds loomed overhead. George pushed his horse to move. "C'mon, before we both freeze to death." The horse bucked at the first flash of lightening. "Steady, boy. Steady, now."

The snow and hail mixed with rounds of thunder, and flashes of lightning danced across the dark horizon. George left his horse and rushed to his barn. The doors were slamming in the wind. As he grabbed hold of one, a deafening clap of thunder rolled from the clouds and a bolt of lightning lit the skies. The electrical charge hit the wet snow where George stood and knocked him down, right outside his barn door. Stunned, George lay on the cold ground, helpless, as icy shards cut his frozen face and hands. The thunder clashed and lightning bolts struck the snow-covered ground as he fought to stay conscious. George prayed to a God he seldom talked to. "Lord, save me. Forgive me." Thoughts of his selfish life and deeds, his greed and sins, including trying to poison his wife, passed through his mind. He called out. "I'm sorry, Lord. I'll change. I'll be a good husband. Give me a chance."

As if the Lord heard him, George's strength returned. His prayers answered, he made it home, all the way vowing to change. He didn't tell Abigale about the experience, but simply promised to try harder. Soaked to the bone, half frozen, shoulders slumped, he spoke, "I haven't been a good husband. From this day forward, as God is my witness, I am a changed man."

The lament went unheard as Abigale dried up the floor, now wet from George's boots and clothes. Lost in thought, she wondered if the lovely Englishman would be inclined more toward a widow than a divorced woman.

XXIX

A Simple Crack

Seahaven, Massachusetts
January 2019

Andrea settled in her favorite chair by the hearth. She sipped a hot cup of coffee with a drop of Bailey's Irish Cream and let the fire warm her feet. She picked up the diary.

March 1870

    I am bereft with grief for the loss of Kitty. Reading and sewing have lost their joy without him purring beside me. There is only one form of justice for a man who kills innocent animals and betrays his wife.

    It was dark when I informed my husband that the storm caused water to leak into the house. He uncharacteristically promised to repair the roof in the morning.

    He lay beside me that night and touched my hand. "I'm sorry, Abigale." I was taken by surprise when he climbed upon me, but in a gentle way. He lifted my dressing gown, and I felt him enter me. He held me close and rocked back and forth, in a slow rhythm, as he repeated. "I'm sorry." When he finished, he kissed my forehead, a first. I may have felt tears on his face.

    I rolled over, my back to my husband, not expecting to sleep without Kitty lying at my feet.

    As promised, the next morning he carried the ladder from the barn, unaware of the small cracks in the rung close to the top. I busied myself sketching a hat of pink silk and pure white linen for my spring collection while George climbed the ladder to the chimney on the highest peak of the roof.

    The scream came first, the thud next, and then silence. I wrapped myself in a heavy shawl and went outside to find him lying on his back on the frozen ground, the ladder, with one broken rung, lying nearby. I sensed a shallow breath and returned inside and finished my chamomile tea. He wasn't breathing when I checked on him an hour later.

The sheriff, who is also the undertaker, concluded right away the rung of the ladder snapped under my husband's weight.

George's body will remain in a dead house until the ground thaws.

In spite of the roaring fire, Andrea shuddered as rows of goose bumps raced up her arms.

XXX

Winter Blues

Seahaven, Massachusetts
Winter 2019

It snowed for two days. A brutal nor'easter dropped ten inches of heavy wet snow on the outer Cape. Power lines fell from the force of the winds and weight of the snow. Whiteout conditions closed roads and the few businesses open through the winter in Seahaven.

Tom stacked extra wood on the new screen porch to see Andrea through the storm. She sat, wrapped in a quilt, the fire in the hearth her only source of heat, listening to the weather forecast on the Panasonic portable radio she and Will bought for the camping trips they never took.

She called Liz in Boston. "I'm conserving my cell phone battery. You're my only call, then I'm shutting it off. It could be days before I get power back. How are you doing?"

"Charge your phone in your car."

"Liz, the snow is flying sideways, and my car is under a three-foot snowdrift. I don't even own a shovel. What if I fall and the snow covers me over? Where are you?"

"Such a drama queen. Andrea, really. I'm home, of course, darling. Just finishing up a project. I still have power."

"Speaking of projects, you haven't sent any lately. What's with that? Business slow?"

"It's more like I'm slow. Just not hustling like I used to. Kinda lost the fire in the belly. You need work?"

"Don't worry about me. You okay?"

"Darling, I'm fine. Just winter blues. They get me every year."

Andrea looked around her house. "I have them too. With so much to do, I sit. Haven't even been painting."

"Well, girl. Get that easel out."

"You know, just today, the beauty of the snow inspired me to paint. I'm thinking of trekking up to the Birch family cemetery at sunrise tomorrow and painting it covered with snow, just the tips of the stones peeking through."

"Andrea, sweetheart, get a grip. You need happiness and joy in your life. Painting cemeteries. Ugh."

"You might be right. I swear I see shadows moving at night."

"I bet you still have that dress form in your bedroom. Get rid of that dead, headless relative. No wonder you see ghosts." Liz changed the subject. "Tell me about the house, sweets."

"The kitchen is taking longer than we expected. Poor Tom. I think he took on too much."

"Yes, but it will be marvelous when it's done. Continue."

"If you really cared, you'd come visit."

"I'm waiting for the grand opening of my private loft."

"Liz, you'll be too old to climb the stairs by that time at Tom's pace. So anyway, work?"

"Now that I'm thinking about it, you can take a job off my plate."

"Sounds good. What's the clinking? Liz, are you drinking? It's only eleven in the morning."

"Darling, it's breakfast, a Bloody Mary, and I'm eating my vegetables, two olives. Anyway, this project. It's right up your alley."

"Tell me."

"It's a promo for a cable television series about DNA. We need two spots, fifteen and thirty seconds."

"Sounds interesting."

"Show's called *DNA Detective*. It follows a scientist who tracks DNA back generations for people looking for their long-lost relatives."

"Wow. I should contact her myself."

"Darling, whose DNA would you use? You don't have any living relatives."

"Good point. Anyway, send me everything you have. After I get power back."

"Will do. By the way, back to your ancestors, there's people who research family lines."

"Liz, that's genius. Quick question. Where would I find such a person here on the tip of the world?"

"Do I detect sarcasm, darling?"

"Of course not. Gotta go. My battery. Kisses."

"That's my line. Kisses to you. Be careful in this storm."

Andrea shut off her cell phone. She gathered candles and flashlights to prepare for an evening in the dark, then busied herself taking apart old pictures she found in the barn. Men, woman, and children stood posed, not touching or smiling, in the black and white or sepia tone photographs. The frames and glass were covered with age. She cleaned them, put them back together and arranged the portraits on the walls of the living room.

Andrea studied the faces, looking for a family resemblance. "I know you're related, but just don't know how." She thought about what Liz said and decided to visit the cemetery as soon as the snow melted and collect names and dates to research her relatives.

The snow continued to fall, covering the skylights, and sliding off. Andrea stoked the fire, surrounded herself with candles, and reached for her favorite books, Abigale Birch's diaries. She was thirteen.

April 1856

I'm done with the schoolhouse. The other children mocked me until I cried. They pointed and teased because my school dress is too tight at the chest. The buttons are about to burst off. The sleeves are too short, and the seams tearing open. Caleb doesn't understand I've grown this last year.

I'm becoming more like a woman. I'm taking apart the old clothes left in this house and making clothes with a proper fit.

I was close to home when two boys threw stones as I walked by them. I thought they were jeering at my dress, instead they shouted my father's name was Cain, that he killed his brother. I hit one with a rock and ran.

Caleb says it isn't true. People made up a story saying my uncle, Roger, didn't fall overboard in the big storm. They claimed my father, Samuel, pushed him and left him to drown. According to Caleb, it was vicious gossip that our father loved his brother's wife and killed him so he could marry her. My mother.

Caleb said it near killed Pa, the way people talked.

I'm never going back to school.

Andrea closed the journal. "Geeze, I think I come from a long line of killers."

XXXI

The Marker

After six months, the kitchen was complete. "It is magnificent, Tom. Beyond my expectations."

Tom shuffled and blushed at the compliments each time Andrea delivered them and launched into a description of the custom features he built into the kitchen.

"You got your extra tall soapstone backsplash, countertops, and sink." Tom pointed up every time. "That pierced tin chandelier is no reproduction, had that in my garage for years. All polished up and rewired." He'd wink and turn to Andrea. "And I noticed you like your wine, so I put in a little rack right up over the microwave." Then he'd qualify, "Course, you can't see the microwave. I saw to that. All that stuff, dishwasher, trash bin," his voice would rise, "even the refrigerator, disguised with custom cabinet doors, the hardware, original to the times." Then he'd nod for effect.

"You deserve bragging rights, Tom. Everything is perfect. Thank you for working so hard. It was a cold winter out in the barn. I felt so bad for you, with just that little heater."

Tom put his hand to his hip. "Yeah, kicked up my arthritic hip, but it will get better. Andrea, if you don't mind, I'm gonna take a couple weeks off. Rest my old bones."

"Of course. I'm glad you're taking care of yourself. I'll catch up here. There's plenty for me to do.

After months of working on it, Andrea was putting the final touches on the painting of the family cemetery in winter. "I'm trying to decide if I should keep this or put it on consignment at the gallery." Andrea touched Tom's shoulder. "What do you think?"

Tom put his hand to his chin and moved his head to the left and then to the right. "Cemetery."

"Yes. Cemetery. A painting. Of mine. Do you like it?"

"Depends if you're going to sell it or not."

"Why?"

"Now, it's just me, but to my mind, you're surrounding yourself with the past here. The diaries, albums, pictures of people you don't even know."

"So, you don't like the painting?"

"Not what I'm sayin'." He pointed to her bedroom. "You even got that dress form in your bedroom. I don't think you need to add a painting of a cemetery with your dead relatives hanging in your living room to look at every day. Move forward…" He stopped, "never mind, not my business."

"That's the longest sentence I ever heard you speak."

Tom changed the subject. "Now, I marked the trees and shrubs with orange paint. The landscapers will take down a bunch of them pitch pines and scrub oaks. They're junk. Big weeds if you ask me." He didn't stop for a breath. "We're not gonna put in a lawn for you to worry about, leaving the bayberry and blueberry bushes, and natural ground cover." He was backing toward the door. "When you're ready, we'll put crushed clam shells in for a driveway. No maintenance." He put his hand on the doorknob. "And, oh, I told them to clear a spot, twenty by twenty for a vegetable garden."

"Oh, did we discuss that? I don't recall." Andrea shook her head. "Never mind. Go, rest your hip. I know where to find you if I need you. Take care of yourself."

He stopped short of opening the front door. "I didn't mean to hurt your feelings."

She hoped her face wasn't flushing scarlet. "No worries, friend."

—⚏—

Andrea tossed about the projects she would tackle in Tom's two-week absence. She considered hanging the wire baskets she found in the barn or cleaning up the metal-framed glass mirror to hang in the bathroom. She also wanted to visit the cemetery and collect more names and dates of relatives.

Prioritizing her goals, she drove into town and for a meeting at Seahaven Gallery. The owner of Seahaven Gallery wore a red and blue silk ascot with anchors printed on it, tucked under his white cotton shirt. "Your tree of life painting hasn't sold yet, but I can't hold that against you."

She thought, *you're right, buddy.* "Yes, I understand you closed the gallery all winter."

"Let's give it the summer and see how it goes."

Andrea unwrapped her latest piece. "It's a family cemetery."

He stood back, one hand on his hip, the other on his chin, studying it. "It's not your usual watercolor."

"No. I tried acrylics. I'm quite pleased with it."

He tilted his head as if to look at it sideways. "It's quite good." He looked at Andrea, and with a straight face informed her. "You won't find a lot of buyers interested in paintings of cemeteries."

Andrea tried to be funny. "Witches, vampires?"

The man seemed annoyed at her attempt at humor. She considered more to see if she could get this stern-faced man to guffaw, *Goths, ghosts, the walking dead?* But restrained herself.

"I'll take it, only because it's quite different from anything else on display right now. You never know."

"How should I price it?"

He tilted his head sideways again, as if it would help him calculate the painting's value. "Let's try fourteen hundred. It has potential."

Potential. Is that a compliment? "Thank you. I'm sure you'll be in touch if there is any interest."

—∿—

Her next stop was the salon for a cut and color and pedicure. She worked her way into the question. "Boy, do I need this. I'm starting to look like Sasquatch." The stylist didn't seem to know about the hairy monster. "Anyway," Andrea continued, "I was talking to a friend about this new show on cable. A scientist tracks long-lost relatives using DNA." The hairdresser began chatting with the stylist working next to her about her boyfriend.

"That's what my husband does, and he doesn't need DNA."

Andrea, her hair now divided into ten sections, each wrapped in foil, turned her chair. "Excuse me?"

The woman, cloaked in black plastic, introduced herself. "My husband is the archivist for the historical society." A hand emerged from under the plastic cape and waved. "I'm Lorraine Prescott."

Andrea's foil-covered head tingled. "Really. An archivist. How interesting."

Lorraine gushed. "Jarrett is the best. There's nothing he doesn't know about most families in town." She clucked her tongue. "The stories, oh my. But I don't gossip. Everything's confidential, of course."

Andrea imagined Lorraine reading Abigale's diaries and telling the citizens of Seahaven she killed her husband by cracking the rung of his ladder. "Can I get your husband's phone number?"

She pulled a cell phone from her purse. "Give me your number, he'll text you."

Andrea thought the day had been productive. Another painting on consignment, a refreshed hairstyle, new red toenails, and an archivist.

"You have arrived at your destination." She remembered the GPS announcement the day she drove down her driveway for the first time. Today, she stopped the car as the house came into sight, admiring the home of generations of her family. The natural cedar shingles, green window shutters, and a bright yellow front door brought it back to life. Trellises, supporting climbing flowering plants, stood on the restored front porch. Rows of Hydrangeas lined her driveway, offering a welcoming embrace. Brightened by the sun, pink pastel blossoms contrasted the vivid purples of others.

After a day of rain, she needed her rubber boots to walk up the hill to the cemetery. She found a stone engraved Samuel Birch with the names of his two wives. Samuel's son, Caleb, lay next to him. There was no stone for Samuel's brother, Roger, who died at sea, or if the rumors were true, was murdered by Samuel.

Andrea dropped to her knees on the mushy soil and after digging through mud, found a fallen stone with the names Edmund and Margaret Birch. She surmised they were the original immigrants from England by the dates of their deaths, Edmund, 1830 and Margaret, 1832. There was another stone, she could only make out the word Abigale. Later, she found what appeared to be a grave marker discarded on the edge of the cemetery, lying loose in the mud. Age covered the name, so she put it aside to bring home. Having enough of the dead for the day, she headed back to the house. Andrea used her easel and a canvas to sketch the names of the family. She read out loud. "Edmund and Margaret had two sons, Samuel and Roger. Samuel had a son, Caleb, and a daughter, Abigale. But what happened after that? Where does the trail go from Abigale? How does Catherine fit in?"

Birch Family

Edmund
1774–1830
Margaret
1776–1832

Samuel Birch
1796–1858

Roger Birch
1798–1841

Caleb Birch
1826–1868

Abigale Birch
1843–1918

Catherine Birch
1918–2013

Mason Birch
1944–2014

Andrea Birch
1984–

XXXII

Best Laid Plans

Seahaven, Massachusetts
April 1870

The Widow Smythe sat in her seat, back rigid, head held high, and hands clasped, on the train ride back from Boston to Cape Cod. A black lace veil covered her pinched face, three rejected hats sat on her lap. She watched out the window, her eyes dry and jaw taut, as trees flew by, until the sun set, and she stared into the darkness. Abigale wouldn't allow thoughts into her mind. Not of the lovely Englishman, Mr. Ellis. Not of George Smythe, her dead husband. She didn't give a thought to the red satin ball gown, the milliner's rejection of her hats, or that her monthly hadn't come since George died.

Earlier that day… It was her second trip in weeks. The refined Englishman, Mr. Ellis, had invited her to tea, and waiting until fall seemed too long. She based her visit on the premise she crafted exquisite fall samples for the milliner to consider. Abigale, now Widow Smythe, consulted the latest fashion magazines before creating her mourning ensemble, choosing black crepe for its dull finish. She made the dress to flatter her own petite body, a bodice with no collar, but gathered crepe trim around the neck. The sleeves were long, covering her delicate arms, puckering at the wrist, and trimmed in black silk. She made the skirt of modest width to accommodate traveling but added delicate silk and lace trim. Abigale finished the outfit with a wide brim linen hat with a cluster of silk flowers, and replete with a six-inch veil of French black lace to shield her grieving face.

She rode the train to Boston with great anticipation, carrying three hastily handmade fall hats. Fantasies of Mr. Ellis's reaction to learning her new status as a widow, filled her mind. 'My dear Widow Smythe, how very unfortunate for your departed husband, but fortunate for me.' None of her romance novels dealt with a widow taking a lover so soon after her husband's death. She would have to write the pages of this scandalous, but passionate romance herself.

Abigale swept into the millinery on busy Washington Street, foregoing her custom of admiring her hats in the windows. In grand fashion she accepted the condolences of the owner and now familiar staff. When the flurry of greetings calmed down, she strained her neck, closing one eye to squint through her lace veil, scouring the store for Mr. Ellis.

With great flourish, she presented her latest pieces to the milliner who seemed sympathetic but underwhelmed by the offerings. "I'm sure the sudden death of your husband has affected your fashion sense. It's understandable."

Abigale dismissed the comments and continued to scan the store, front to back, side to side.

"Widow Smythe," the milliner handed the hats back to Abigale. "These are not representative of your best work. Perhaps in the fall when you've had time to grieve…"

She interrupted, raising a black lace gloved hand, "Is Mr. Ellis here today?"

"He's expected." The milliner checked the clock on the wall. "Soon."

"Yes. You are right. It's too soon." Abigale snatched the sample hats from the milliner's hands. "It's several hours before my train leaves."

Abigale strode about the store, touching the flower on one hat, adjusting the ribbon on another. The milliner served customers, while at the same time, watching Abigale move from one display to another. Abigale visited each hat in the store three times and was about to again when Mr. Ellis appeared at the store's entrance.

She darted to the door. "Mr. Ellis. Such a pleasure. I never expected to see you today. It's not my regular time for a visit."

The Englishman, dressed in an elegant three-piece gray suit, bowed and took the fragile hand of the widow. "My deepest condolences. Such a young man. A tragedy."

Abigale dropped her eyes as if agreeing George Smythe's death was tragic, then got right to the point. "Now that you're here, I'll remind you, on my last visit, you invited me for tea. Such a sweet gesture. I'm pleased to accept."

Mr. Ellis straightened his back and tapped the floor with his walking stick. "Jolly idea." He hesitated and dropped his voice. "Are you up to it? Perhaps it's too soon," he winked, "or perhaps not."

"I think tea with you would do me a world of good."

"Very well. You know I had given up on the idea after hearing of your loss."

Flushed at the flattery, Abigale countered. "As you can see, I'm not a woman to give up on. Am I? My timing is exactly right, isn't it, Mr. Ellis?"

He burst with enthusiasm, banging his cane again. "Righto."

Abigale fought back the urge to cheer.

"It will positively thrill my wife to have you take her measurements. It's a Christmas ball she's planning for. She's yearning for a gown of red satin or perhaps velvet."

Abigale inhaled the words 'my wife' into her brain. She processed the other words one at a time. 'Measurements,' then, 'Christmas ball,' and, 'red satin.' The black French lace veil covered her red splotched face and the fury in her eyes. She spoke with purpose. "You invited me to tea to measure your wife for a ball gown?"

The distinguished Englishman seemed unflustered, "Yes, of course. Hadn't I mentioned that? Oh my. Yes, she's looking forward to meeting you." He rolled his eyes. "Mad for your hats."

Abigale's ears burned. Her neck stiffened, and throat tightened. She spoke through pursed lips, "Yes, Mr. Ellis, you are right. It is too soon for me. Your wife," the word wife pronounced louder than the others, "will have to find another seamstress for her red satin or velvet Christmas ball gown."

It took all she had to exit the milliner's store with grace.

XXXIII

Follow The Trail

Seahaven, Massachusetts
September 2019

When archivist, Jarrett Prescott, texted he would not be available for months because of a commitment to a book he was writing, Andrea emailed the attorney who informed her of the death of Catherine Birch and her inheritance of the Birch family homestead.

> **Dear Attorney Swain:**
> I have several questions regarding the property I inherited from Catherine Birch. I'm interested in learning who held the title to the property before Catherine. As we discussed a few months ago, I am renovating the property and, most importantly tracing the Birch family ties to determine my relationship to them. This brings me to my most pressing question. How did your law firm determine I was the heir? Thank you. Andrea Birch

The reply came the following day.

> **Dear Ms. Birch,**
> In compliance with Massachusetts laws governing title searches, the obligation of the Swain Law Firm was

to determine for the past sixty years the deed was free and clear of liens, and Catherine Birch was the current deed holder. My title search concluded Catherine Birch was the title holder of the property since nineteen ninety-two, when, as the sole survivor of her mother, Iris Birch, she inherited it.

On a personal note, it is my experience that photo albums, correspondence, old tax bills, bibles, etc. are a treasure trove of family history. You should also either contact an expert in genealogy or search one of the websites for tracing family members.

Your question regarding how we determined you are the heir to the property deserves a personal conversation.

A minute after Andrea read the email reply, her cell phone rang.

"Ms. Birch, this is Attorney Joseph Swain."

"Yes, Mr. Swain."

"First, let me clarify that the Swain Law Firm represents the town of Seahaven and we took this case as a sort of favor to them. They were concerned with the deterioration of the property after Catherine Birch went into a nursing home."

Andrea grabbed a pen and paper. "I understand."

"We fulfilled our duty, locating and notifying you." He cleared his throat. "Now regarding the matter of how we determined you were the heir ..."

"Mr. Swain, it sounds like there's a story coming."

He chuckled, "Very perceptive."

"I'm all ears."

"Ms. Birch, my father, the principal of this firm is ninety-one years old. Up until last year, he came to the office once or twice a week."

"Did he handle this case?"

"He did, but unfortunately, my father, quite old-school, put everything in writing or stored it in his head. He never used a computer."

"And so…"

"My father determined independently that, due to his fading memory, he would no longer take cases. There were a few he left in process, yours was one of them." There was a pause. "Ms. Birch, being totally confident in my father's competence at the time he worked on your case, we mailed you the letter he prepared."

"So, Mr. Swain, you're trusting your father's search was valid, but don't know how he determined it was?"

"That's one way to put it."

"I'm annoyed."

"I understand, Ms. Birch. As we speak, I have a paralegal dedicated to researching all the paper folders in my dad's office so we can either put them in the archives or log active cases into our computer system."

"What does that mean to me?"

He cleared his throat. "It means, let me think, it means we will prioritize your case and when we find the file, we will notify you."

"Do you expect that to be next week, next month?"

"Hard to say, and I won't commit. As I said, we met our legal obligation. Anything beyond notifying you is a courtesy."

Andrea turned different replies over in her mind. "Very well, Mr. Swain. I'll expect notification soon and look forward to any documents verifying I am the heir. I'm sure you look forward to peace of mind, given your father's memory issues."

They said their goodbyes and hung up. Andrea spoke out loud. "I guess I'm on my own."

Andrea researched the Chain of Title document on Seahaven's Town website and identified deed owners of the Birch homestead as far back as nineteen forty-four.

—◊—

As promised, Tom returned after two weeks.

"God, I missed you." Tom stiffened when Andrea hugged him. "I made coffee, and bacon and eggs."

"All set right now." He nodded. "How are the kitchen and bath working out?"

Andrea handed him a mug of coffee, anyway. "Love, love, them. That shower, mmm, mmm."

Tom sipped his coffee. "Gonna get to that loft this month. I'll be framin' it out this week." He set up a worktable and laid out his tools. "I want to finish up before the end of summer."

—w—

A weary Tom descended the ladder after eight hours working in the loft.

"Guess what?"

"Oh, I don't know. You want a hot tub? In-ground swimming pool?"

"No. Silly. I tracked down the deed owners to this house before Catherine Birch."

"I coulda told you that. Hope you didn't pay money to find out."

Andrea shuffled a pile of papers she printed off the Registry of Deeds website. Tom's words stopped her. "What do you know?"

"I don't go too far back. I'm a washashore, just like you. Came here when I was five years old 'cause my father got a job building houses. There was a building boom on the Cape in the sixties."

Andrea took the tape measure out of Tom's hands. "You've been holding back on me. Why didn't you tell me you knew the people who lived here as far back as the nineteen sixties?"

He took the tape back. "First, you never asked, and second, it was more like the seventies when I was a little older. My family bought eggs from Nelson Birch."

"Tom, we have to talk. According to what I learned, Nelson lived here with his wife…"

"Mrs. Birch. She was my fourth-grade teacher. Died young. Something about her blood."

"What about kids? Did they have any?"

"Now, I was just a kid myself, but I remember when I was working in the hardware store in town, Old Mr. Birch would come in. After he left, the others, the older men, would shake their heads and say he was never the same since his son got killed in the war."

"Name, Tom, what was Mr. Birch's son's name?"

"That I don't know." He tapped his temple, "James Doyle."

Andrea was accustomed to Tom's short spurts of speech. "Yes?"

He pointed at her. "Write that down. Father James Doyle. He'll know all about the Birch clan."

Andrea knew better than to push Tom too hard, especially at the end of the day.

—◆—

"Coffee?"

"Thanks."

"James Doyle?"

"Huh? Oh, sure. Father Doyle. He was one of the parish priests back throughout the sixties, seventies… God, he retired only a couple of years ago."

"Okay, so you think I should speak with him. He's alive, I take it."

Tom moved up the ladder. Andrea stood at the bottom. He turned and looked down. "Now do you think I'd be tellin' you to talk to a dead priest? Of course, he's alive, far as I know. He lives in the rectory at St. Joan's. Give him a visit. If anyone knows the secrets of the people in this town, it's Father Doyle."

Birch Family

Edmund
1774–1830
Margaret
1776–1832

Samuel Birch
1796–1858

Roger Birch
1798–1841

Caleb Birch
1826–1868

Abigale Birch
1843–1918

Nelson Birch
1901–1979

Iris Birch
1903–1992

Catherine Birch
1918–2013

Mason Birch
1944–2014

Andrea Birch
1984–

XXXIV

Will's Secrets

Boston, Massachusetts
September 2019

Will Rossi had secrets. He was skimming pills from customers to pay off gambling debts to loan sharks who threatened his life. He'd almost forgotten about the affair.

—m—

Carrie Fazio still lived in the North End neighborhood where she and Will grew up. It was the winter of 2018 when they ran into each other for the first time in years. Carrie just ended a long-term relationship. Will and Andrea's marriage was strained by the stress of the infertility. Will stopped by Carrie's apartment a few times. Their affair didn't last long.

Today, she dropped in to the pharmacy and introduced him to his son. "Say hi, Daddy."

"Carrie, what the hell?"

"Look at him, Will. Brown eyes, curly dark hair. He's yours."

"You have brown eyes and curly dark hair. This entire neighborhood has brown eyes and dark hair. Don't try to hang this on me."

Carrie picked up her son. "I don't want to talk here, or in front of Billy."

Will looked around. "Billy? Jeesuz."

"Hey, I'll give you his spit. Test the DNA all you want. He's yours."

"What do you want?"

"Come to my apartment tonight. We'll talk." She turned to leave and looked back. "You remember where it is, right?"

—⁓—

"Could you put out the cigarette? It's choking me."

Carrie took another drag and snuffed out the Marlborough Light in the tin ashtray on the kitchen table. "Want a beer?"

Will shook his head. "What do you want?"

Carrie got up to get a beer for herself. "It's not rocket science, Will. I need money."

"Why now?"

She had the nasal voice of a smoker. "I tried to do it without you. My parents own this building, so I pay hardly no rent. I work, nurses make decent money."

"So?"

"I can't do it. Daycare costs an arm and a leg. My ma used to help, but she's gettin' too old. I have to pay family medical, that's six hundred a month."

She lit another Marlborough.

"Cigarettes are ten bucks a pack, plus you're killing yourself." Will stopped and took the baby from Carrie. "And Billy."

Carrie squeezed off the lit end of the cigarette and saved the rest. "I don't need a lecture from you. Let's get down to business. I need two hundred and fifty a week."

Will ignored her and spoke baby talk to Billy. "Tell your mama, no more smoking. It's bad for babies."

"Will, you listenin'? Either start paying or get a lawyer. And that's gonna cost you big time."

"Do you give him vitamins? Fresh vegetables? That kind of good stuff?"

Carrie stayed focused on money. "You can test the DNA. Trust me, you're paying. We can do it legally or as friends."

Will turned to Carrie. "So, if you didn't need money, I'd never know I had a son? Do you think that's fair? Kids need fathers, you know."

"Ah, excuse me. I called your cell five times. Remember? When you were married?"

Will was walking the floor with Billy. "Yeah. But still, I would have stepped up, married or not. My old man wasn't there for me, too busy working all the time. I would have stepped up."

"Yeah, nice to hear. I'll believe it when you start paying money every week, like a real father."

"So, you know, Carrie, if he's my son, I want to be in his life. It's not just about the money. I want to spend time with him. Be a real dad."

"Sure, sure. We'll see. When you gonna spit in the tube so you can start paying?"

"Forget the DNA. He's mine. I knew it the minute I saw him."

Will took a picture from his wallet. "Guess who?"

"God, that looks just like Billy."

"Except it's me. He's my kid. I know it."

"So, you'll pay?"

Will was bouncing Billy on his lap and singing to him. "Of course. He's my son. I'll take care of him. First I got business to take care of."

—⚖—

Will left Carrie's and walked back to his store. He lived in the room on the second floor where his grandfather and grandmother stayed when they first established themselves in America and opened the little grocery. He made a call.

"Rick, it's Will Rossi. What can I get for the store, you know, the building?"

Rick assured him it was worth a small fortune. "I'll do comps in the neighborhood. But, yeah, lots of developers would kill for that spot."

"Okay. Let's move fast on it."

Rick had been after the sale for years. "Why now? You dying?"

"No. Just doing what my old man should have done years ago."

XXXV

A Widow's Child

Seahaven, Massachusetts
April 1870

Abigale kept her pregnancy to herself as, with a forceful hand, she attended to the business of the farm. She hired back her most trusted farmhand. "Jason, take care to see the cows and calves on Mr. Smythe's ranch are cared for. Their owner is eager for his tenderloin steaks."

Afternoons, she stole time for herself, and her new view of the world, smiling as the green shoots of crocus poked through the hard earth, and touching delicate blooms of red and purple tulips. She walked along the beach, lifting her face to the spring sun, inhaling the salt air, counting the months.

Evenings, she sewed hats to bring to the dry goods store in town. She informed the clerk, "The first ever Easter Parade will take place in New York this year." The shop owner furrowed her brow. Abigale stammered with excitement. "Hats, ladies' hats are the rage, featured in all the fashion magazines." She emphasized, "For the very first Easter Parade."

She spread the magazines on the counter. "I've copied the most fashionable. Look," she produced three of her best creations, wide brim straw hats, with caps surrounded in tulle ribbons of pink, orchid, yellow, and blue. The ribbons were long enough to form a bow under the lady's chin. "I've decorated each hat with silk flowers in a pastel rainbow to match their ribbon." She winked at the confounded-looking clerk. "For the most daring and younger customer, willing to expose part of her face, I've tacked up one side of the wide brim and topped it with a large satin bow."

Before the clerk protested, Abigale made the sale. "I'll leave you eighteen. Just put two in the window and they'll sell."

The hats sold out of the dry goods store in days. Customers demanded more, but Abigale's supplies were diminished.

Abigale attended Easter services, surrounded by women wearing her elegant hats. Dressed in widow's black, she accepted condolences on the death of her husband, and compliments on her festive creations. She rode home basking in the praise, without a thought of George Smythe, and wondering how the townspeople would react to her news.

—❀—

By late summer, the life inside Abigale was apparent. She spent evenings sitting on her porch, rocking and singing to her baby. She spoke in gentle terms. "In time we will meet, my little one." Placing her hand on her swollen belly, she felt little hands and feet move about. She limited human contact to the farmhands and fellow worshipers at Sunday services, and hid her growing middle in generous skirts, confiding her secret to no one.

Abigale knew the novel, *The Scarlet Letter*, by heart. She often compared herself to the heroine, Hester Prynne, a strong, independent woman, living in a small Puritan town in New England. She became pregnant, although her husband was presumed lost at sea. The townspeople punished her for adultery, sentencing her to wear a scarlet A on her chest. Abigale feared the same fate. *I'm a widow,* she reasoned. *The nine months between George's death and the baby's birth will confirm he is the father.* She fretted to herself. Would the people of Seahaven suspect otherwise, shame her, brand her with a scarlet A, demand she disclose her lover?

—❀—

Abigale visited the mid-wife in town in early November. Her examination confirmed a healthy baby, approaching full term. Abigale, still dressed in widow's black, whispered to the mid-wife. "My husband died just after we conceived the child."

The mid-wife put her finger to her lips. "It's not for me to ask questions. I'm here to deliver a healthy child, I don't get involved in the gossip."

Abigale protested. "Count the months. My husband died in late March. It's been almost nine months. The child is his, a legitimate baby, not deserving scorn."

Again, the mid-wife shushed her patient. "Pay no attention to what others think or say."

"What? People are saying things about me? What are the rumors? Tell me, I must know. Am I to face a public shaming and sentenced to wear a scarlet-colored $\mathcal{A}$ on my chest?"

The mid-wife, a German immigrant in her sixties, tried to calm Abigale. "Dear mother, I've delivered every baby in this town for over thirty years. It's not for me to say, but I can guess that many are being raised by men who didn't father them. You and your baby are not alone."

Abigale became inconsolable. "George Smythe is the father. He's the only man I've been with. Mr. Ellis from Boston was a mere acquaintance, a business associate, it turns out. He's not the father, no matter what the gossip."

The mid-wife winked, and nodded. "Of course, he's not. There's no need to protest so much. Is this Mr. Ellis a married man?" She patted Abigale's great belly.

Abigale was near hysteria. "Yes, I learned of his wife when I last visited him in April. Before then, I didn't know. All he wanted of me was to sew a new dress for his wife. A red gown. How was I to know?"

"You couldn't have known, I'm sure. The cruel man manipulated you to get his way."

Abigale tearfully agreed.

"Now go home, rest. Send for me when the pains start or there is a burst of water."

An exhausted Abigale wrote in her diary that night.

George Smythe cursed me. He left part of his despicable, greedy self to grow inside me. I'm to bear a child whose parents' union was based on lies and deceit, who didn't share a speck of love between them, parents filled with evil and hate. What can I expect from this child whose mother and father plotted to kill one another, but wickedness and obstinance?

Now, just as the townspeople recognize me for the beauty I create, for my talent, they will cast me as a whore raising a shunned bastard.

I am about to lose all hope. If I could keep this child from being born, I would.

—w—

January 1871…Abigale began pacing the floor at dawn, feeling no pain, but consumed by anxiety. Her time had come and gone. The mid-wife visited earlier in the week, and after pressing her stethoscope to Abigale's great belly, assured, "Your little one is a bit reluctant to enter the world, or perhaps your dates are off." She added wood to the fading fire. "Is someone staying with you? You'll need a messenger."

"A farmhand, Jason. A good man, I've known him for years. He'll get to your house when it's time."

"I'm only two miles down the road."

The mid-wife packed her leather bag. "Have Jason bring his wife, too. Now, stop fretting. It's not good for you or the baby."

Abigale held her belly and hauled herself up from her chair. "The pain? Will there be pain?"

The mid-wife, a tall, big-boned woman, handed her a small brown bottle. "Drink this. It will encourage the baby. The pain, my dear," she lifted both hands, "it's the price we women pay for the love of a child."

—w—

The storm started with slow falling delicate flakes, melting as they drifted from the sky. Within hours, blinding sheets of wet snow blew sideways, disguising the roads, ruts, and trees as one glaring white sheet. The castor oil took effect, and by dark, the labor pains came every ten minutes. Abigale called to the farmhand sleeping in the attic. "Jason, Wake up. Go now to the mid-wife."

The man scurried from his blanket, down the ladder and out to the carriage. He returned within minutes. "Miss Abigale, it's a hell of a storm. I got the carriage from the barn, but I don't know..."

A voice even Abigale didn't recognize screamed out. "Go. To hell with the snow. Go, now."

"I won't be fetching my wife tonight. It's dangerous, but I'll do my best to get to the mid-wife."

Abigale grabbed her belly and bent forward. The voice screamed again, "Go. Now."

An hour passed before Jason and the mid-wife appeared at the door, both red faced and drenched from the blowing wet snow. Abigale, curled, clutching her legs, sat in her chair by the fire. Her face, white, and streaked with perspiration.

The mid-wife tore off her soaking hat and cloak. She pointed to a straight-back chair. "Jason, bring that here." As Jason fetched the chair, the mid-wife prepared Abigale.

"What are you doing?"

"You can't birth a baby in layers of clothes. It's not sanitary." She removed Abigale's boots and stockings, opened the dress at the top and peeled it off.

Abigale, weak and in pain, protested. "Jason."

The mid-wife tossed Abigale her shawl. "No time for modesty, dear." She pulled Abigale's bloomers off, leaving her only in a chemise, and stood her up. "Get in that chair, Jason." The bewildered farmhand sat in the straight-back chair. She ordered, "Open your legs."

The mid-wife plopped Abigale onto the chair between Jason's legs, and gave an order. "Now wrap your arms around her and don't let go."

Sitting in a chair opposite them, the mid-wife spread Abigale's legs and peered between them. "Won't be long. Where's the clean nightdress I told you to have ready?"

Abigale sat between the legs of her farmhand, struggling to cover herself with a shawl, her legs spread. "I object to all of this."

The stern mid-wife would have none of her protest. "It's not your choice. There's a child about to come out of you, and I'm going to see it's born healthy. Now where's the clean nightdress and the swaddling?"

Drained of energy and helpless, Abigale pointed to the cradle she found in the attic. She'd stripped the fabric away, replacing it with muslin, and trimmed it in white lace. "There." And then she screamed so loud, Jason let go of her.

"I told you, don't let go," shouted the mid-wife.

Jason put his hands between Abigale's swollen breasts and bulging belly and held on. Abigale cried out as she pushed her feet against the mid-wife's shoulders. The mid-wife buried her head between Abigale's thighs and demanded, "Push, bare down. I can see the head. Push with all your might."

Abigale heard the mid-wife's calls and thought about her might. She thought about her brother Caleb bribing George Smythe with land in exchange for marrying her. And her husband's stinging betrayal, killing her Kitty and trying to kill her. She thought about charming Mr. Ellis, who flirted with her as a means for his wife to have a red gown. And then she thought about the townspeople gossiping that she was an adulterer. Abigale snapped back her head, grasped Jason's sweaty hands, and wailed as she pushed with every bit of her might.

Jason's arms locked Abigale in position. He turned his head away from the sight of her half naked body and the bloody birth.

The mid-wife cut the cord and wrapped the newborn in swaddling. She cleared the baby's airways with her fingers and gave it to Abigale. "I still have business here."

Abigale uttered a cry as her uterus contracted and the placenta emerged. The mid-wife finished attending to the afterbirth. She took the child from Abigale's arms and placed it in the cradle. "Jason, you can let go, now."

A pale Jason released his trembling arms and retreated to the attic. The mid-wife washed Abigale down before dressing her in the clean white nightdress. "Go to your bed. Keep your legs up for the night."

"The baby?"

"I'll bring him to you." *Him.* Abigale thought. *A son.* When she held him and felt his warmth, a piece of her heart opened. "So tiny, helpless. You won't be like other men. I'll see to it. You won't lie and cheat and treat women like brainless idiots."

At the mid-wife's instruction, she held him to her breast. "You'll be honest and true, as a man should be. Ernest, I'll name you Ernest."

XXXVI

The Journal

Seahaven, Massachusetts
October 2019

Andrea took the lawyer's advice and opened an account on a website tracking ancestors and records of births, deaths, marriages, immigration, and military service. She had no problem locating Nelson Birch's son.

"I found Nelson Birch's son. John L. Birch. Died in France, October, nineteen forty-four."

Tom didn't wait for more. "Battle of Normandy."

"How did you know?"

"It was the turning point of the War. We attacked the Germans on the coast of Normandy in France." He hesitated. "I'm a bit of a history buff."

"I wonder why the Army didn't notify my father's mother, Rose, when John got killed."

Between hammering nails into the stairs to the loft, Tom offered a reason. "Andrea, the military would have notified John's father, Nelson, as next of kin, here in Seahaven. The reality is, maybe John and Rose," he stopped and took his hat off. Scratching his head. "This is hard to put into words. It was wartime. It's possible John and Rose only knew each other for a month, or a week." He put his hat back on. "Maybe…," he slammed a nail, "just a night."

"Hmm. You think that's why John didn't list Rose as next of kin? They hardly knew each other? Plus, he didn't know she was pregnant?"

"Could be. During wartime, people lived for the day. One of them was shipping out, risking his life for our country. Think about it, if Rose and John were close, she would have been in touch with John's family."

"True. Funny, Rose always told my dad that story about how much she and John loved each other, and that he was coming back for them."

Tom shrugged. "Whatever helps you sleep at night, I guess."

I found John's birth certificate. "Parents, Nelson and Florence Birch. They had another child, a baby in nineteen twenty-eight. Death certificate says it was stillborn. They named her Pearl."

Tom commented, "Lots of infants died at birth in those days. Wasn't uncommon."

Andrea added Nelson and his stillborn daughter to her list of relatives.

Tom stopped his work. "You're not gonna let up till that trail leads to you, are ya?"

"Why should I? I'm almost there." Andrea finished writing in the names. "According to what I can see, Abigale died in nineteen eighteen. She had a child. A son I suspect. Based on the timeline, he's the missing link between her and Nelson."

Tom looked at the list and pointed to Catherine. "All right, Miss Stubborn, I'm giving you fair warning. If you want to know about the woman who left you this house, and her mother, Iris, you better get to Father Doyle soon. He's old as dirt, may not be around too much longer."

Father Doyle agreed to meet with Andrea. An older woman led her into a room with the longest dining room table she had ever seen. "Father, you have a visitor. And I've brought your tea."

A small old man, with a rounded back, sat at the head of the table, a walker by his side. He nodded toward it. "My legs. Can't get around without it." He shifted to one side to pull a folded white handkerchief from his pants. He wiped his mouth. "I have tea at two o'clock and my nap at two-thirty every day."

Andrea hadn't seen the inside of a priests' rectory before. Father Doyle offered her a seat. He must have caught her look because he tapped the tabletop with his gnarled knuckles. "Nineteen forties. Real walnut. You don't see furniture like this at that place, you know, Bernie and Phyllis's. Now do you?"

"Certainly not." Andrea was going to agree with just about anything the old man said as long as he had information about Catherine and Iris. She tried to start the conversation, but he took over.

"Young lady, I understand you're livin' in the old Birch homestead."

Andrea sat back in her chair as the priest stirred sugar into his china cup. She tried to answer, but he continued. "This is a schedule of our Sunday Masses." He pushed the pamphlet toward her. "There's Saturday confessions listed there, too."

"Thank you, Father…" She was estimating the value of the crimson Oriental carpet beneath the dining room table.

"So, you're here to find out about Catherine, is that it?"

"Yes, Father. I inherited the house, as the last of the Birch line, but I'm trying to learn about the Birch family."

"Fair enough. I know my grand nieces and nephews are all over that thing about searching for DNA. They made me spit in a cup. Wanted to trace any long-lost relatives." He shook his head. "Foolishness."

Andrea talked fast before he interrupted again. "This isn't about DNA, Father Doyle. My father, Mason Birch, didn't have any living relatives. I'm trying to trace how I fit in to the Birch line. I know I share their DNA."

"Well, good." He tapped the table again. "Catherine."

Andrea thought perhaps the old priest was lonely and dragging this meeting out for the company. "Yes. My friend, Tom Whelan…"

"Tom. Good man. Tell him we miss him at Sunday services."

She nodded and took a deep breath. "I will, sir. Yes, Catherine Birch. Did you know her?"

The old man pointed a crooked finger. "You're lucky I kept all my marbles. I've been around here since the sixties."

She tried to get him to focus. "What can you tell me about Catherine?"

"So, you want to know about Catherine?"

The priest looked straight ahead. "I remember poor Nelson Birch. Used to visit him and his wife when she was dying."

"Yes, their son, John, was my grandfather. Killed in World War II. I found his birth and death certificates, but then I thought you'd be my best resource to learn more about the family."

"Died in the war, that's what I understand." He looked up. "You say he was your grandfather? Didn't know their boy had a child."

Andrea annunciated each word, "Yes, John went off to war. He left a woman behind who gave birth to his son, Mason. I'm Mason's daughter."

As if she had said nothing, the priest kept talking. "Folks here said Nelson stopped comin' to church after John died. The wife did, though, right up till she couldn't anymore."

This was all old news to Andrea. "Father, Catherine?"

He lifted his head from a bent neck. "Catherine Birch?"

She sat up straight. Was he about to give? "Yes, Father. What do you remember about her?"

"Nothing. I didn't know the woman. Heard of her, never met her."

Andrea sputtered, "But, I thought…"

"The woman was a recluse. Can't remember her ever comin' out of that house, except maybe once, and then when they took her away."

There was a gentle knock at the door. "That's my housekeeper reminding me it's time for my nap."

The priest got up and pushed his walker over to a bookcase. "I knew Catherine's mother, Iris, well. Nelson's sister."

"Nelson's sister." Andrea leapt from her seat. *Now we are getting somewhere.*

He pulled a leather-bound book from the shelf and looked at the spine. "This is it. Birch. Nineteen seventy-eight to nineteen ninety-two."

Andrea suppressed the urge to exclaim 'holy shit' out loud. She moved toward the priest, taking the book from his trembling hands. "We had many conversations about her life." He tapped his forehead. "I just can't remember them anymore."

Andrea held the dusty book against her chest. She hesitated but asked anyway. "Father, are your notes confidential?"

He took one hand off his walker and waved. "No, no. These are notes I made to help me remember. There were so many women coming to talk back then. It's confession that's sacred. These are just conversations."

Andrea wanted to jump up and down but contained her excitement. "Thank you, Father."

He snapped his walker around toward the door. "I'm off for my nap. You'll find what you want there."

Andrea called out, "Father?"

"What's say?"

"Iris and Nelson's father. Who was he?"

The priest looked forward as if the answer were written on the wall. "Before my time."

He turned and, looking impish, winked at Andrea. "See you Sunday."

Birch Family

Edmund
1774–1830
Margaret
1776–1832

Samuel Birch   Roger Birch
1796–1858   1798–1841

Caleb Birch   Abigale Birch
1826–1868   1843–1918

Nelson Birch   Iris Birch
1901–1979   1903–1992

John Birch   Pearl Birch   Catherine Birch
1926–1944   1928–1928   1918–2013

Mason Birch
1944–2014

Andrea Birch
1984–

XXXVII

Meeting Iris

Andrea settled into her chair, a glass of wine by her side, and called Liz. "You don't return calls, now?"

"Sorry, darling. If I don't write things down these days, I forget. Too much on my mind, I guess."

"You okay? Is it work?"

"Work, people, politics, the world. You know how it is. Enough about me."

"I'm sipping Pinot. You?"

"Not tonight, sweets. Talk to me. I miss your voice."

"Well, the good news is the loft is coming along. I mean, your private quarters are almost ready for your visit."

"Lovely. What do you think? An autumn visit? After the tourists?"

"Perfect. I'm holding you to it. We'll sit on the porch and reminisce like two old ladies."

"One old lady and one hot chick. Any new men in your life? Come on. You know I live vicariously through your romances."

There'd been no work from Liz for several months, but Andrea didn't bring it up, assuming business wasn't good. "One romance. And that's long over. Nope. Spending my time doing a little painting, searching ancestors, finishing the house."

Liz rushed Andrea off the phone. "Well, darling, thanks for the call. Kisses to you."

"Okay, I'll let you go. Love you."

———m———

Satisfied she reached Liz after two unreturned calls, Andrea settled into her chair and opened Father Doyle's journal. He wrote in distinctive, precise handwriting, perfectly punctuated, and marked with the day and date of each visit. Andrea raised her glass to him. "You may be losing it at eighty-six, but you had it together back in the seventies. I'll give you that, Father Doyle."

Monday, May 1, 1978
    Reached out to Iris Birch today at the May Day Celebration. She declined my invitation for tea. I understand from some older parishioners, she disappeared from town when she was a girl.

Monday, January 1, 1979
    Iris Birch was at Mass this morning. From what I hear, she is living with her brother, Nelson, who does not attend church. I'll plan a visit to the house when weather permits.

Tuesday, May 1, 1979
    Visited the Birch home today in the afternoon. Nelson Birch is feeble at eighty years old. His sister, Iris, a small, fragile woman, looks to be younger. Both appeared to need a good meal. I offered them confession and Holy Communion, but they declined. The house was tidy.

Thursday, July 12, 1979

Word came today, Nelson Birch died. They put him in the ground by the time I heard. I visited his grave and said prayers for the dead.

Wednesday, August 1, 1979

Visited Iris Birch today to extend my condolences on the death of her brother. I found her to be quite withdrawn, probably mourning the loss of Nelson. I invited her to join me at the rectory for tea whenever she felt ready.

Saturday, December 29, 1979

Doctor Fields let me know he's treating Iris Birch for pleurisy.

Sunday, January 20, 1980

Doc Fields assured me it was safe to visit Iris. I found her sitting up and looking well. She promised to come for tea in the spring. I thought it best not to press her to say her confession or come to Mass.

Andrea got another glass of wine, thinking this was boring reading compared to Abigale's murderous tales. She read on to find out how Nelson and Iris were related to Abigale.

Monday, May 5, 1980

Iris Birch visited the rectory today. She looked quite healthy compared to her appearance in January as she recovered from pleurisy.

She spoke in a childlike voice, informing me she did not intend to confess her sins, but to clarify if she had sinned at all. That was an interesting distinction, not one I'd been asked to make before.

She started by telling me a man forced himself on her and she gave birth to a child out of wedlock.

I explained that even if she consented to relations with the man, with confession and absolution, God would forgive her. She became defensive, interpreting I suggested she gave consent to the man.

I changed my approach, fearing I alienated her, and stated I was sure God is pleased that she gave one of His children life.

Ms. Birch seemed satisfied with my reply and bid me good day. I wanted to ask about the child who I assume is an adult, given Ms. Birch is in her later seventies, but reserved the question for another visit, should there be one.

It was almost midnight. Andrea spoke out loud to herself as she set the journal aside. "Geeze, murder, rape… what other secrets do the Birches have?"

XXXVIII

Finding Ernest

Andrea put aside Father Doyle's journals and went back to Abigale's diaries. She wanted to learn about her child, the connection to her grandfather and father.

January 25, 1871

The birth of my son was a harrowing experience. The pains stabbed like a dozen swords piercing my body all at once. Heat ignited me from within. I was sure all my innards would soon expel themselves from my body. And I didn't care.

It is a mystery to me that women have a second child. I suspect their uncaring husbands don't control their urges and force the act upon them.

I lost all hope of dignity when the German general, claiming to be a mid-wife, tore off my clothes, exposing my naked body to the farmhand, and forcing me into his lap. Such humiliation. Bloomers and stockings thrown about, my hair loose and drenched with perspiration, me hurling curse words, condemning God, with my legs sprawled apart. Jason will never see me the same.

If I had my way, today I'd be keeping company with Mr. Ellis, but, to my deep disappointment, the wretched man has a wife. I'm blessed that George Smythe met an early death. If ever I imagined a husband for myself, which I did not, he would not have been it.

The infant, Ernest, is learning the virtue of patience. I am raising him to be a man who respects women and treats all people with dignity and honesty.

He is showing signs of strong intelligence. It took several weeks, but after letting him cry between feedings, which I offer every three hours during the day, and every six hours at night, he now waits in silence, without even a coo. The child is not much of a bother, except that he does linger at my breast, which I allow on occasion. It's too cold to put him out, so I move his cradle to the south window for afternoon sun.

January 31, 1871
    The German general came by to check on my recovery. I didn't let her in the house for fear she'd tear my legs apart and examine my most private part.

Andrea put her flip chart up on to her easel. She added Ernest as Abigale's son, and father of Nelson and Iris.

Birch Family

Edmund
1774–1830
Margaret
1776–1832

Samuel Birch
1796–1858

Roger Birch
1798–1841

Caleb Birch
1826–1868

Abigale Birch
1843–1918

Ernest Birch
1871–

Nelson Birch
1901–1979

Iris Birch
1903–1992

John Birch
1926–1944

Pearl Birch
1928–1928

Catherine Birch
1918–2013

Mason Birch
1944–2014

Andrea Birch
1984–

XXXIX

Like Mother Like Son

Seahaven, Massachusetts
October 1873

Abigale Birch searched her son's face, looking for resemblances to George Smythe. She didn't find any, nor did she find similarities in their personalities. Instead, she thought of Ernest as she thought of herself, kind and honest, gentle, not scheming and crude. She devoted every living moment to grooming him and sheltering him from the evils of the world.

Abigale poured heated water into the metal tub. "You must bathe often, Ernest. Cleanliness is a sign of refinement, purity, and virtue. Now sit for your bath and scrub until your skin shines like pure white fine porcelain."

At nearly three years old, Ernest complied and scrubbed his skin raw.

"Isn't it warm here by the fire? Mother would never let you get a chill."

Ernest offered a compliant smile.

The mother and son existed as companions. Abigale consulted Ernest on every decision, despite his young age. "Shall we have chicken stew for dinner?" "Would you like to take a walk on the beach?" "It's our bedtime. Are you ready?"

She read to him from Aesop's Fables and offered her own interpretation. "In the story of *The Ass in the Lion's Skin*, we learn the Ass revealed his true self to the fox when he brayed." She'd shake her finger at Ernest. "If the Ass stayed silent, he would not have been discovered. What does that teach you, Ernest?"

Ernest learned the answer after hearing the story over and over. "We shouldn't speak to other people, Mama. Just to ourselves. You and me."

—⁂—

Demand for hand-sewn clothing and hats diminished with the invention of the industrial sewing machine and assembly lines. Clothes were mass-produced and sold ready to wear. Even the women from Seahaven made trips to Boston department stores or ordered through catalogues. Abigale no longer sewed hats for sale in Seahaven or Boston. Instead, she took in clothes for alterations, and when requested, created a special occasion dress. She hand-sewed all of Ernest's clothes.

At eight years old, he raised his first protest against his mother. "I refuse to return to school tomorrow. The others call me names."

This was an offense to Abigale. "Don't be foolish, Ernest. You're the only boy, or girl, for that matter, who has clothes styled from the latest New York fashion magazines. Kilt suits are the height of fashion in England and France."

"No, Mother. I'm the only boy or girl who looks the fool. Seahaven is not England or France. You must allow me to dress like the others."

Ernest tore off his kilt and shirt. He found the burgundy velvet suit Abigale made him for church. "And I'm burning this."

It was their first contest. Determined to make it one of few, she pulled her apron to her face. "I've tried so hard, for you, Ernest. My hands bleed from sewing for others so I can make us money to live on. And you reject my work." She sobbed and wept.

The last of the velvet suit and kilts burned in the hearth. Ernest wrapped his arms around his mother's waist. "Forgive me, Mother. Please don't cry."

"You know we only have each other, son."

Ernest tried to hold on to his mother, but she stepped back. "You can't love me and hurt me at the same time."

Now Ernest cried. "Mother, please. Hold me."

Abigale walked to the hearth and poked the fire. Velvet embers escaped into the air. "This is the thanks I get from you who I've sacrificed everything for."

Ernest dropped like a puddle to the floor. "What shall I do, Mother?"

Abigale won the battle and now took her prisoner. "We shouldn't argue, ever. What would you do without me?"

The puddle spilled onto the floor, arms and legs out. "Don't leave me, Mother."

Satisfied she made her point, Abigale lifted her son. "You may wear the tasteless clothes the poor commoners wear. I'll concede to that."

Ernest's sobs slowed.

"But I will make them myself. No store-bought clothes."

Later that evening, Abigale sat in the soaking tub in her room and called out. "Ernest, another pitcher of hot water, please." The boy brought the water. "Now, pour gently, and wash my back."

Ernest proved to be a talented student. At age eleven he was tall, with thick blonde hair and brown eyes. A normally shy boy, he made friends with several others. "Mother, may I play with the boys after school today?"

Abigale offered excuses for requiring Ernest to return home after school for several weeks. When he asked for the fourth time, she relented. "I don't know those boys, but I've heard they are trouble. Be home before dark and don't do anything you wouldn't do if I were watching."

A delighted Ernest played for two hours and hurried home around dusk. His mother didn't reply when he called out. He searched the house, and as darkness fell, walked the property, discovering her in the barn lying helpless after tripping on a bucket.

"Mother…"

"I fell. Been laying her for two hours. The bucket…"

Ernest last used the bucket to milk the cow. "I put it away, I swear."

"It's all right. Just help me to the house, son. Did you enjoy playing with your friends?"

Abigale made an entry in her diary that night.

XL

Making Acquaintances

Seahaven, Massachusetts
October 2019

Andrea searched the diaries for entries about Ernest, finding Abigale became more obsessed with controlling her son.

January 1882

At eleven years old, Ernest is showing signs of independence. I fear he will leave me. The world is cruel and cold and unforgiving. I won't let liars and frauds hurt him. He will soon learn that his place is here. Schoolboys are not true family. A mother is.

I reminded my son that despite several opportunities to marry, I chose to devote my life to him. He was very grateful when I reminded him a husband would cause me to spend less time with him. After my fall in the barn, we both felt it safer if I schooled him at home.

April 1885

Ernest and I finished his homeschooling today. The days together, reading, and learning about world history, brought us closer than even mother and son. Because he showed an interest and a talent, I taught him to sew, and he is quite good.

July 1886

Ernest is a genuine reflection of me. Except for his golden hair, he shares my fine features and slight frame. He has grown to his full height of five feet, ten inches. A quite handsome man to keep company with. No husband could have given me such satisfaction and fulfillment.

We discussed his future today. He agreed, for now, he is content here. He is experimenting with creating rudimentary patterns for his own clothing.

January 1890

We rarely see other people. The summers are busy with keeping up the house and barn, and winters, too cold to venture out, except for church. I expect there will come a day when Ernest will want to take a wife. I have a few women from church in mind. I prefer someone shy, not inclined to an opinion, and certainly not one who is critical of my son or me. Only a woman who meets our specifications will share our home.

May 1894

Ernest is corresponding with several New York based pattern companies. They are impressed with his talent. McCall's, in particular, expressed an interest in seeing his men's designs as they are planning to branch out from exclusively women's wear.

September 1896

We entertained several ladies from church for tea. They understand the fortunate woman who Ernest chooses to marry will reside here on the farm with us. The one both Ernest and I pursued declined an invitation for dinner. It quite surprised me as she seemed shy and compliant, an excellent choice. I've learned modern women don't take to living with their mother-in-law. One other acknowledged a willingness to hear more about our arrangement, however, I told Ernest she was too anxious and probably not trustworthy. He concurred.

September 1898

Unknown to me, he sent several of his designs to McCall's. They are trying to influence him to move to Boston and take a position as a pattern maker for their new line of clothing. Ernest accepted an invitation to travel to Boston to meet with a representative from McCall's of New York.

I declined his invitation to go along, instead disclosing my fears of becoming blind as my eyesight fails me. I confided my angst at losing the ability to read and sew, my only pleasures, except for his company. After a short discussion, he agreed to rethink his Boston trip.

November 1899

I can't hold him off any longer. McCall's has been relentless in their seduction of my son. He agreed to meet with a New York hustler on Friday in Boston. I disappointed him, refusing to accompany him on the trip.

Andrea sat surrounded by a pile of old diaries. She thought, *Wow, that Abigale was some piece of work, manipulating and controlling poor Ernest from the time he was born. He's almost thirty, and she's still holding him back. There's nothing but trouble for any wife he takes.*

XLI

Art Works

"Andrea, come here, you gotta see this."

Andrea put her paint brush down and rushed to the ladder. Tom never raised his voice and rarely called her by name.

"What's up, no pun intended."

Tom called down from the sweltering second story. "Very funny. Now come up here."

Andrea muttered as she climbed to the oppressive second floor. "I cleared everything out, so don't you be complaining I left a sewing machine or trunk behind."

She stopped at the top to see Tom standing at the back wall. "I was using a strong cleaning solution, my own recipe, to clean this wall. Figured I'd keep the original wood."

"What the...?"

"Another artist in the family."

They gawked at the wall covered in one large painting.

"That must have taken years."

Tom moved the construction lamp up and down and back and forth. "Looks like painting runs in the Birch family."

"The more I look, the more I see." Andrea pointed to the left side of the mural. "There's the family cemetery, set on a hill, facing the ocean. Amazing."

"And look here." Tom shined the light on the highest part of the wall. "People. Probably portraits of the Birch family. My God. Who do you think did this?"

"Is there a signature anywhere?"

"Haven't got that far. My suggestion is, if you want to keep the house original, we don't cover this up."

"Of course not. It's a work of art, more than that, it's family history. There's a story in here, somewhere."

"I thought you'd be interested. I'll finish cleaning it up. Once we have power up here, we'll get a better look."

"Let me know if you find any initials or a signature."

"Sure thing. Thought this would make your day."

Andrea backed down the ladder. "Sure did." She added. "I'm going out to the barn to see if there are any paintings buried under all the junk I hauled out of that attic."

A phone call distracted her. "Ms. Birch, this is Jonathan Hall, from Seahaven Gallery."

Andrea did a little dance, a shuffle ball change, the only step she remembered from seventh grade tap lessons. "Hello, Mr. Hall. What can I do for you?"

"A gentleman expressed interest in one of your paintings, the seascape, as I live and breathe."

Now she was twirling. "How lovely."

"Yes, lovely. In any event, he's made an offer of thirteen hundred dollars."

"Our full price."

"There is one contingency."

"Contingency?"

He cleared his throat. "He wants to meet the artist."

Andrea stopped her silent celebration dance. "Is that unusual, Mr. Hall?"

He replied after a moment of silence. "Let's just say, it's not usual."

"What do you suggest?"

"We artists must be prepared to be in the public eye if we want to sell. Ms. Birch, look at it this way. If you had a showing you'd meet all the guests. If you had a magazine spread, readers would meet you through print."

Mr. Hall challenged Andrea's patience. "So, Mr. Hall, you're suggesting I agree to meet with this person? Is it a man or woman, by the way?"

"A man."

"Will you be there?"

"Yes, Ms. Birch, I will be here at the gallery and you'll meet him in front of your painting."

"Well, it sounds safe enough. Will you set up the meeting?"

"The gentleman suggested a week from Thursday when he'll be back in the area. Four in the afternoon."

Andrea hesitated, "I'll be there. Thank you."

—⁂—

The thrill of selling one of her paintings sent Andrea back to her latest piece, rows of the purple and pink Hydrangeas and the crushed clam shell road leading to her home.

That evening she wrestled with her choices of reading more about Abigale and her son Ernest, or Father Doyle's notes about the intriguing life of Iris Birch. She chose Iris.

Sunday, August 10, 1980

Iris Birch stopped by today after Mass. The extreme heat seemed to bother her, as she removed her hat and used it to fan herself through our visit.

She mentioned her discomfort confiding in a man. I'm assuming she meant me. I assured her I listened as a trained counselor, not as a man, and she is in control of the information she shares.

She asked me if intending to blackmail a person is a sin. I told her I'd need more context to render an opinion. I quote, "I went to his house intending to demand money to support myself and my baby."

I waited.

"A child of fifteen, myself, and four months with child."

I repeated her last words, "... a child of fifteen."

"Yes. I needed money. I was put out."

Iris told me, although she intended to demand money from the father of the child she was carrying, his wife answered the door.

"She thought I was replying to her ad for a nanny. She was so welcoming."

The woman served Iris tea, and after it was clear Iris and her child were well suited, hired her.

"I didn't mention I was carrying her husband's baby."

The afternoon heat was affecting me as well, or perhaps it was hearing the hardships this poor woman suffered but, feeling exhausted, I ended our visit.

Andrea thumbed through the journal for references to Ernest.

XLII

A Tale Of Two Women

Seahaven, Massachusetts
September 1900

Abigale was not happy when Ernest accepted the position with McCall's. "What do you mean, you'll be sleeping in your office?"

"It's a new venture, Mother. McCall's isn't paying me enough to rent a room. Boston is expensive."

"Which is why you shouldn't be taking this job. What's wrong with home?"

"I'll be home every weekend. I'll read to you then and help with the chores. Please, Mother."

Abigale relented rather than lose. "I suppose you need to at least try if this is what you want. You'll know when it's time to give up and come home for good."

—⁓—

Ernest worked hard for his New York boss, Ryan Taylor, and brought tales of his accomplishments home to his mother every Friday night. "Ryan's a Scottish chap. Lovely man. Very smart. Quite charming, as well."

"Listen to you. Been in Boston a few weeks, and you're using words like chap and lovely. Don't let charm fool you, Ernest. I didn't bring you up to be taken in by a fast-talking New York swindler."

He started to protest but stopped. "I'll be cautious, Mother. You could be right."

Ernest stopped describing his adventures in Boston. He didn't tell his mother about the bars he drank in, or the restaurants where he ate his supper. He kept his infatuation with an alluring blonde beauty who worked in his office to himself.

The two dined together each night and soon Ernest took to sleeping in her rented room. After a few months, he invited her home to Seahaven to meet his mother.

Abigale dashed that plan. "... a floozy from Boston?"

Ernest argued. "Mother, you are being unfair. Alice is a wonderful woman."

"Older than you, I understand."

"I never should have told you about her."

"And married before. Really, Ernest. Of all the eligible women..."

As it had many times before, Abigale's disappointment in her son reduced him to a puddle on the floor. "Stop, Mother."

"Get up. Be a man, not a foolish boy. Give up the woman or give me up."

Ernest didn't give up Alice. He gave up telling his mother about her, and split his time, staying in Boston on alternate weekends, claiming his boss, Ryan, was coming in from New York for a meeting. He and Alice spent every night together. Their relationship grew to mirror Ernest's relationship with his mother. She, controlling and manipulative, he, compliant and malleable.

A year into their relationship, Alice announced she was pregnant. Ernest offered to marry her and make their child legitimate. He embraced the idea of a family. "I'll move you and the baby to Seahaven with my mother. Boston is no place the raise a child."

Alice flexed her muscle. "I'd rather be a single, scorned woman than live with your mother. She hates the notion of me. Tell Ryan Taylor it's time he promoted you to take charge of the Boston office. He's been stringing you along for over a year now."

"I will, dear, but first, let's take the rail to Seahaven this weekend and surprise Mother with the news."

The bride-to-be had a quick answer. "You take the rail, and you tell your Mother. I won't deal with her wrath."

"Of course, dear. It won't be hard to convince Mother we are better off living in Boston, at least for the time being."

"Forever. And Ernest, before you go, we'll get married."

—⁂—

It was the first time his mother hit him. "Idiot," she screamed as her hand cracked the side of his face.

Abigale struggled to catch her breath. She clutched her chest and stumbled to her chair. "Fool. Stupid fool." Anger burst from her. "Stupid, stupid fool."

Ernest stood stone straight as his mother railed on. "She's pushing a child on you. What are the chances it's yours? She's a tramp." She inhaled deeply and exhaled. "You've ruined my life."

Abigale went to her bedroom and slammed the door. Ernest spent the night in a chair. If his mother came out of the room, he'd be there.

When morning came, Abigale emerged, contained and calm, her arms crossed over her chest. "You'll marry the woman and she and the child will live here with me. You'll stay in Boston, except for weekends."

Ernest tugged at his crumpled clothes and pushed the hair from his face. He cleared his throat. "I married her, Mother. I thought it best, given her condition… with child."

Abigale's jaw tightened and her fist curled. "Bring the slut here. She can give birth in this house where you were born." She stopped and, for the first time, looked at her son. "That's my final word, Ernest."

Ernest breathed a sigh. "That shouldn't be a problem, Mother. Alice is fond of you and I'm sure she'll appreciate the slow pace of Cape Cod, rather than the busyness of the city."

—⁂—

Ernest returned to Boston and his new wife. "Mother rejoiced at the news of our marriage and, of course, the baby."

"So, it went well, better than you expected?"

"Perfectly."

"Any talk about us moving to Cape Cod?"

Ernest embraced his wife. "Never mentioned it, dear. I'm sure she'll welcome an occasional visit. She sends her love and congratulations on our marriage."

XLIII

The Prince

Seahaven, Massachusetts
October 2019

Andrea checked in with Liz the night before her meeting with the gentle-man interested in her painting. "I hope he's not a serial killer."

"The famous Cape Cod Serial Killer? Darling, they caught him years ago."

Andrea shouted into the phone. "What? There was a serial killer on the Cape?"

"You are so easy. Serial killers don't drive to the Cape, too much traffic."

Andrea heard congestion in her friend's cough. "Liz, that doesn't sound good. You got a cold?"

"Oh, just the tail end of one."

"Anyway, I'm picturing an old bent over skinny guy, hairless, of course."

Liz came back with her own idea. "Perhaps a troll who crawled out from under the bridge."

Andrea stopped the fun. "Enough. As it is, I see ghosts lingering here at night; I don't want to dream of an ugly, short, stubby guy with pointed hair."

"Naked. Trolls don't wear clothes."

"Stop it. How am I gonna sleep now?"

"Just having fun, darling. You'll be fine. The gallery owner will be there, right?"

"Yes, as if he isn't creepy enough."

"Listen, girl. You need to calm down. You've walked into rooms and made killer presentations before twenty men stuffed in three-thousand-dollar suits. This is a cake-walk."

"You're right. I'm a little rusty, that's all. Too much time in this house reading old diaries and going through thirty-five-year-old notes made by an ancient priest."

"Sounds riveting."

"It's interesting. From what I can figure out, Abigale's son, Ernest, had two children. One of them, Iris, ran away when she was just fifteen. Pregnant."

"And who is Abigale?"

"Edmund's granddaughter."

"Who's Edmund? Never mind. I've got my hands over my ears. Too much information for me. Now I'm convinced, you desperately need to get out."

"Chances are slim to none I'll meet my Prince Charming tomorrow. At least we got a few chuckles over the whole thing."

"Darling, if he's a troll and offers to buy you dinner, order the filet mignon."

"We'll see."

"Time for me to hang up. Just one thing, any word from your ex, Will? What's he up to?"

Andrea's neck muscles tensed. "Funny you should ask. I was thinking about him just the other day. I don't know what he's up to."

Andrea didn't know Will had a team of four, filling fraudulent prescriptions, and cleared thousands of dollars a week for himself or that he gambled most of it away and was two hundred thousand dollars in gambling debt.

Andrea questioned herself as she dressed that morning, wondering why there was so much anxiety attached to meeting a person who liked her painting enough to buy it.

She stood in front of the full-length mirror in her bedroom, inspecting herself from head to toe. Her hair was a beautiful shade of blonde, cut to her chin. Her makeup, subtle enough to bring out her hazel eyes. She chose a navy-blue linen, belted shirtwaist dress, and gave herself an extra spritz of her favorite cologne.

Andrea strolled into the gallery, looking her best. The owner was nowhere in sight. A handsome older gentleman, stood in front of her seascape painting. He turned as she walked toward him.

"Andrea Birch, I presume." He reached out for her hand.

Andrea fumbled, moving her purse from her left to her right hand, and accepted his gesture. She spoke, hearing the tremble in her own voice. "Yes, and you are?"

"Brian Evans. I thought Jonathan would have mentioned my name when he set up this meeting."

Jonathan Hall appeared. "I apologize. I didn't know I was at liberty."

"Not a problem, we all know each other's names now, don't we?"

Andrea thought about the conversation with Liz the night before. *Who is Brian Evans, troll, serial killer, Prince Charming?*

Brian got right down to business. "Pardon the cliché, Andrea, but your painting spoke to me."

Andrea waited, suppressing a smile.

"I spent every summer of my childhood in Seahaven at my great aunt's cottage. The view was so much like your painting."

"Actually, it's the view from a house in Maine where I vacationed once. I took pictures so I could paint it."

As Brian Evans spoke, Andrea assessed him. She decided he was in his early fifties, fit, tanned, and, by the way he carried himself, probably wealthy.

"So, Andrea, what do you say?"

"Excuse me?"

"Will you sell me the painting? I promise to give it the home it deserves."

"Of course," she hesitated. "Brian. I'm flattered."

"Do you have other paintings here?"

Andrea turned to look for Mr. Hall, who disappeared again. "Yes, over there." She pointed across the gallery. Brian put his hand on Andrea's back and ushered her toward the cemetery painting.

"Acrylics?"

"Yes, it's my first. I've been faithful to watercolor until now." Before she mentioned her tree of life painting, he interrupted.

"Fascinating."

Andrea inhaled his cologne. His hair looked professionally coiffed. He wore what appeared to be an expensive, fitted blazer. "I'm glad you think so." She wondered if he was sizing her up.

The gallery owner returned to the showroom, wrapping the painting with paper, and securing it with twine. "This is all set for you, Mr. Evans."

"Well, Andrea. Again, I thank you for the artwork. It will forever remind me of my Cape Cod summers."

Andrea turned up the charm, extending her hand. "It is my pleasure, Brian." She walked toward the gallery's exit, thinking, *how cute is he? Ask me out, ask me out.*

Just like in the movies, she heard, "Andrea?" and turned.

"Do you teach?"

"What?"

He repeated, "Teach. Do you give art lessons?" His voice dropped to a humble tone. "I'm a wannabe painter."

She tried to be coy. "I could, for the right student."

Brian clapped his hands as he walked to her at the gallery's exit. "Give me your number."

Andrea settled in her chair with her glass of Cabernet and called Liz that night. "Did I wake you?"

A groggy voice replied. "No, darling, just napping on the sofa."

"He's a prince."

"Wonderful. Who are we talking about?" Liz sat up and grabbed her martini. "Ugh, the ice melted. Let me get another drink."

"Liz, the guy buying my painting, remember? We laughed last night that he might be a troll."

"Yes, of course, sweetie."

Andrea heard ice clink. "Adorable. He is adorable. Handsome, older, smells divine."

"Okay, I'm awake now. Did he ask you out, or at least take your number?"

Andrea took a sip. "I think so. Well, sort of."

"Tell me everything. I'll interpret."

"Yes, my relationship consultant, tell me what you make of him asking me for painting lessons?"

"Code for a roll in the hay, I'd say."

"Roll in the hay? How old are you?"

Liz snapped back. "None of your business. Anyway, roll in the hay is ageless, universal. He wants to bed you, dear."

Andrea sat in her stuffed chair, diaries and the priest's journal piled on the floor. "Liz, to be truthful, I need the distraction. My mind is getting as dusty as these old books I'm going through every night."

"Then have him. He's yours for the taking."

"You sound tired and hoarse. How's that cold?"

Liz cleared her throat. "Darling, hearing from you is the best medicine for me. I want every detail of the bedroom goings on."

"Liz, never."

"Okay. Just a broad brush, for an old lady."

"Maybe. But first, he has to call me and worst of all, I have to give him painting lessons, and my only experience teaching is with children."

"Darling, it's not art lessons he's after. Good night. Love you."

XLIV

Gram Abigale

Seahaven, Massachusetts
November 2019

A week passed. Andrea's only company was Tom, by day, working at a snail's pace on the loft, and by night, Abigale's diaries and Father Doyle's notes on Iris Birch. With nothing to report, she didn't call Liz, instead choosing a glass of Barolo, an expensive red, reserved for special occasions, and Abigale's telling of Ernest's marriage. The entries were clear, Abigale simmered with anger.

1903

It gets dark early now in winter. The hands stack wood in the fireplace and get a good blaze going for the night. If Ernest cared, he'd be here, seeing to it the mother who sacrificed her life for him, was warm and safe. It's the harlot holding him back.

I knew he was too naïve for the world, in just months, seduced by a whore eager to spread her legs to secure her financial future.

My fingers are painful gnarls from years of sewing, my eyesight, that helps me escape into other worlds, dimmed. It's the rare book I can read under the best light.

Ernest salves his conscience, sending money each month, but I long for his company. The wretched pig of a wife further shackled him, giving birth to another child. Knowing her proclivity for promiscuity, I tried to remain unattached to her children, Nelson and the infant, Iris.

Ernest confided regretting the marriage. Alice keeps a tight rein, limiting visits to his own mother. When she allows him, she saddles him with the children. Nelson is not tall like his father and bears no resemblance to the Birch family. The infant, Iris, has light eyes, unlike my own. I confess, she does have a certain charm that draws me to her. More than anything, I treasure the evenings Ernest and I spend together.

XLV

A Date With The Prince

After two weeks, Andrea went about her business pretending she didn't care if Brian Evans called. She walked the property every day, taking in the autumn colors, planning to incorporate them in her next painting. The new and used furniture she selected was in place, and the kitchen almost complete.

Tom took the last sip of his morning coffee. "Once I put on the baseboard, I'm done."

"When are you going to give me a bill? I haven't seen one for three months."

"I leave you invoices for materials."

"I'm talking about you. I must owe you a load of money by now."

Tom waved her off. "This is fun. Keeps me out of trouble."

Andrea lifted a green and yellow plate from a box. "You need to bill me."

Tom took a step back. "Whatcha got there?"

"My dinner set. The boxes arrived yesterday." She unwrapped a bowl. "You like?"

Tom looked from the yellow bowl to Andrea. "What's that painted on it, blueberries? For God's sakes."

Andrea stood, her feet surrounded by crumpled packing paper, and stacked blue, green, and yellow stoneware into the dishwasher. "The pattern is Farmhouse." She examined a dinner plate. "Perfect. Can't wait to have a dinner party."

Tom mumbled something about fancy dishes and headed for the loft. "I'll call the landscapers to clean up all them leaves in the front of the house. Your weeds need cuttin' back, too, before they take over the house."

Andrea was about to shout a thank you when her cell phone rang. She didn't recognize the number and answered, expecting a Robo call. Instead, she heard the deeply masculine voice of Brian Evans. Her stomach fluttered.

"Am I speaking to Andrea, the famous artiste?"

She conjured her witty side. "It depends on who's calling."

Brian dropped the pretense. "You got me. How have you been? Are you painting?"

Andrea flopped into her chair and threw her legs over the arm. "I'm just fine. And am I painting? I'm always either imagining a piece or painting one." She stopped. "More imagining than painting, lately."

"A creative mind never rests."

Andrea didn't know if she could match this guy's enthusiasm. "What have you been up to?"

"Oh, the usual. Living my dull life. But I am excited about starting lessons. Are we still on?"

"Brian, let me explain. I've never taught adults. Just kids."

He changed his tone. "Listen, Andrea, I understand. Let's make this an adventure for both of us. Painting lessons for me, teaching a hopeless, no talent for you. Consider me a kid."

He made it easy for her. "Sure. I'm game. Fixing up an old house hasn't tested me enough."

"Perfect. I'm on the Cape every other Wednesday and Thursday. Can you squeeze me in on a Wednesday afternoon?"

She wanted to ask him where he was the rest of the time, but it wasn't her business. "Okay, sounds good."

"Is next Wednesday good for you? I want to paint the ocean from atop the hill, like you did."

A red flag went up in Andrea's mind when Brian mentioned coming to her property. "I guess that would be okay. I don't know how much daylight we'll have at four."

"Let's try. Text me your address. I'll see you at four on Wednesday. You take care."

It all happened so fast, she heard herself say. "Sure," before they ended the call.

She dialed Liz. "I may have made a date with the Cape Cod serial killer."

"Shut up."

"No, really. This guy, Brian, just rushed me into agreeing to teach him to paint, but he plans on coming to my house and then up to the cemetery."

"Oh, dear. That sounds homicidal."

"Liz, come on. I don't know him. Wait, I'll Google him and see what I find."

"Listen, Andrea. You're a big girl. Call him back and tell him the plans don't work for you. You'll meet him on the beach out in public."

"I could. I'm Googling as we speak. Wait, Brian Evans. Whew, he's a podiatrist. It says on his website he works on the South Shore and Cape Cod and the Islands."

"So there. What's he gonna do, whip out his nail clipper and slash you?"

"Or maybe he'll saw me in half with his emery board."

The two women howled. Liz gathered herself. "One more, one more. Maybe he wants you to sell your soul to him, get it, sole? Wait, wait, he's gonna want you to toe the line."

By now, Tom was down from the loft, standing with his hands on his hips, facing Andrea. She was wiping tears from her eyes and trying to compose herself. "Gotta go, Liz. Someone's staring at me."

"Get a pedicure before Wednesday, he's into feet." Liz shouted into the phone before hanging up.

"I could hear you cackling from upstairs. Are you finally losin' it?"

Andrea got up from her chair and went into the kitchen to clean up the boxes and packing paper. "No, no. Just having fun. God, I needed that laugh."

Energized by the prospect of meeting Brian again, Andrea spent the rest of the day stacking the linen closet with her new towels, arranging and re-arranging her living room furniture, and hanging artifacts she found in the barn on the walls. She placed a soapstone foot warmer against the hearth, sure one of her ancestors warmed their feet by it.

Tom stood in the bathroom's doorway. "What in the heck are you doin'?"

Andrea placed three antique apothecary bottles, cobalt blue, amber, and green on a shelf in her bathroom. "In homage to my ex-husband, the pharmacist. I found them in the barn and cleaned them up."

Tom shook his head. "I don't know. I really don't. And you put them old bowls in the sideboard?"

"Those old bowls, my friend, are from the nineteen thirties. Yellow Ware. Those and the Spongeware mixing bowl are another find from the barn."

She stood back. "There. Lots of progress made today."

Tom packed up. "To each his own, I guess."

"Wait. Check out my bedroom." The week before, she hung two hats over her bed. She'd found them wrapped in tissue paper in a trunk. One, a wide-brim straw hat with green satin ribbon and purple and white silk flowers; the second, also straw, but ivory and decorated with blue ostrich feathers and black lace. In between them she placed four ornate hat pins she mounted on a scrap of aged lace and framed.

Tom peeked in. "Like I said, not my taste. Hats are for wearing, not hanging on a wall. But, whatever."

—⚬—

Andrea turned in early, abandoning her ritual of reading Abigale's diaries or Father Doyle's journal about Abigale's granddaughter, Iris. Instead, she drifted off to sleep planning her outfit for the following Wednesday.

XLVI

All About Iris

Even as a small child, I worried about my parents' marriage. Father and Mother were either arguing or not speaking to each other. We lived in Boston, but most every weekend, Father brought me and my brother, Nelson, by train to visit his mother on Cape Cod. At first, I felt unsure about Gram Abigale, that's what she told us to call her. I remember her being distant to me and Nelson, but affectionate to our father. "Ernest, come kiss your mother," she'd say as soon as we walked through the door.

I was eight years old when I took an interest in Gram Abigale's hats; that's when we became friends. She taught me to use the sewing machine. She'd put her hand on my shoulder. "Be patient, Iris, take your time, you're doing fine."

I knew my mother and Gram didn't like each other. Every Christmas, we'd open our gifts in Boston, and take the train to Cape Cod in the afternoon. Mother rarely joined us, and Gram never asked about her.

When I was ten, Gram Abigale invited me to spend the summer on Cape Cod. We picked blueberries and blackberries, and Gram taught me to make her famous jam.

"It's my own recipe. It took years for me to perfect it."

On summer evenings we'd peruse pattern catalogues and pick out the dresses I liked best. At Easter and Christmas, Gram surprised me with those exact dresses. I loved Cape Cod and spending time with Gram. We made a secret plan. "After you finish school, you'll come live with me." Father always smiled when he saw Gram and me whispering and giggling.

Once I asked her about her gnarled fingers, and she pointed to her crooked back. "Hard work, Iris. I spent years bent over a sewing machine and squinting by candlelight to support myself and your father."

—⁂—

I remember the first time I met my father's new boss. He came all the way from New York to Boston several times a month. My father often invited Mr. Taylor to take supper with our family, because as Father said, "The poor man stays in a rented room. It's the least we can do to feed him a good meal."

Although Nelson and I were fourteen and sixteen, he spoke to us like children. "Candy for each of you. Now brush your teeth after you finish and don't be leaving any around for the mice."

In the beginning, Ryan's thick red hair and Scottish accent fascinated me. I looked forward to his visits and entertaining stories. I liked his sweet-smelling cologne, different from Father's. That's how I figured it out. One Sunday evening, Father, Nelson, and I returned from Cape Cod. I went to Mother's bedroom, only to be struck with the fragrance. In spite of my young age, I knew Ryan Taylor visited my parents' bedroom. I cried myself to sleep that night, fearing Mother would run off with Father's boss. I rehearsed confronting Ryan and scolding him for interfering with my parents' marriage. I planned to banish him from our home with a swift push to his chest.

My chance occurred when Ryan arrived at our house while my parents were at the doctor's with Nelson. My hands sweated and my stomach tied into a knot.

"Mr. Taylor…"

"Ryan's the name to you, darlin'."

He walked to our parlor and invited me to sit on the settee. I tried again but couldn't conjure the anger I rehearsed. "I know you like my mother…"

Ryan moved next to me and placed his hand on my knee. "Of course, I do, sweet child. I like your father, as well, and you and your brother, for that matter. You're family to me."

I could smell his cologne. "Don't you want my mother and father to stay married?"

Ryan assumed a concerned expression. "Now, now, young lady. There's nothing to fear."

I fought the urge to cry and wanted the conversation to end. My body had only recently taken the form of a woman, but a child's tears still came easily. I exhaled a sigh of relief. "Very well, then."

Ryan repeated. "Very, very well, then." He opened his arms as if he saw I was about to cry. "Come here, my sweet lassie."

I welcomed the comfort and leaned into his chest. He placed a gentle kiss on the top of my head, and I knew I could trust his word.

I still remember the deep sense of betrayal the following month when the sweet scent of Ryan's cologne lingered in my parents' bedroom. Determined to save their marriage, I watched the street and intercepted him before he arrived for dinner.

"I smelled you."

Ryan threw back his head and roared laughing. "It was fine, I'm hopin.'"

My face flushed red, and I didn't care if I cried. "I smelled you in my parents' bedroom. I know what you're up to."

Ryan became somber. He put his hands on his hips and face close to mine. "Do ya, now. And what is it you think I am up to?"

I screamed, "You're up to my mother's skirts. That's what you're up to. And I'm about to tell my father."

He moved his face closer. "And I'm your father's employer. Now where would that get you?"

I weighed the question and sobbed. "Please, Mr. Taylor. I want my ma and pa to stay married. I want Pa to keep his job."

He pulled me to him, and I buried my face in his chest. He wrapped me in his arms. "Now, now. You know, my pretty lassie, it's that your mother looks like you I'm drawn to her."

I didn't understand him.

Tall, red-haired Ryan Taylor made it clear. He placed his palm on my small breast. "It's the likes of you I'm drawn to, not your mother."

With his touch, I understood how I could save my parents' marriage. I pressed his hand closer to my breast.

It was summer, and I declined spending it with Gram on Cape Cod. Ryan brought me to his rented room on each of his visits. I didn't understand sex and found no pleasure in the act, or when his hands explored every part of my body. I endured it for the sake of my family. Each time I demanded assurance. "And my mother?"

"My hand to God."

Each visit diminished me more. The scent of his cologne sickened me. When he whispered in my ears, I retreated into my mind, singing the *Battle Hymn of the Republic* to block out his words. *Mine eyes have seen the glory of the coming of the lord; He is trampling out the vintage where the grapes of wrath are stored.* When he mounted me, I drifted away to the rides on the train, imagining the trees and clouds speeding by and being embraced in the warm open arms of Gram Abigale.

I thought about confiding in her but knew she would lash out at Ryan and certainly my mother. Instead, I stayed in my bedroom, taking meals with the family when forced. Ryan's visits to our home became less frequent. When he did come, Mother turned a cold shoulder.

Father chastised her. "Alice, for the love of God, Ryan is my boss. He puts the food on our table."

She'd lash back. "He has a wife in New York, let her cook for him."

Father begged. "Pretend you like him for the sake of my job."

I kept it to myself when I missed my monthly in September, October, and November. When he visited in early December, I told Ryan.

"You stupid, careless child."

He cut me off, ignoring me, refusing any of my attempts to talk to him. My belly puffed out, and I could not stifle the child growing inside.

I'd soon be found out. The truth would break up the family, and I'd be to blame. I decided to wait for our Christmas visit to Gram Abigale. I'd tell her I was pregnant from a boy at school, and ask her to take me in.

A week before Christmas, my father prepared us. "Gram Abigale has taken to her bed."

I didn't believe illness could befall my Gram. "She's resting. Preparing for our Christmas visit, I'm sure."

My father tried again to prepare us as we traveled to her house on Christmas day. "This may be our goodbye to Gram." I saw the tears in his eyes and became alarmed. It was even more telling that Mother was along for the visit.

The house was quiet and dark, the fire only warm embers. Father loaded wood and started a roaring fire. Gram, a wasted form in her bed, requested to see 'My Iris,' as she called me. I gathered the first hat she and I made. It was brown linen with a wide green lace ribbon wrapped around the cap, and long enough to make a large bow under my chin. I knelt by her bed. "Remember this, Gram?"

Gram's lips turned up. She touched the hat and looked at me. "You were eight years old."

"Yes, and I wanted the hat to look like a bird's nest on my head."

"You piled silk flowers on the top."

"I rummaged through all your ribbons and bows and found a garish bird."

Gram Abigale lifted a frail hand and touched my chin. She looked at me with longing. "My Iris. We had some good times, didn't we?"

Tears streaked down my face. "And secrets and giggles."

"She moved her hand to my belly," and smiled. "You'll be all right. Now, send me your father."

"Mother," was all he said before dropping to his knees and resting his head on her chest. I watched from the doorway as Gram lifted a weak hand to Father's head.

"I lived for you."

He sobbed, clutching his mother's hand. "How can I go on without you, Mama? How?"

Gram released a deep sigh, her last.

We put Gram to rest the next day. The mild December left the ground soft. My father placed a marker at his mother's grave site, promising a proper stone in the spring.

Abigale Birch
1843–1918

XLVII

Lessons

Seahaven, Massachusetts
November 2019

Andrea struggled more with what to wear than how to teach. In the end, deciding this was an art lesson, not a dinner date, she chose one of her better fitting pairs of jeans and a black sweater. She topped the outfit off with a pink and gray cotton scarf, which she thought made her look more artsy.

Brian Evans arrived promptly at four p.m. He was as handsome as she remembered. "Welcome, Brian. Come in." He chose the same outfit, good fitting jeans and a sweater.

One step inside the house and he swept his arms around her for a quick hug.

"Wow, I didn't expect that."

"Oh, I'm a hugger. Besides, this is exciting." He rubbed his hands together. "Aren't you excited?"

Andrea stretched to meet his exuberance. She raised her voice an octave. "Of course, yes. You're my first."

Brian gave her an odd look. "You're a virgin?" and winked.

Andrea flushed. "God no, I mean. Oh my God. I meant first student. I didn't mean... never mind."

He pulled her into him again. "Hey, we can joke. No need to blush. Where do we go from here?"

Andrea felt frazzled after the hugging and talk of virgins.

"Do we drive or walk up to the site?"

"Oh, painting. Sure. I got you an easel and paper and some paints. Grab them and we can walk."

As they walked to the cemetery, Andrea wasn't sure she liked Brian. He was too over the top for her. She wondered if he had too much personality, if that's possible, or if he was a phony.

Once they set up, there was only an hour of daylight left. Andrea started with the basics. "We are using dry paper today. It helps to define more precise and defined shapes." She wet her brush and painted a blue horizontal line. She quoted from the Internet. "The opacity of your paint will depend on how much water you mix in."

Brian followed her directions, moving his wet brush across his paper. "Oops. Mine's dripping."

"That's okay. We're experimenting. Now try using less water."

The hour passed quickly. Brian's technique improved with practice. Andrea noticed he stayed focused on the task with no enthusiastic chatter.

As they arrived at the house, Andrea mentioned, "You know we didn't need to hike all the way up there just to practice the basics."

"I kind of realized that when I lost feeling in my feet."

She laughed. "It was cold standing in the mud with that ocean breeze. Next time, we'll stay in the house."

Brian added wood to the fire. He rubbed his hands together once the flames took off. "Works for me."

—⁓—

Brian seemed more relaxed now, so Andrea took a chance. "Can I get you a cup of coffee or hot chocolate to warm you?"

"Believe it or not, I'm over twenty-one."

"Okay, then, red or white?"

"I'm a red man. But don't go to any trouble."

Andrea poured two glasses of her reserve Barolo. "Excuse me for a sec."

She went into her bedroom to check her hair and makeup, sure there was mascara dripping down her face after standing in the wind. She plumped her bob and applied a touch of lip gloss and returned to the living room. Brian stood in front of the stone foot warmer on the hearth. "You have cold feet?"

"Oh that, no. It belonged to my ancestors. I'm finding all sorts of treasures in the barn and giving them a new life."

He looked around. "I love old houses. Lots of my patients live in old places, but don't keep them up. You wouldn't believe what I see."

"Patients? You're a doctor?"

"C'mon, Andrea. I know I Googled you."

She took a too big gulp of wine. "Well, a girl has to be careful these days. You're a podiatrist."

"I am. And you work in advertising and used to live in Boston."

"*Was* in advertising. I inherited this old house and changed my life." She joked, "You could say we're both in rehab."

Brian shook his head. "That's okay. You're young, attractive, and bright, I'm sure. I know you're talented. Change is good. Are you happy?"

The conversation flowed, along with the wine, for two hours. Brian listened with intent. "I'm in awe of you. Changing your life for the better."

At seven o'clock, he stood up. "I've bored you enough for one night. I honestly didn't intend to take up your entire afternoon and evening. I apologize."

Andrea stood as well. "Nonsense. I enjoyed every moment, especially showing off the house. I almost never have company."

They walked to the door. "I think I scared you with the hug earlier, so I'll just wish you a good night."

Andrea tried to laugh it off. "I'm braver than I look. Shall we schedule another time to paint lines across our papers?"

"Sure. Two weeks from today. Four p.m. Indoors."

"For sure. I'll even make us dinner if you paint your lines straight."

"Deal. I'll practice."

Andrea flipped on the porch light and watched as Brian drove away. "Hmm, a black Lincoln BMX, impressive."

She decided not to call Liz and report on her date or painting lesson. Instead, she went to bed and replayed every moment in her mind.

XLVIII

Life Without Tom

Still in her bathrobe, Andrea called from the kitchen. "Coffee's almost ready."

Tom went to the loft stairs. "Before the day gets too long, come here, I want to walk you around the loft."

"Third time's a charm."

Halfway up the stairs, Tom snapped his head. "What's that?"

Andrea poured his coffee. "It's my third tour." Concerned she'd hurt Tom's feelings. "Each time I see more progress. You are such a craftsman."

He reached the top. "You comin' or not?"

She climbed the stairs to see Tom, dressed as usual in L.L. Bean coveralls and a navy-blue long sleeve jersey. "It's finished. Ready for you to spend a fortune on furniture."

Andrea handed her friend his morning coffee. "Very funny, Tom. I'll have you know, I'm an excellent bargain hunter."

Tom ignored her response and continued. "Now, you got a built-in bed, full size, comfortable for one." He looked at Andrea and adjusted his cap. "Or two best friends," and winked. "Underneath the bed," he pulled out drawers, "you got storage for linens and blankets. I put skylights above for light.

"Now pay attention. I won't be around forever. You need to know these things." He demonstrated how to open and close the skylight.

"Nice, Tom."

"I know." He pointed to an end wall. "You got this tension rod here so you can hang a curtain. Give your guest privacy when gettin' dressed."

"Geeze, I never thought of that."

"I know."

She slapped him on the shoulder.

"Your floors are original, all restored. Same with the beams. This back wall we left with the painting. If you ask me, it's kind of weird, but it's your house."

"You calling me weird?"

Tom remained on focus. "No, just kind of weird."

"You got plenty of electrical outlets. I know how you like lamps and all that electronic stuff."

"We call them computers."

"Yup."

Andrea hugged her friend. "Once again, you've exceeded my expectations. I couldn't have imagined all this. You're right, I'm going to go crazy decorating."

Tom stepped away from the hug. "I knew that. Now, I hope your friend Liz will come visit."

"She will. Are you worried?"

"No." He looked at his coffee mug.

"You're drinking the first cup of coffee from my new dishes."

"I see. Mexican, right?"

"No, I told you before, the pattern is Farmhouse."

"Not from no farmhouse I ever saw."

Tom settled into the chair of Andrea's new kitchen set, an old round mahogany pedestal table she refinished in black before she distressed it. The slat back dining chairs were new, painted white with black seats.

Tom cleared his throat. His habit before making an announcement. "Like I said, I won't be around forever."

Andrea stood at the kitchen counter pouring her coffee. "What's that supposed to mean. Are you sick?"

"No, no, nothin' like that, thank the lord." He cleared his throat again. "I'm leavin' for a while."

Andrea's left eyebrow arched. "What's going on, Tom?"

He lifted his yellow mug and took a slow sip. "Remember last summer when I took two weeks off? Well, I visited my son in Ohio."

"That's wonderful, Tom. How is he? You never talk about him."

"I generally keep my business to myself, but you need to know this. My boy hasn't seen or spoken to me since he finished college."

Andrea started to speak, but Tom put up his hand. "It's no secret around this town. I was a drunk for years. Drove away my wife and son. No fault of theirs."

Andrea sat down across the table.

"Anyway, before the summer, my ex-wife, God bless her, let my boy know I been sober for more than a year."

"That's wonderful, Tom."

He looked at Andrea, tears welling in his eyes. "It was this house, and you. Chances are I would have started drinkin' again, happened before. But when I got the chance to, I'll use the word rehabilitate this house, home, I took it as a chance to rehabilitate myself. You gave me purpose, Andrea. I've been so broken. I needed purpose."

Now she was wiping tears.

"Last summer my son invited me out. We looked for land for him and his wife and two young babies."

"You have grandchildren?"

Tom took his wallet out and showed pictures of twin boys. "That's them at one year." More tears came as he smiled at their photo.

"Anyway, my boy and I agreed, if I made it to two years sober, I could come out and help him build his house." He nodded. "And that's where I'm goin'. Ohio."

"Wow. Amazing. And I thought this house brought me back to life."

Tom chuckled. "I guess we both got what we needed."

"We did. I want to hug you."

One hand went up. "Won't be necessary."

"Okay, I'll hold back. When do you leave?"

"Tomorrow. It's been on my mind to tell you, but..."

"I get it. That's why you mentioned Liz visiting. Don't worry about me, Tom." She hadn't told him about Brian Evans.

Tom put his cup in the sink. "Still look Mexican to me." He faced Andrea. "It won't be forever. I got my house here, and you."

"I'm gonna hug you, like it or not."

"I might cry."

"Me, too."

—m—

Later that afternoon, Andrea started to call Liz, but felt the tears coming and put the phone down. She went on the Internet and shopped for bedding, lamps, and end tables for the loft. Shopping usually made her feel better, but not today. Her buddy, her friend was leaving. She'd be on her own for a few months.

XLIX

The Seduction

The house felt different without Tom's truck parked in the driveway, his tools spread out, and the sound of hammering. Andrea didn't bother cooking breakfast, and the morning coffee didn't taste as good. She lost the motivation to hang the old black and white photos of her ancestors. It didn't seem fun alone.

It was a few days before Andrea realized she'd filled her time fixing the house and depending on Tom's company instead of dealing with the reality of her life. She was a divorced, thirty-six-year-old woman with no job, living in a remote old house in a sleepy town on Cape Cod. She spent evenings reading a dead relative's diaries. She thought about calling Liz to complain, but Liz didn't seem to want to talk lately.

Andrea took Abigale's grave marker from the mantel and put it on the table next to her chair where she piled the diaries. "It's you and me now, Miss Abigale." She opened a diary.

Winter 1911

I'm sure it's the coldest winter in history. There's a layer of ice on my house, covered with six inches of snow. I fear the roof will fall in on my head. If it does, so be it. This miserable life will be done.

I thought sure after missing Christmas, my Ernest would visit, but the ice covers the train tracks. I'm trapped here, alone. Not that I'd travel out even without snow. It's only when Iris is here in summer that I leave the house, and that's as far as the blueberry patches in the garden. God, I miss that girl.

Spring 1911

Ernest and Iris visited. Iris lights up the house. She and I baked a loaf of bread with zucchini squash from the root cellar. Perhaps it was the overdose of baking powder that rendered it hard. She doesn't understand sadness and brings Ernest to a smile when she jumps onto his lap with a book for him to read with her.

My son is an unhappy man, sullen and withdrawn. I offer affection and he pulls away. That woman, Alice, broke him with her drinking and whoring around. My heart aches knowing after all my sacrifice to give my boy a life with morals and virtues he married a woman with none.

They left today, and the house is once again cold. Thank the lord, they brought candles and oil.

I don't think my brother Caleb intended for me to live in solitude and disappointment in life.

Andrea closed the diary and imagined Abigale enduring a winter living in the house alone with only oil lamps and candles for light. She thought, *I gotta get a life.*

As if he read her mind, Brian called on her cell phone. "Hey, what's cookin', good lookin'?"

"Nice to hear from you. I'm just hanging. Contemplating life."

"Your life, or life in general?"

She didn't know him well enough to confide her real thoughts. "Life in general, I guess."

"Listen, I know it's a Sunday and not our lesson day, but I'm heading to the Cape, meeting with a possible new client tomorrow, a nursing home, and, anyway, how about dinner later?"

Andrea hesitated.

"I know it's short notice. You're probably busy."

She rolled her eyes and looked at herself, still in her bathrobe at two in the afternoon. "I could do dinner."

"Great. Is six okay? I can pick you up."

She moved toward her closet. "Sure. Where are we going, so I know how to dress?"

"Sweetheart, I know every little hole-in-the-wall on the Cape. I travel it up and down visiting clients. You like seafood?"

"Of course." She pulled a pair of brown cotton suede pants from the closet.

"I'll take you to a casual spot. How's that?"

She grabbed a black turtle-neck sweater. "Sounds like my kind of place."

"See you at six."

Brian was the first man Andrea was excited about since Paul. He was handsome, charming, smart, and happy. She told herself, *Time to put your big girl pants on and start living again.*

He knocked on her door at six. "Bonjour, for you, Beaujolais."

"Wow, thanks. Was that supposed to be a French accent?"

Brian attempted a James Cagney imitation. "It's the best I got, Sweetheart."

"Well, thank you again."

Andrea got two glasses. "Beaujolais. I'm not familiar."

Brian settled on to the sofa. "It's very nice, light body, best served *un peu* chilled. Did I mention it was French?"

Andrea laughed as she handed him a glass. "Gee, no. I don't think I heard that."

"Chin Chin." They clinked glasses.

—⁂—

The ride to Provincetown was twenty minutes. "The views are spectacular in the daylight. I love the rows of sand dunes and artists' shacks."

"You know how it is, Andrea. I travel up and down the Cape so much, I forget to look anymore. Have you found a favorite spot?"

Andrea thought how easy the conversation flowed and how much she enjoyed sitting beside a tall handsome man. "Hmm. To be honest, I've been so wrapped up in the house, I haven't gotten very far, but a few years ago I toured a lot of Provincetown's art galleries. I could do that all day."

"And we will. If you like the beach, I'll show you some of the least popular, spectacular ones with the most amazing sunsets."

"Love it."

The evening passed with conversation, laughter, great seafood, and wine.

It was still early, and it seemed natural to invite Brian in to finish his bottle of Beaujolais. "Are you in a hurry?"

"Not at all, I have all night."

"Did you just wink?"

Brian ushered her through the door. Andrea found the music channel on the television. Faith Hill sang, *Breathe*.

Brian stood up. "Faith Hill? C'mon. Put on real music." He changed the channel. "Now this is dancing music." Brian took Andrea in his arms and slow danced her around the room to the Righteous Brothers' *Unchained Melody*.

Brian sang, "*Oh my love, my darling...* Oh, oh. Am I dating myself? You were probably still in diapers in nineteen-ninety-one."

"No, but the tooth fairy left me a few quarters that year."

"Ouch. I'm robbing the cradle."

Andrea pressed herself against Brian's body. "I'm a big girl. Don't you worry."

Andrea found Brian a thoughtful, gentle, and sensual lover. The love making lasted two hours before they fell asleep in each other's arms. Brian woke first. He kissed Andrea on the head. "I have to run, early appointment."

It was still dark. Andrea touched his hand. "I loved last night."

"Me, too. Be good. I'll call you."

L

Discretion is the Better Part Of Valour

Andrea sorted through boxes of Abigale's fashion magazines from the eighteen hundreds, trolling the Internet to see if they had any value. The caller ID on her phone read 'Liz.'

She picked up to hear her friend's familiar voice. "Long time, no speak."

"I thought I'd wait and see how long it took before you called. For all you know, the slasher podiatrist may have cut off my toes and left me limping around in the woods."

The raspy voice brought a smile to Andrea's face. "Darling, I know he didn't because you answered the phone. Now that you brought it up, how was the date with Mr. Nail Clipper?"

"Liz, do you think early editions of *Harper's Bazaar* have any market value?"

"Don't try to throw me off track. The date. Details."

Andrea grimaced and kept her response light. "I like him."

"How much did you, ah, um, like him?"

Andrea pushed aside the cardboard box of old magazines and laughed out loud. "You don't miss much, do you, Liz?"

"Sweetheart, I'm past sixty. And yes, I'm ashamed to admit, I live my sex life vicariously through you."

"That's a joke. Anyway, I liked him a lot, a whole lot. We've had a couple of dinner dates, and he's got some talent."

"In the sack, I assume."

"Liz, stop pushing. I don't kiss and tell. I meant his painting is coming along. I'm a little surprised."

"Is he painting feet?"

Andrea used her free hand to throw a log in the fire. "Stop it. Podiatry is a noble profession, he helps people. Anyway, he's painting a seascape. We both are. Not outside, it's too cold. We do it from a photograph in the house."

"Okay, I'll stop. Other than you've got a lover, what else is going on in your life?"

Liz hadn't mentioned work in months. "I hate to admit, I don't have much of a life. The house is done, except for a few little final touches I'm working on. I've been digging around the barn to see if there is any hidden treasure. What about you? How's that cold?"

"Oh, that was nothing. But I am thinking of retiring, closing the business altogether. Between the economy and my advanced age, it seems like this is the time. We've only had little projects trickling in the last six months or so."

"Wow, the end of an era."

Liz hesitated. "This may be too personal, but you know I have no boundaries, anyway. I'm feeling guilty. Are you okay for money? I promised you work and haven't been able to keep you busy."

Andrea moved to the kitchen and started emptying the dishwasher with one hand. "Lucky for me, Dad was a good money manager. My financial advisor called last week. He said if I don't buy a yacht or a castle in Austria, I'll be okay, even if I don't have another income. Sooner or later, I'll get a real job. I'm starting to climb the walls."

Liz was in the midst of a coughing fit.

"You okay? I thought that cold was all gone."

"Fine, fine. Dry heat in this condo. Gets to me every winter. Anyway, good news for you. We should all have such wonderful fathers. God bless Mason."

"Yes, God bless my dad, but I'd rather have him here than live on his money."

Not one to commiserate, Liz changed the subject. "Listen, I took a gig I'm not the least bit interested in. Any chance you might take it on?"

Andrea did her tap steps. "Sure. Did I mention how bored I am? Brian is only on the Cape a couple of times a month. Other than dating him and sorting through stuff in the barn, I spend my time reading old diaries and notes about my strange ancestors. Watcha got?"

Liz cleared her throat. "It's a fascinating challenge."

"Oh, Oh. I've been around you long enough to know 'challenge' is code for impossible."

Liz chuckled. "Right on. I'll just spit it out. It's a men's incontinence product."

"Yup. Go on."

"No, listen. The client wants a TV ad that almost subliminally suggests to men, and their wives, of course, that men need products to manage their incontinence. How's that?"

"Good pitch. Why don't you do it? How's that?"

"Funny. I don't feel like it. The client wants three fifteen second TV spots, all discreet. No man wants to watch a long commercial about what kind of diaper he needs."

"I got one."

"I couldn't have guessed. Let me have it."

Andrea scribbled. "Okay, here goes. We get an old basketball legend to look into the camera and bounce a ball. He says, 'Dribbling is for the basketball court, not your pants.'"

Liz howled. "See, I knew this was your kind of job. My turn. A muscle man type of guy is sitting at a bar, there's a football game blasting on the TV in the background. He raises his beer and looks into the camera, 'Wet your whistle, not your pants.'"

Andrea screamed. "Stop, I'll never be able to think of a straight ad, now."

"You will. I'll send you all the stuff I have on it."

"Okay. I'll take a look this week."

"Did I mention there's a two-week deadline?"

Andrea slapped the kitchen counter. "No, you did not."

"Ta, sweets."

"Wait. Don't hang up. I want you to come visit, you promised months ago. The loft is all set up, just for you. Did I tell you we discovered one wall covered in paintings from one of the late occupants of this house?"

A weary voice replied. "Oh, sweetie, I'll get there sooner or later. Right now, I'm busy closing the business. Another painter in the family, you say?"

"Quite possibly. That's why I'm digging through the barn. I'm thinking there's more."

Andrea stood facing the loft. "Listen, how about Thanksgiving? Do you have plans? I could cook a turkey, mashed potatoes, the works. When was the last time you had a home cooked dinner?"

"Sorry, sweets. My sister and her husband are coming in from New York. We made reservations at The Four Seasons. Why don't you join us?"

Andrea tried to sound positive. "That's okay. I'll talk to you when I have something nice to say about men's diapers."

"Love you, darling."

LI

A Day of No Thanks

With nothing to do until Liz sent the materials on the project, Andrea bundled up with a heavy coat, hat, and gloves, and spent the early afternoon rummaging through the trunks and boxes in the drafty barn, setting aside the junk she wanted hauled away. She tackled a section in the furthest corner, moving trunks and boxes to the other side of the barn, clearing her way toward the back. She spotted an old easel. Encouraged by the find, she thought, *where there's smoke, there's fire,* and kept moving dress forms, hat boxes, and three old suitcases out of the way.

It took more than an hour and a lot of muscle, but she found a pile of paintings leaning against the barn wall. *Eureka,* she thought, and carried as many as she could from the chilly barn into the house. She ran back for the easel. The day approached four o'clock, and Brian was due for his lesson. Andrea put the paintings aside and hopped in the shower.

When he arrived, she pointed to his partly painted canvas, propped on the old oak easel. "What do you think? Today's barn bounty."

"Wow. Not the work of a skilled carpenter."

"Not at all. Someone took a few scraps of oak and nailed them together. But I bet the person who painted the loft wall is the artist, or was the artist, I should say." Andrea walked toward the sofa where she piled the paintings on the floor. "Check these out. What do you think?"

Brian flipped through them. "You're the artist. What do you think? Are they good?"

They sat on the floor, staring. "I'm an amateur painter, not an art expert. Besides, they are so dirty, who could tell?"

"Isn't the value of art based on what appeals to the person? You know, beauty is in the eye of the beholder?"

Before Andrea answered, Brian kissed her. "Is it considered improper for a student to kiss his teacher?"

"Not in my book."

Brian shook his head. "Somehow, when I'm this close to you, painting lessons don't seem so important."

Andrea's heart fluttered. She said out loud what she was thinking. "Sometimes I think this is all a dream."

Brian stood and helped her to her feet. "You pour the wine, I'll put on some music. Lessons be damned."

She called from the kitchen. "None of the eighties stuff."

The lovemaking was more sensuous and satisfying for Andrea each time. Brian didn't fall asleep right after, but faced her, staring into her eyes. "What are you thinking?"

"Oh, just things."

"Tell me."

"About you, for one."

"And I you. What else?"

Andrea had never been with a man who was so attentive to her feelings. She felt safe enough to be honest. "I'm finding my way, I guess you could say."

"Tell the doctor more."

She pulled the sheets to her shoulders. "I feel stupid."

"I'll get you a glass of wine to loosen you up."

The two sat in bed, covered by Andrea's new pale blue satin sheets, reserved for nights with Brian. She sipped her wine. "This is the story of Andrea." She cleared her throat. "After I got my degree to teach art, I moved in with a guy for four years."

"Should I be jealous?"

"No. Paul and I planned to move to the West Coast and get our graduate degrees, but unfortunately, my dad got sick. He had a devasting heart attack."

"Sorry about that, Andrea."

"No need. It's been a long time. Anyway, the love of my life went off to the West Coast alone. I stayed in Boston and cared for my dad and went to grad school part time."

"Sounds like a long road."

"It has been. My father was disabled for three years before he died. But I don't regret it at all. He devoted his whole life to me and my mom."

"I want to hug you."

"No need. Enough of that story. Whew. On a happier note, did I tell you I got a project from Liz?"

"I'm still stuck on your journey."

"I'm okay, really. You'll love this new project. I have to come up with three fifteen second TV spots, one of which has to convince men to buy diapers for their incontinence."

"And you're telling me this, why?"

She slapped his chest. "It's not about you, silly man."

"Good to know. Sounds challenging."

"That's how Liz described it. I call it impossible, but I'm gonna try."

"Go for it."

Andrea leaned back on the headboard. "You know, Brian. We talk a lot about me. You're a wonderful listener. I want to know more about you."

He nodded. "Fair enough. Well, you know I'm a podiatrist."

"Aha. And you live on the South Shore."

"I do. It's my parents who keep me there, mostly. My dad is seventy-six. He's in good enough shape, but it gets too much for him to care for my mom."

"I understand. My father cared for my mother for years. She had MS, Multiple Sclerosis."

"Terrible disease."

A chill went through Andrea. "Enough of these sad stories. This room is always a little cold. Let's sit by the fire."

—⁓—

Brian flipped through the pile of paintings from the barn again. "I have an idea."

Andrea sensed he didn't want to talk about his sick mother. "About what?"

"Take these paintings, the best of them, to Jonathan Hall at the gallery. See what he thinks."

Andrea moved closer to Brian. She put her head on his shoulder. "You're so smart. I'll call him in the morning."

Brian jumped up, something he did often. "I'm hungry. Want to head out for dinner?"

Andrea looked at herself, wearing her bathrobe. "You mean get dressed and go out in the cold? No thanks. Let me make cheeseburgers."

—⁓—

Brian was about to leave around midnight. "Listen, I'm going to Martha's Vineyard the day after Thanksgiving to meet with the administrators of two nursing homes who want the regular service of a podiatrist. Come with me. We can bundle up and walk around. Spend the night. There's bound to be a few shops and restaurants still open."

Andrea did her little dance. "Absolutely. I love the Vineyard."

"I'll get ferry reservations and call you next week with the details."

She wanted to ask about his plans for the holiday, but assumed he'd spend it with his parents.

Andrea cleared the dishes and blew out the candles. She loaded enough wood to heat the house almost until morning. She slid under her silk sheets and down comforter.

Thanksgiving came and went, and Andrea spent it alone. The phone never rang.

LII

Nanny Iris

New York
January 1919

With my only hope, Gram Abigale, dead, I had no other choice. I traveled to New York to find Ryan Taylor. I didn't expect him to welcome a fifteen year old, four months pregnant with his baby.

I knocked on his door, intending to destroy his life and demand money to support myself and the baby. A pretty young woman answered and offered a wide smile and greeting. "Please, dear, come in."

She poured tea. "I don't mind that you just stopped by without a call."

Puzzled by her welcoming, I took in the woman with styled blonde hair, curls piled on the back of her head, and long, wavy pieces on the sides. I sat up straight. "Is your husband home?" I asked, preparing for an uncomfortable encounter.

She grimaced. "No, no. Ryan travels a lot. And, frankly, I'm just not a homebody. That's why I need a nanny." She gestured to a young child playing in the corner of the room. "For Belle." She turned back to me. "What's your experience, dear? And your name, by the way?"

I opened my mouth and said, "Iris Birch," while thoughts raced through my mind.

Ryan's wife didn't seem to notice my confusion. She carried on. "I'm Teresa Taylor. I trust you have experience with children?"

I thought about leaving, but with nowhere to go and no money, my survival seemed more important than confronting Ryan Taylor. I stayed seated, hands folded on my lap. By the appearance of the home, the Taylor's were rich. I spoke as if it were the truth. "My mother died after giving birth to my brother. I took care of him as an infant right up until he went off to boarding school this year."

Teresa seemed eager to secure help. "My sister and I are traveling to Florida next week. This damn flu has kept us all locked up for too long." She didn't take a breath. "I'll pay you two dollars a week and you'll live in our guesthouse. Don't worry about food. Our cook always makes extra."

My naivete showed. "You have a cook and a nanny?"

Teresa smoothed her hair. "Iris, I'm twenty years old. My father wanted more for me than to be a housewife."

I nodded, waiting to hear more. "And yet, here you are."

"Yes, indeed. Here I am. It's not that Father wants to support Ryan, it's that he wants me and his grandchild to have the life he can give us." She paused, "It's complicated."

"Will I be meeting your husband?"

"Oh, yes. He comes and goes. It's his business to travel."

With that, Teresa opened the front door. "Follow me."

She brought me to a small, but adequate guesthouse. A warm and safe home, suiting my needs for the time.

Two days after I moved in, Teresa summoned me to the house. The fear on Ryan's face is forever in my mind.

"Iris, this is Ryan."

I extended my hand and made a small curtsy. "Mr. Taylor, thank you for welcoming me into your home."

Ryan offered a damp, limp hand. Red blotches climbed up from his neck and scattered across his stunned face. Teresa explained my experience raising a younger brother after my mother died giving birth.

He uttered a weak, "How impressive."

I made him squirm. "Yes, you would have liked my mother, Alice. A sweet, wonderful woman."

Ryan excused himself and left the room. Teresa assured me. "He's never around." She looked at my dress. "You've been wearing that since you arrived. Tomorrow I'll sort through my clothes and make you up a wardrobe." She winked and smiled at me. "We have to look our best."

Teresa made good on her promise. As I was leaving her house after I put Belle to bed, I found a sack of clothes at the front door. For the first time in months, I felt joy as I sorted through the gaily colored stylish dresses, bloomers, stockings, and hats. She even included a winter coat, which I desperately needed.

I enjoyed caring for Belle, a fair-skinned redhead, like her father. Ryan traveled several times a month, and with World War I winding down, Teresa and her sister took frequent trips, often as local as Niagara Falls and New York City. I took extra pleasure imagining the fear my presence instilled in Ryan. I'm sure he wondered if I ended my pregnancy. A month after my arrival, it became apparent I did not.

Teresa never asked but left a sack of maternity clothes at the front door for me. Even they were stylish, with wide white collars and bows in the front. She was tall, so I sewed hems on the dresses to avoid tripping. I kept Belle in the guesthouse when Teresa traveled. This night, she stopped in on her way to the theatre in New York City.

"The blue dress suits you."

My throat tightened as I faced discussing my pregnancy. "Will you be putting me out?"

She wore a fur jacket and long rose-colored velvet dress. Her perfume filled the little guesthouse. "Of course not, Iris." She started and then stopped, "Not long ago, I..."

Teresa turned to the door and put her hand on the doorknob. "Take care of my pumpkin, we will talk more when I'm home in a few days."

Teresa returned with a plan. "Do you have a doctor?"

"I don't."

"I'll arrange for mine to visit you. You'll have the baby here." She thought out loud. "Clothes…I have baby clothes for a girl. We can wait and see."

—⁂—

For the next months, Teresa and I prepared for the baby. We hauled Belle's cradle and a rocking chair through the garden from her house. She gave me Belle's infant blankets and gowns, a supply of nappies, and her large pan to clean them. "Boil them hard and hang them in the sun. Too many germs around these days." After Teresa put the last touches on the blanket she knitted, she plopped into the rocking chair. "Now we wait." And I did wait with great anticipation.

She never asked about the father or even why, at fifteen, I was on my own, pregnant. Instead, she concerned herself with my well-being. "The Spanish Flu is killing thousands of young people. You'll stay safe in the guesthouse until the baby is born."

Her doctor visited me at the house and assured I and the baby were healthy. In my last months, Teresa made tea, and ordered me to rest when my ankles swelled. I worried she spent more time with me than her husband. Teresa confided. "We have little in common with him being fifteen years older."

It occurred to me, only a few years before, Ryan seduced a fifteen-year-old Teresa.

Catherine's time to enter the world coincided with troubles in America. World War I ended, but the Flu continued to take the lives of young people, and the economy suffered. I questioned Teresa why Ryan was home more.

"It's his business. Americans can't afford new clothes right now. The Flu is keeping everyone home." She whispered as if he were nearby. "It's only my family money that is supporting us now."

—⁂—

Catherine came into the world on a warm spring day in May. Teresa assisted the midwife. She handed me my child.

"She reminds me of my Belle. We'll raise them like sisters." I wanted to tell her they were sisters but couldn't risk the consequences. Catherine was a quiet baby, an exuberant breast feeder, and solemn sleeper.

When the Flu pandemic came to an end in the summer of 1919, Teresa and her sister traveled more. They left for months on a transatlantic cruise to England and France. Ryan stayed to himself in the big house while I kept Belle and Catherine with me in the guesthouse.

I didn't know if my parents were together or even in Boston. Only Ryan could tell me, but I couldn't bear to see his face, save speak to him. I imagined the conversation. "Ryan, tell me, is Ernest Birch still in your employ? Are you still sneaking around with his wife, Alice, my mother?"

In my fantasy he replied, "Yes, Iris. They are both well. I'll convey your regards when I visit the Boston store next month."

I'd offer, "Here, hold your daughter." He'd reach for Belle and I'd say, "Not her, this one." I'd pick up Catherine and place her in his arms.

In my heart and mind, I knew I'd never speak to him or allow him to touch my daughter.

—⁂—

There were times over the years when I felt restless, but the world is a dangerous place, and living in the guesthouse, homeschooling Belle and Catherine, isolated us from the troubles affecting other people. Teresa knew more about the economy and politics than I did.

"People are afraid to spend money. No one is buying clothes or goods. Factories are closing and putting thousands out of work."

"I thank goodness I'm here. What would happen to me and Catherine if I worked in a factory?"

"You'd be on the streets. There're thousands lining up just for a bit of sugar or a loaf of bread. Even the wealthy lost everything. Men are jumping off rooftops in despair."

"Is your family affected?"

"My father is a brilliant investor. He's buying up real estate for pennies from those who lost everything in the stock market."

I confided my fear of going out into the world with Catherine. She reassured me. "Iris, this is your home. I need you. Belle needs you."

It never seemed the right time for me to ask Teresa why she married Ryan. There were moments I felt brown-eyed Teresa knew full well Belle and Catherine shared Ryan as a father. She'd say, "Look at them. Both tall and slim with red hair and blue eyes. A rare combination, you know."

It seemed the right time to leave when Catherine turned fifteen. The girls completed their home schooling, and Belle left for college. I'd saved my wages for years to give us enough for a start. Still a young woman of thirty, I dreamt of a future including marriage and more children. Catherine didn't seem excited about the prospect of a new home. Already a quiet girl, she became withdrawn and sullen.

Teresa and I discussed it. "She's never known another home. Stay here. Go out, find a job in a shop, but, please, stay."

I wanted to be away from Ryan Taylor and the memories. "I'll find a place nearby. We'll still be friends. Please, support me. I'm a bit afraid. Never been on my own."

Teresa agreed. "And don't concern yourself with Catherine. Belle fought moods around the same age, I'm sure you remember."

I searched for several months before I found affordable housing, a flat with two bedrooms in a building with six other families. I thought it held possibilities for making new friends. With our modest belongings, we planned to leave after Teresa and Belle, home from college for the weekend, returned from a two-day shopping trip into New York.

—m—

A calm Teresa brought the news. They were still dressed in their travel clothes. "Belle and I returned from our trip this afternoon." She stopped and looked at her daughter and back to me. "Ryan seems to be dead."

Catherine retreated to her room without a word. No feelings of sadness came to me, nor did I detect any in Teresa.

"Iris, dear. Belle and I are exhausted. A cup of tea would do wonders."

I offered to attend to the more urgent matter. "What about your husband?"

"We'll have the tea first. There's no rush. He is very dead. His face is gray and drawn." Teresa left it to me. "Iris, you go, after tea. You're better at this sort of thing. Do you have any biscuits?"

I had no experience dealing with dead bodies. "What do you suppose happened? Is the house tossed about?"

She stuttered, "I don't know. I didn't see blood. The house looks put together, except for his dirty dishes and half empty glasses of whiskey. Normal for Ryan."

"We'll call a doctor. If he says Ryan is dead…" I stopped. "If he says he is dead, we'll follow his instructions."

Teresa agreed. "After tea." She thought out loud. "I haven't even unpacked. I need to call my parents. God, I have a cruise booked for next month. Do you think I can still go?"

"Finish your tea. When you're finished, we'll go to your house and phone up the doctor."

—⚌—

The doctor pulled the blankets off Ryan, stared for a moment, and announced, "Stress." He covered Ryan and turned to Teresa. "I've seen a lot of this. Undisturbed bed clothes, sudden death while sleeping."

Teresa nodded. "I see."

"Has Ryan been worrying about the economy? Smoking cigarettes? Drinking too much?"

"All of those, Doctor."

He removed the stethoscope from his neck and put it in his leather satchel. "Exactly what I suspected. Ryan succumbed to the stresses of life. We call it 'natural causes.'" He put his soft hat on. "Good day. Contact the undertaker. He'll take over from here." He walked to the front door, turned around and tipped his hat. "Condolences, Teresa."

—⁓—

Teresa went on her cruise a month later. She offered to take me as a guest, but I didn't feel I should leave Catherine, and we were about to move to our new apartment.

Teresa begged me, "Please, Iris. I can't bear the empty house. I don't sleep or eat. I'm miserable. Belle is off to college. I've done so much for you. You can't desert me in my time of need."

Teresa's desperate pleas convinced me to stay. She had, after all, saved me at fifteen and pregnant and given me and Catherine a home. I got a job in a dress shop. Catherine worked in the same shop, preferring to stay in the back room, unpacking boxes.

LIII

Indebted

1942... The years passed quickly. We lost our jobs when the shop closed at the start of World War II. By then, a remarried Teresa had two young children. I resumed my role as a nanny with Catherine at my side. Teresa traveled to New York City several times each week to volunteer as a bandage roller for the Red Cross.

After the War ended, Teresa increased our weekly pay, insisting Catherine and I were better off living in the guesthouse than most. Although we never saw them ourselves, she described the outside world as tainted with dirty streets, crowded with noisy automobiles and streetcars, men lined up on sidewalks begging for employment to support their families, and decrepit apartment buildings, standing side by side, overrun by poverty-stricken families.

—⬥—

1960... I raised Teresa's children as if they were my own. They satisfied my longing for more children. When they went off to college, I tried to separate Catherine and myself from Teresa.

"I've saved enough money, and Catherine and I are going on a cruise to England." My intention was to move away when we returned.

She insisted on joining us. "My husband is leaving me for his young mistress. You can't abandon me now."

After that, I resigned myself to staying with Teresa, at least for a while. Her husband, Ryan, trapped me at fifteen, and now, at fifty-seven years, she held me, indebted, as she frequently reminded. At her insistence, I moved into her home. I wished for Catherine to go out on her own, or at least move into the house, but like a wounded bird, she stayed close to the nest, preferring the solitude of the guesthouse.

Teresa paid us each week. I was never sure of my role. She confided her woes to me like a friend, ordered me around like a handmaiden, but expected companionship on her trips.

She announced the plans, never consulting me first. "I've arranged a trip to Florida for February. We can't suffer the winter in New York."

I packed the bags and arranged transportation. We stayed in the same hotel room, not to save money, but so I'd be at her beck and call. "Iris, draw my bath, lay out my clothes. Make dinner reservations."

There were a few times over the years when I gathered the courage to tell her Catherine and I were leaving. She always created a crisis to keep us from going.

"My doctor says I'm suffering from depression. He says it's out of the question that I should be alone. Dangerous, even."

Another time, she offered a veiled threat. "If you go, I don't think I'll survive."

And there was Catherine. Teresa pretended to care about her. "Catherine will never adjust to the outside world. Can't you see the way she keeps to herself in the guesthouse? Don't be so inconsiderate of your daughter."

It was nineteen-sixty-five when Teresa played her last card. She didn't have to, I'd resigned myself to staying. The stroke was massive. It left her paralyzed on her right side, and unable to speak. She lived that way for ten years. Catherine and I took care of her until the end, just as she planned.

I wanted to go home to find my parents in Boston but didn't know if Catherine and I were welcome. Gram Abigale's house was our other option. The day I left there, my brother Nelson took me to the train. I was fifteen years old and four months pregnant.

It was December, we buried Gram the day before, and the weather turned bitter cold. Mother was in a sour mood. She'd turned angry over the years, giving up her beauty for cigarettes and too many nights at the local taverns. My father, always passive, tolerated her behavior, like me, for the sake of the family.

She'd drank her way through the day, and as she often did, turned on my father. "Ernest, you fool. What is the point of moving your mother's rubbish to the attic? It needs a good fire."

Gram collected in her later years. There were piles of magazines, stacks of newspapers and books, and boxes filled with scraps of material, bows, ribbons, and buttons. We moved about the house through paths of her possessions. My father made more room, moving piles of them to the attic.

"These are my dear mother's treasures, Alice. I won't burn them. You wouldn't understand because you're only loyal to your whiskey."

Their fighting went on. Nelson and I moved to the corner of the room because Mother threw glasses and pots when she drank too much.

Even with Gram dead, Mother didn't want to stay in the house. "I'll take the train to Boston tomorrow. You can stay here, crying in your piles of rubbish."

My grieving father, an even-tempered man, did not have tolerance for Mother's comments. "Go. Pack your belongings when you get there. My mother's death has opened my eyes. I won't spend another day in your miserable company."

Nelson and I watched in awe. We were accustomed to Mother's drunken rants, but Father never said a harsh word. A naïve fifteen year old, I thought I could stop the arguing if I told them about my condition. I didn't consider the consequences of making such an announcement. "Father, Mother, stop," I shouted. They turned their attention to me. "I'm having a baby." All the stress and pain I harbored for months burst from me at that moment, and I fell to my knees, sobbing.

Neither of my parents spoke. Nelson knelt next to me and put his arms on my shoulders. The only sound was my gasping for air.

My mother moved toward me. "Stand up," she screamed. The rage on her face terrified me. "Who? Who?"

I didn't anticipate naming Ryan Taylor as the father, but I didn't expect being shaken and slapped by my mother, who continued screaming.

"Who? You tell me who." Her face turned a bright red, and tears spurted from her eyes. If I named a boy from school, she would surely kill him and that wouldn't be fair.

I looked to my father for relief. He stood, a box of magazines in his arms, on the second step of the ladder to the attic.

Mother continued. "You won't move from this bloody spot until you give me a name." She put her face to mine. "Give me a name, give me a name, you little slut." She slapped me across the face, again.

Afraid, I blurted out, "Ryan."

"Ryan. Ryan who?"

"Ryan Taylor. He told me if I let him do it to me, he wouldn't do it with you anymore."

Mother released me, and I crumpled to the floor, exhausted. She turned to look at my father. Her tone a whisper. "Ernest…"

Father dropped the box of magazines, straightened his shoulders, and walked out the door into the frigid night. Mother turned to me and hissed. "Pack your clothes."

Nelson followed me to the bedroom. "Where will you go?"

"I don't have anywhere. I planned to stay here with Gram, but…" I cried on Nelson's shoulder. "She's gone."

Mother interrupted our moment, she slurred, "Nelson, take her to the train." She gave him money. "Buy her a one-way ticket for someplace far away."

She turned to me, her face distorted from whiskey and rage. "Don't come back. Ever."

Nelson and I waited at the end of the road for Father, sure he would send our mother off, rather than me. When he hadn't returned after midnight, we left for the train station where I bought a ticket to New York to find Ryan Taylor.

My brother wept as he hugged me. "I'll be here. I'll wait for you to come home."

LIV
Show And Tell

Seahaven, Massachusetts
December 2019

The client liked Andrea's submissions for the men's incontinence product. She called Liz to report. "I didn't embarrass you. They loved it."

"Tell me you didn't use words like dribble and nappies."

Andrea sat in her favorite overstuffed chair, the fire roaring, and candles lit on the mantel. "You sound hoarse. What's with you?"

"The usual winter sniffles, I guess. So anyway, the pitch?"

The story board sat on the old easel she found in the barn. "It's simple and discreet, just like they asked. I've got an average-looking man, around sixty-five, standing in the drugstore aisle in front of shelves of the product. He's got a box in his hand and turns to the camera, 'My doctor told me he used these after his prostate surgery. That's good enough for me.'"

"Bravo. Perfect. Doctor recommended. Nice touch."

"Thanks. I learned from the best. I don't hear ice clinking. It's after five o'clock."

"Not tonight, dear. Slowing down on the gin. But, by all means, drink up."

"Oh, I have my trusty glass right here. Listen, they asked if I'd take on a couple of projects on a freelance basis. Any problem with that for you?"

"Darling, it's what I hoped for. You deserve it and you'll do a wonderful job. Congratulations." There was a pause. "Oh, what the hell, I'll just have a little glass of wine while we chat. How's the romance?"

"Romance is good." Andrea took a sip of her Merlot. "There's not much to do around here in the winter. Brian sees patients on the Cape every other week. It's basically dinner, sex, dinner, sex. You know, same ole, same ole."

"I'd kill for that same ole. Don't knock it."

"Oh, Liz, don't get me wrong. I love his company. He's great and we still manage to have fun. I'm just not sure where it's going."

"Where do you want it to go?"

"Good question, but I'm trying not to obsess, just enjoy it for what it is."

"Whatever it is, huh?"

"What's that supposed to mean?"

Liz didn't answer. "Listen, darling, I'm so pleased you did well with the pitch. We'll talk again before Christmas, ta ta."

"Wait. Not so fast. When are you coming for a visit? Do I have to beg?"

"Spring. When the daffodils sprout. I promise."

Andrea tried to get in the last word. "I'm holdin' you to it," but Liz had hung up.

—⁓—

Andrea emailed Jonathan Hall, the gallery owner, during the winter. He called her April first when he opened the gallery. "I understand you have old paintings you want to display."

"No, no, Jonathan. They are far from being displayable. I found them in the barn, and I'm not even sure they are salvageable."

"No sense bringing them to me, then. I'll email you the contact information for a guy who restores old art."

Andrea loaded her Prius with six of the paintings and kept her appointment two towns east of Seahaven with Cape Cod Art Restoration.

The man's name was Mark Rosen. "Your artist made good use of acrylics, I see."

"I thought they were acrylic but wasn't sure."

"They are not copies of famous art, which I see a lot. These are painted from the artist's eye. Obviously, focusing on the ocean."

"I think my cousin did them, probably in the nineteen fifties, but I can't be sure. Can you restore them?"

Mr. Rosen used a loop to focus in on the damaged paintings. He made sounds like, 'hmm,' and then, 'umm.'

"Are those positive or negative noises you're making, Mr. Rosen?"

He looked up from a blue, gray, and white painting of waves crashing against rocks. "What sounds?"

Andrea waited with no more questions.

"I can clean these up. It's mostly accumulated dust that's aged and hardened. I can take care of most of it."

"Wonderful. Can you estimate the cost to restore these six? And I'd love your opinion of the quality of the work."

Mr. Rosen stood from his stool. "Give me your contact information, I'll email you a quote after I look them all over. As for the quality… you know the adage…"

"Beauty is in the eye of the beholder?"

He nodded and added, "But I wouldn't be ashamed to hang one of these in my living room. Let me put it that way for you."

Andrea headed home. It was Wednesday, and Brian was due for dinner. It was his turn to pick out a movie. Their relationship had become routine over the winter. Brian surprised her with a gold bangle bracelet several days before Christmas, but she spent the holiday alone.

Once they settled in and he told her about his week, she mentioned her visit with the art restoration shop.

He looked his usual handsome, happy self, except less tanned. "I have a brilliant thought."

Andrea imitated his enthusiasm. "Oh, do tell your brilliant thought, Dr. Evans."

"You're making fun of me, so now I won't tell you." Brian frowned, looking hurt.

Andrea played the game, sitting on his lap, petting his head, kissing his neck. "I'm sorry. Forgive me?"

"Okay, okay, you're forgiven. Here's my idea. Jonathan Hall has a show at Seahaven Gallery every July Fourth weekend. Lots of tourists around then. He rents space to artists to show or sell their work."

"Are you suggesting I show my work?"

"I'm suggesting you show your work alongside the ones you found in the barn. I think that's a cool juxtaposition, seascapes, old and new."

"Hmm," Andrea rubbed her chin. "I like it. If you keep working on your piece, maybe I'll give you a spot."

Brian clapped his hands. "You'd do that for me?"

"I'll connect with Jonathan and secure a space for us. Now this is something to look forward to. July Fourth."

—⁂—

Andrea did her daily check of email and found two messages. She read the email from Mark Rosen, quoting the cost to restore the paintings, and approved it. There was a message from Jarrett Prescott, the town archivist, too.

Ms. Birch, I find myself with idle time as I await the editor's red pen marks on my book. There's little in the town records regarding the Birch family, however, if we meet soon, I might have enough memory left to help you out. I'll be at Town Hall on Friday morning at 9:00 a.m.

Andrea had yet to put the pieces together about what happened to the Birch family after Abigale died. She knew Abigale's grandson, Nelson, lived in the house for a time, and his son John died in World War II and was probably the man who fathered her dad. Father Doyle's notes made it clear Abigale's granddaughter, Iris, and her daughter Catherine, returned to Cape Cod after years of being missing, and lived out their lives in the house.

There were still missing pieces. Did the Birch family know their son John had a child? What happened to Abigale's son Ernest?

Birch Family

Edmund
1774–1830
Margaret
1776–1832

Samuel Birch   Roger Birch
1796–1858   1798–1841

Caleb Birch   Abigale Birch
1826–1868   1843–1918

Ernest Birch
1871–

Nelson Birch   Iris Birch
1901–1979   1903–1992

John Birch   Pearl Birch   Catherine Birch
1926–1944   1928–1928   1918–2013

Mason Birch
1944–2014

Andrea Birch
1984–

LV

Give And Take

"I'm not really an official archivist, Ms. Birch."

"Andrea."

"Please to meet ya." The chair scraped the floor as the old man half stood to extend his hand to Andrea.

"Please, sit." Andrea took a seat at the old oak wooden table in a small room at Town Hall. The floors were aged oak as well. The overhead light fixture was post World War II, original to the old building. "If you're not an official archivist, Jarrett, what are you?"

The man leaned back in his chair, his belly pressuring the buttons on his blue striped shirt. "Grew up in Seahaven. Went off to college and worked my entire career as a high school history teacher. Came back every summer." He leaned in. "History fascinates me."

"I see."

"Came home to retire and found myself bored to death. Figured I knew all about Seahaven and the people. Knew how to research what I didn't know, and, well, here I am."

"Good for you."

The old man removed his cap and placed it on the table. "Now, when did you say you moved into the Birch house?"

"I didn't say, but it was over a year ago."

"And where did you say you were before that?"

Andrea was beginning to understand how this gentleman knew about everyone in town. "I didn't mention that." She folded her hands on the table. "What can you tell me about Nelson Birch? I understand he was Abigale Birch's grandson and lived in the home for his whole adult life."

"That's my understanding. How did you learn that?"

Andrea feared the meeting would serve Jarrett's need for information more than her need for family history. "Jarrett, did you know Nelson?"

Jarrett took a pair of black-framed glasses from his shirt pocket and peered across the table at Andrea. "I did."

The man seemed starved for details. She offered him a tidbit. "I found a diary written by Abigale Birch."

He sat upright and pressed his hearing aid. "Is that so? Abigale. She died way back. Nineteen eighteen, I believe."

"She did. She wrote about her son, Ernest. Did you know him?"

"Ms. Birch. There's a tragic story behind Ernest's death. Don't suppose you heard it?"

She had the sense he was now competing with her for details about the Birch family. "No, no, no, Jarrett. That's why I've come to you. People say you're the expert on history in Seahaven. I've just been poking around."

Jarrett fished in the pocket of a cardigan sweater he hung on the chair next to him. "I wrote some notes." He looked over his glasses. "Mind's going."

Andrea laughed. "You seem sharp as a tack." And then she thought, *and as nosy as an old maid.*

"I had a little landscaping business in summers when I came home after school let out. Extra money for the family. Teachers don't make much, you know. What did you say you do?"

Andrea ignored Jarrett. "Did you mow Nelson's lawn?"

He nodded. "Did. For years. Got to know the man."

"Did he ever mention his son, John?"

"Oh yeah. Said John signed up. Didn't have to go, but it was wartime. Nelson never forgave himself."

"For what?"

Jarrett looked at Andrea as if she should know. "That he got killed. Last battle of the war and the kid died. Just got there."

"Why did Nelson blame himself?"

"Nelson was a war buff. Talked about the Germans nonstop. My guess, John wanted to please his dad, be a war hero." He shook his head. "Killed Nelson's wife."

Andrea hated to disclose her own personal information to nosy Jarrett, but she realized this was a give and take kind of meeting. "Did Nelson know John had a girlfriend in Boston before he shipped out?"

Jarrett furrowed his eyebrows and then thumbed through his notebook. "Rose?"

Andrea mentally slammed the table, but outwardly remained composed. "Yes, Rose."

Jarrett pushed his glasses closer to his eyes. "See that? Wrote this down last night and forgot it already this morning. Oh, boy. This is what I got." He squinted at his notes. "They got one letter from John after he shipped out. He died his first week in Europe." He looked at his notes again. "Here it is. I'll read it, 'told his parents he was in love with a girl named Rose, pretty as her name,' is exactly what he put in the letter, and he couldn't wait to get home." Jarrett closed the little book.

"Good thing you got me now, these old memories are fading fast." Jarrett yawned, as he looked at the round clock on the wall. "I'm beginning to fade, myself."

The old history buff turned out to be a wealth of information. Andrea thought fast. "What about Ernest, Abigale's son? I found notes about his children, Nelson and Iris, but not much on him."

As if Andrea knew the characters, Jarrett told the story. "Nelson hated to tell her, but when his sister Iris showed up after almost sixty years being gone, she wanted to know about her father."

Andrea waited, wishing she were taking notes. "Tell her what?"

"Now this is a story I'll never forget. I'd sit with Nelson summer nights on the porch, and he'd reminisce, goin' on forever. I think I was his only company until his sister came back.

"It was the night after they buried Abigale. Freezing cold. Ernest, his wife Alice, and Nelson and Iris were all together at the house." He lowered his voice. "Alice was, well, Nelson called her 'flighty,' but I've heard it was worse than that. Anyway, Ernest and Alice were arguing, and all of a sudden, fifteen-year-old Iris announces she's pregnant." Jarrett stopped as if waiting for Andrea to gasp.

"According to Nelson, who was seventeen at the time, all hell broke loose. Alice was screaming and slapping poor Iris. Ernest was standing there, all stunned." Jarrett got up and got himself a bottle of water. "Want one?"

Andrea shook her head. "Go on."

"Evidently, the big bombshell was that Iris swore it was Ernest's boss, Ryan Taylor, who got her that way, and he'd been messing around with Alice, too."

"Geeze."

"Yup. And mind you, this was back in nineteen eighteen or so. Times were different. This scoundrel, Ryan Taylor, went for Ernest's wife and fifteen-year-old daughter."

"What happened to Iris?"

"Nelson told me this story so many times…" Jarrett looked at Andrea, shaking his head. "It was an awful night all around. Right in the middle of Alice wailing on Iris, Ernest stomped out. Alice was so furious with Iris for spilling the beans on her, she sent her off."

"She banished a fifteen-year-old girl from her home?"

"Alice was a nasty woman. Nelson always cried when he got to this part of the story. It was him who took Iris to the train that night."

"That answers some of my questions."

Jarrett put his hand out as if to stop Andrea from talking. "There's more."

"Go on."

"Morning came and Ernest hadn't come home. The temperatures were in the teens, and the winds were whipping off the ocean. Tree branches sagged with ice."

"What happened?"

"They searched, Nelson and Alice. Just after noontime, they found him, laying right across his mother's grave, frozen to death. Guess he couldn't leave old Abigale."

Andrea sat back. She was sweating. "God." She looked over at Jarrett. "And Iris?"

"Poor Iris never knew what happened to her father till she came back with her daughter, Catherine, in the seventies. Never knew he died that night. All those years away, Iris didn't know her brother, Nelson, was in the house, waiting for her to come home." Jarrett peeked over his glasses at Andrea. "Kept it just like it was when she left. Never changed a thing in that old place. Drove is wife nuts."

"What happened to Alice?"

Jarrett shrugged and pushed back his chair. "Don't know. No one does."

He put on his jacket, tucked his glasses and notebook in his shirt pocket. "So, that's all I got for you, Miss Birch. Hope it helps."

He asked another question as he approached the door. "Who did you say you were married to?"

She smiled at this man's persistence. "I didn't." And then she thought he'd been generous with his knowledge and time. "I'm dating Brian Evans."

Jarrett's left eyebrow arched. "Dating?"

"Yes, do you know him? He's a podiatrist."

Jarrett put his hand on the doorknob. "I know he's a podiatrist. Give him my regards, although he probably won't know me. I think he's my wife's second or third cousin."

Andrea walked to Jarrett and shook his hand. "Can I pay you? You've been so helpful."

"Nope. I'm a volunteer. Pay would make it work. Good luck to you, now."

—⁂—

Andrea called Liz to share her progress. "Ah, hello. I saw a daffodil today, sprouting right out of the ground."

"Nice to hear your voice. Daffodil, huh? The streets around here still have mounds of grimy snow on them, hard to spot the little yellow flowers."

"I have news. I've made progress tracking the Birch family line." She looked at her easel. "Turns out, John Birch was in love with Rose. He wrote to his parents when he got overseas. He never knew he was going to be a father."

"Interesting, except I can't follow you with all these Birch people."

"Liz, the long and the short of it is my grandmother Rose was right. John loved her and if he hadn't died at Normandy, he was coming back. She knew it in her heart. That's why she told my dad the story every night. It gives me such peace. I wish Dad and his mom were here now so I could tell them."

Birch Family

Edmund
1774–1830
Margaret
1776–1832

Samuel Birch   Roger Birch
1796–1858   1798–1841

Caleb Birch   Abigale Birch
1826–1868   1843–1918

Ernest Birch
1871–1918

Nelson Birch   Iris Birch
1901–1979   1903–1992

John Birch   Pearl Birch   Catherine Birch
1926–1944   1928–1928   1918–2013

Mason Birch
1944–2014

Andrea Birch
1984–

LVI

An Eye For An Eye

Andrea spent the rest of the weekend and following week putting the finishing touches on the three seascapes she chose to exhibit at the gallery showing. She moved her sofa an inch to the left and then an inch to the right, refolded all the clothes in her dresser, and made sure the forks and knives all lined up in the silverware drawer. She had little else to do, except wait for Brian's visit.

He was on time, his usual exuberant self, and went straight for the CD player. "C'mon, dance with me." Brian put on *The Great Pretender* by The Platters and latched onto Andrea's waist.

"Hey, I have food on the stove. Do you want burned steak or a dance?"

Brian finished his glass of wine and followed Andrea to the kitchen. "What's going on? You seem distant."

She turned from checking the broccoli. "It's not you. I'm learning so much about my family. I'm distracted tonight, I guess."

Brian nodded and brought her in for a hug. "I'll take off. Let you think about your relatives."

Stunned, Andrea called out. "Brian. You don't have to leave." He didn't turn around but picked up his keys and walked out the front door. "Temperamental bastard."

The song ended. *I seem to be what I'm not, you see, I'm wearing my heart like a crown, Pretending that you're still around.*

The steak dinner went uneaten, wrapped in the refrigerator for another day. It was only nine o'clock, but she went to bed, the words repeating in her mind. *I seem to be what I'm not, you see...*

—⁓—

Andrea brightened up the following morning when Mark Rosen from the art restoration store called. "Ms. Birch, good news."

"About the paintings? Were you successful?"

"I'd say so. They cleaned up very well. Acrylic is forgiving. Definitely by an artist with an unusual view of the world. Or in this case, the ocean."

"When can I pick them up?"

"They're ready now."

"I'll be by today and then run into the gallery to see what Jonathan thinks of them."

—⁓—

Jonathan Hall didn't have a lot of facial expressions. He either looked disinterested or mildly interested. Today he seemed mildly interested in the paintings. "Interesting."

"Jonathan, when you say 'interesting' that could mean these are so terrible they are interesting, or these are so good, they are interesting."

Andrea detected the sides of his mouth curling upward. "Is that a smile?"

"You can call it that. What I'm seeing is work by a self-trained artist. That's what makes them interesting, if you will. They are not your run-of-the-mill seascapes, no offense."

Andrea laughed. "None taken."

"They are pure, in a way. A view from the artist's eye, no standard technique, just raw vision. Interesting."

"They'd be great to mount in contrast with my run-of-the-mill seascapes, do you think?"

He nodded, employing his mildly interested expression. "A notion. A notion."

"Well, that's my plan."

"I can go along with it. I'll reserve you the right space so you can contrast these three with three of your paintings."

"Oh, and room for one of Brian's. He's been working on a beach scene in watercolor."

A harrumph sound came from Jonathan's throat. "I'll ponder that."

———

Brian sent flowers with an apology. He added he wouldn't be visiting during the week, so Andrea spent her time hanging a few more old relatives' photographs. Evenings, she spent reading more of Father Doyle's notes on his visits from Iris Birch, hoping to learn the artist's identity.

Monday, April 6, 1981

Iris Birch visits less now, and when she does, she confuses time and dates.

She still questions if she is a sinner. I invited her to confess but she insisted on asking me if her deeds were truly sins.

She has deep remorse about her daughter, Catherine. She told me Catherine remained in a small guesthouse when she moved into a modern home with their employer. "Catherine became more and more withdrawn. She lived like a hermit, and cluttered the tiny guesthouse with books, clothing, and food."

I advised Iris I didn't think it was her sin. Catherine was an adult, with her own free will. She continued to blame herself, exhibiting deep guilt and remorse, "Father, I lived in comfort, even traveled, while Catherine ate herself to a shameful size and allowed her gray hair to fall straight down her back. I couldn't control her behavior."

Again, I counseled to her deaf ears. "Catherine has free will."

Iris wouldn't let it go. "She seems content to be alone and paint, paint, paint."

Aha, I knew it. The paintings are by Catherine Birch. I bet she lived in the attic and painted the walls.

She read on.

July 10, 1981

Ms. Birch visited today, unannounced. I am finding her visits tedious, I confess. She continues to confuse dates and times, even people. Today she asked another question about sins. I believe she has a psychological condition, and it is worsening. She obsesses on her own past behaviors, questioning if she's sinned.

Today she asked about murder. "Father, is there anything that justifies killing a person?"

My patience frayed due to the July heat, I told her outright she'd have to give me context, as I've told her many times before.

She became agitated. "If a man harms another? If a man destroys another's life? If a man must be stopped from hurting others? Is it a sin to stop a man from sinning?"

Now this question gave me pause, but with Iris being confused often and asking confounded questions, I wasn't sure if I should continue the conversation. I made a decision, one I'm afraid was driven by my own impatience and the grueling heat.

I told her I was hearing confessions the following day from one p.m. until four p.m. and I would answer her question then.

Iris stood and gathered herself. Her face distorted with, I imagined, anger. She railed at me. "Death is justice for a man who takes the innocence from young girls, robs them of their futures, and leaves them in a state of shame." She left before I could respond.

Saturday, July 11, 1981

It was near four p.m. today and I'd given up hope Iris would visit me in the confessional. I concluded she was suffering from senility and her rantings were baseless. I'd taken off my glasses, and removed my confessional stole, when I heard someone kneel. I slid open the door between us and bowed my head to listen.

"Father, I've sinned by killing a man."

Right away I suspected it was Iris, but the voice was a whisper, and I couldn't see through the screen. I tested her story. "Tell me how you killed a man."

There was a long pause, and I heard a release of breath.

"Is it a sin? I question it because he was hurting others."

Again, I suspected senility in Iris and probed for details. "How was he hurting others?"

She was vague, as I expected. "Many ways. For too long."

It was late and hot in that confessional, I probed again for details. "And how did you kill this man? It must have been difficult for a woman to overcome a man."

Again, a long pause. I was about to offer her absolution and tell her to say a few Hail Marys, hoping it would satisfy her need to repent.

"A hat pin, Father."

I bowed my head, praying to the dear Lord for patience. "A hat pin? Did you say a hat pin?"

She started talking rapidly, her voice a hoarse whisper. "Bless me Father, I stuck a hat pin in the corner of a man's eye, straight into his brain, and it killed him. Forgive me Father, for I have sinned."

She didn't stay long enough for me to ask another question, absolve her, or give her a penance. When I realized she was gone, I pounced from the confessional and looked around the church. It was empty save for two women kneeling at the altar rail. One was Iris, I recognized her dress. Next to her was a heavy-set, taller woman with long straight gray hair.

Father Doyle's notes on Iris Birch ended. Andrea was stunned, *Holy shit, either Iris or her daughter, Catherine, stuck a hat pin in Ryan Taylor's brain. This family can't stop knocking people off.*

This was news Andrea wanted to share, but Liz and Brian made it clear they weren't interested. Tom Whelan emailed he was coming home in August. *I'll fill Tom in. He'll listen,* she thought.

The following day, another piece of the puzzle appeared in the mail. It was an envelope from the Law Office of Swain & Swain. A brief letter explained that the enclosed letter was in the file of documents related to the search for the heir to Catherine Birch. Andrea found an envelope inside with a return address of the U.S. Army, Washington, D.C. The elder Attorney Swain scribbled a notation on it:

"This envelope from the U.S. Army was unopened among the belongings of Nelson Birch. I opened it and read the enclosed letter, which assisted me to determine that Andrea Birch Rossi is the rightful heir to the Birch property."

The letter was in a woman's handwriting, addressed to John Birch, U.S. Army, Washington, D.C.

To Whom It May Concern,

I am trying to contact John Birch, however, I have not heard from him since he shipped out in June of nineteen forty-four. If you have information about his whereabouts, possibly an Army hospital, if he was wounded, please tell him we have a son. Mason Birch is the image of his father, and we both await his homecoming.

Sincerely,
Rose Emery
24 Walden Terrace
Boston, Massachusetts

Andrea thought, *so John Birch never opened the letter from the Army. If he had, my father may have had a family.*

LVII

Elation

July 2020

Andrea planned out her day. Wrap six paintings, pee on a stick, head to the gallery to mount the paintings. She put off the pregnancy test and wrapped the six paintings. She'd missed her period twice, and decided it was time she knew for sure. With nothing else to do before heading to the gallery, she took the test.

Andrea arrived at the gallery parking lot at three p.m. A young man met her at her car. "I'm here to help bring in your paintings."

She suppressed the urge to say, "Good for you, I'm pregnant."

When Jonathan met her at the door, she pushed back the urge again. "Good day, Jonathan. What a pleasant, sunny summer day." She nodded toward her helper. "And thanks for the muscle."

"I do it every year. These kids are grad students in a Master of Fine Arts program. It's great experience for them, and they work cheap."

Jonathan was unusually cheerful, considering the stress of setting up the showing. "You're the chipper one, today, Andrea. Excited about the show?"

Again, she resisted shouting out, "Hell, no. I'm excited about being pregnant," and instead agreed, "Yes, this is so fun, I can't tell you."

"I've given you prime space. Follow me."

They walked from the front door to the middle of the gallery. "Your three paintings will hang here, vertically." He pointed up and moved his hand down. "One, two, three."

"Okay, I'm trying to envision."

"There's a channel of wires and attachments running up and down."

He pointed. "To the right is a second channel of wires and attachments for the older seascapes to hang vertically, as well."

"And the space between the hanging paintings, people walk through?"

"Exactly. They make it halfway through the gallery and then pass between three paintings on each side of them, the highest, just above their eye level."

"I like it."

There was activity all around. The college kids were asking Jonathan for direction and artists were searching for their designated spots. Jonathan excused himself. "Andrea, you've got help. I have to move on. This is a big day."

"Of course, Jonathan. Just one thing, where's the space for Brian's painting?"

Jonathan walked two steps away. He turned back. "How do I say this? I have a reputation."

Andrea nodded in understanding.

"I just couldn't use it."

The moment of disappointment passed when her college helper asked her to put the paintings in order so he could hang them. Once she gave him direction, she excused herself. "I'll be right back."

Andrea ran to the car for a sign she'd painted for her exhibit. "Can you hang this from the ceiling above the paintings? Center it right between them." She handed him the sign, painted in the blue and white colors of the seascapes.

Her helper read it. "Tides that Bind, hmm, cool."

Again, she held herself back from saying, "You think that's cool, I'm pregnant." Instead, she watched until she was satisfied with the arrangement of the paintings, checked to see that both sides were even, and left the gallery.

Andrea drove home, thinking less about the gallery showing and more about telling Brian her news. She rehearsed her words out loud. "This is the happiest I can remember being in my life." In her fantasy, he'd smile and cup her face as she assured him, "Now, I don't expect anything from you. I'm an independent woman. It's up to you if you want to be in our lives."

She pictured his face breaking into a huge grin. "Honey, I can't imagine my life without you. And now a baby? That's fantastic."

Andrea was smiling to herself as she approached the curve a quarter mile from her house. The gravel road was narrow, and the curve always seemed to surprise her. She hit the brakes and turned the steering wheel. *Focus, girl, focus.*

Andrea arrived home and baked a batch of oatmeal raisin cookies for the gallery showing. She grabbed a few and with a hot cup of ginger tea, sat in bed and watched television. She noticed a missed call on her cell phone and saw there was a message from her ex-husband, Will. She spoke to the phone. "Perfect timing, Will. Now you call after months? You'll have to wait because you're not gonna ruin my gallery show and day with Brian."

LVIII

The Showing

The early morning July sun woke Andrea. She read the paper and relaxed. By ten a.m. she was anxious and jittery about the big day and called Jonathan. "Can I run in and bring my cookies for the gallery showing? I have time to kill before one o'clock."

"Of course, there're a few people here milling around, putting their final touches on their exhibits."

Andrea put off her shower and primping and hopped in the car, cookies in hand. The walk from the parking lot to the gallery left her dripping with sweat. Even her hair, pulled back in a ponytail, went limp.

She found Jonathan. "I think my cookies wilted between here and the parking lot."

Jonathan responded to Andrea's attempt at humor. "We have the air conditioner cranked as high as it will go. Let's hope it holds up, or we'll all dissolve into little puddles."

"I'll just drop these on the goodies' table and head home. I'm a mess; have to shower and pretty myself up."

Jonathan moved on to settle a minor crisis. Andrea circled the gallery, cookies in hand, searching for the table with the bakery offerings for the gallery visitors. She stopped by her exhibit as a double check, and saw several people milling around it, including Brian.

"Well, hello. Aren't you the early bird?"

Brian turned toward the voice. "Look at you. Yes, I thought we'd get an early peek."

"We?"

He turned toward a tall, tanned blonde woman. "Yes. Andrea. This is Suzanne, my wife." He put his arm around her waist. "Hon, this is my art teacher, Andrea. Although I don't know if she considers me a student or a charity case, given my lack of progress."

Suzanne nodded toward Andrea. "Oh, yes. Brian gave me one of your paintings for my birthday. So nice to meet you. Your exhibit is outstanding. I love the contrast you've created between the two styles of the artists."

Andrea's heart pulsed blood to her face. The veins in her temples bulged from the rush. All her adrenalin ascended to her brain, leaving her body weak and trembling. Her attempt to speak failed. Her jaw locked, she could feel her ears burn and was struck by an instant headache. Brian took over.

Andrea stood numb, her mind racing to put this scene in context. She forced two words. "Excuse me."

Andrea adjusted the air conditioning in the Prius as high as it would go, but the flush in her face continued to burn. She gulped for air to breathe; her head pounded. She drove with intention, pushing the Prius to fifty miles an hour on the road winding back to her house. Her mind focused on one word, married. She repeated it over and over, not conjuring any other thoughts. "Married, married, married." Then, "Bastard, bastard, bastard. Lying bastard."

Andrea slammed her keys on the floor as she walked through her front door. Her first instinct was to call Liz, but she hadn't sorted her own thoughts. Incensed, she paced the living room, no longer minding the July heat. She went to the kitchen and emptied the dishwasher, checked the dryer for clothes, opened and closed the refrigerator, all the while, fuming.

There was so much to sort out, but she was out of energy for the day. She didn't give the one p.m. gallery showing a thought.

Drained by the emotional roller coaster, Andrea retreated to the bathroom for a cool shower. She changed into a nightgown and turned on the window air conditioner in her bedroom, hoping for sleep.

The ringing of the phone woke her at seven a.m.

"Andrea, Will."

She was gathering her thoughts, putting the pieces together, remembering her early bedtime, Brian and the wife, the gallery show she never made. And now, Will on the phone.

"Hey."

"I've called you a few times."

"Yeah, sorry. I was going to call you today." She lied.

"Listen. How are you, by the way? Did I wake you?"

Andrea sat on the side of her bed, feeling impatient. "What's up, Will?"

"Not much. It's been a while. Wanted to catch up."

At seven a.m., don't think so. "Nothing new here." *Except I'm pregnant and the daddy is a scumbag.*

"Well, I have news."

She jumped on him, "Listen, if you need money…"

"No. It's not that. Part of my news is I'm in GA, Gamblers Anonymous. Kicking the habit for good this time."

She didn't believe him. "Great. But I'm not in the position to lend you…"

"I sold the store. Paid off my gambling debts. I'm all set for money. Got a job in a hospital pharmacy. I like it. Working regular hours like a normal person."

"Good for you." There was an awkward silence. "Really, great news. You take care, now."

"Wait, Andrea. I have a son."

Andrea stood up and looked at the phone in her hand. "Well, I guess I should say congratulations."

"Yes, thanks. He's a wonderful little guy. All Rossi."

Andrea sat back down on her bed.

"Yeah, he's walking like a champ; starting to talk up a storm, although we don't understand him yet."

"Talking? How old is he?"

Will's voice dropped, "Going on two. Two next month."

Andrea counted on her fingers. "But…"

"Yeah. I'm sorry about that. Didn't want you to hear it from someone else."

Andrea's body shook all over. Her hands trembled and her stomach flipped. "I'm hanging up now, Will."

"Okay. I get it. You take care. Okay?"

Andrea didn't reply.

"I'm gonna do a better job with Billy than my father did with me. You know what I mean?"

She disconnected the call and counted again. *The son of a bitch screwed around while I was getting infertility treatments.*

That Will conceived a child during their marriage was the final blow. Her initial rage dissolved into pain and deep, anguished sobs emerged.

She dressed and got in her car and drove east to Provincetown, on the tip of the Cape. It was Fourth of July weekend, and traffic was heavy. With nothing else to do, she inched along and after finding a parking space, took herself for lunch. Forgetting she was pregnant, she ordered a Bloody Mary, which sat on the table untouched.

After a long day of walking around Provincetown, even buying a few infant outfits with lobsters on them, she headed home. It was a slow ride. She used the time to process, realizing she rushed into marriage with Will because she wanted to be settled, and she thought she could fix what was broken about him. Both he and Brian sensed her vulnerability and took advantage of it. She smiled, thinking, *Lucky for them I'm more civilized than my ancestors. Abigale Birch killed George Smythe for less, and one of my cousins finished off Ryan Taylor.*

She thought about her next conversation with Liz. "So, my cousins, Iris and Catherine, killed a man by sticking a hat pin through his eye. At least my great-great-great grandmother, Abigale, would have been pleased they used a fashion accessory."

Andrea felt at peace when she arrived home. It was dark but still hot and humid. She opened her shopping bags and smiled as she examined the baby clothes she purchased. She took a shower and put on her nightgown, planning to settle down for the evening with a cup of Chamomile tea. A chill ran through her when she heard the familiar three little taps at the door. *Brian,* she thought. *Go away.* She didn't answer and waited, hoping he would leave. The taps came again, and he called out her name.

She took three deep breaths and reminded herself she was moving on. She opened the door.

"Hey, hon. I thought you might be sleeping."

"Hon? Did you say 'hon'?"

He walked in, a broad smile across his face. "Happy Fourth. What happened to you yesterday? You never showed at the gallery."

She gathered her thoughts to reply. "Why are you here?"

"It's Sunday. I'm working on the Vineyard tomorrow." He sat on the sofa. "Doesn't look like we'll be going out to dinner unless you plan to wear your nightgown." He pointed to her feet. "Most restaurants require shoes."

Andrea stood, arms folded. "You're married."

Brian's pleasant expression changed. "Of course, I'm married."

"You say that like I'm supposed to know."

Now his face turned angry. "Don't play this game with me, Andrea."

She reminded herself to remain calm, *moving on.*

She cleared her throat. "What game, Brian? You never said you were married. You probably have a bunch of kids, too."

"If you don't mind, I prefer not to share my personal business. By the way, you never asked if I was married. You know why? Because you knew."

"I didn't." She took a deep breath. "Guess what, I don't need another woman's husband."

He stood. "Apparently you do. Otherwise, you wouldn't be sitting around night after night, waiting for me to take you to bed once or twice a month."

Only two days before, Andrea envisioned this moment to be one of celebration of her baby. "Get out, you bastard. Find some other naïve woman to screw around on your wife with." And then it occurred to her. "I'm sure I'm not the first or the last."

"Or the best," he added and slammed the door behind him.

The calm abandoned her. She screamed after him. "Not the best? You bastard. Now you're gonna pay. Your little wifey's gonna boot your ass to the curb and you're gonna have to clip a lot more toenails to make the child support payments every month."

A quick Google search, and Andrea had Brian's address. Despite the holiday traffic, she set off mid-morning, thinking of Iris, pregnant at fifteen, walking up to Ryan Taylor's home, prepared to ruin his life. Today, she would do the same to Brian. She spent the hour in the car practicing her speech out loud. "Hello, Suzanne. Do you remember me? I'm your husband's, ahem, art teacher." She imagined Suzanne would acknowledge her with a curt 'hello.'

The practiced conversation continued. "I'm here because your husband and I had an affair." She'd wait for Suzanne's surprised reaction, the incredulous expression on her face, the sputtering in disbelief, and continue. "It's over, but there's one lingering matter." Another pause. "I'm pregnant, and your husband is the father." *So there,* she thought. *I've ruined his marriage and possibly his life.* She'd walk away, offering, "Have a good day." She didn't take the time to imagine Suzanne's response.

The GPS directed her down a tree lined street with large colonial homes and sloping green lawns. She stopped at the house with the mailbox numbered fifteen and the name Evans. Two young boys, no more than ten years old, played basketball in the driveway. Andrea felt her determination waver for an instant as she watched them chase each other around, vying for the ball. She took a moment and imagined her words again. *Hello, Suzanne. Your husband and I had an affair. I didn't know he was married.* And then Suzanne entered Andrea's imagined scenario.

Then you must have ignored the signs.

Andrea replied with indignance. *Signs? Like he only saw me twice a month? Never on holidays? That he never mentioned a family? That I never asked? You mean those signs?*

Imaginary Suzanne came back. *Why are you here? Don't you see those boys in the driveway? Will it give you pleasure to destroy our family? Do you think you're the first woman to knock on my door?*

Now Andrea was sputtering. *No. Of course I don't want to hurt those boys. Or you. It's Brian I want to make suffer.*

Suzanne's voice didn't waver. *My father was a cheater and my mother divorced him. I spent every other weekend of my childhood visiting him in the dingy apartment that was all he could afford. My mother was bitter and miserable. I'm not putting my boys through that. Brian will have his day, but, for the sake of my children, I'm turning a blind eye, just like you did.*

The July sun beat on the car, making it too hot to bear. Andrea turned on the ignition and waited for the air conditioning to cool her down. She rethought the scenario that just played in her mind. *No, I don't want to ruin a family. Yes, I did turn a blind eye,* and set her GPS for Seahaven, Massachusetts.

LIX

The Odd Alliance

Andrea's first appointment with the doctor confirmed she was pregnant. "Looks like you'll have a New Year's baby, Ms. Birch."

"And all's good? With the baby?"

"Absolutely. Healthy mom and healthy baby. Just what I like."

Andrea shared the news with Liz. "Guess who hasn't had a glass of wine in a month?"

"I know it's not me, so it must be you. What's going on? Did your liver finally give out?"

"Guess again."

"Darling, I don't play guessing games. Tell me. Are you all right?"

"Better than all right, Liz. I'm pregnant. Due just before New Year's."

There was a moment of silence on the telephone before Liz spoke. "I'm so sorry, Andrea."

"No, no, no, Liz. Don't be sorry. I'm thrilled. Feel great, except the idea of a cup of coffee makes me nauseous, and you know how I love my Colombian brew."

"Can I ask?"

"It's Brian's, of course." Liz didn't reply, so Andrea kept talking. "Listen, if this doesn't get you to visit, I don't know what will. Please, come. I really need the company."

"Can you wait a bit. How's the end of September? I love the Cape in the fall."

"So, you're coming, really?"

"Yes, darling. Get my bed ready."

—⁂—

Andrea and Tom walked around the garden. "Almost time to harvest our tomatoes. I can't wait."

"We'll pick 'em in due time. Don't wish your days away, kid. Life passes by pretty quick. Take it from me."

Andrea hadn't told Tom about the baby. "You are so right. I'm living every day, more aware of how quickly time passes than I've ever been."

Tom was putting the hose and bucket of weeds in the wheelbarrow.

Andrea walked with him to the barn. "I guess I'm treasuring each day more because of a new life."

Tom kept walking, pushing the wheelbarrow.

"Tom, did you hear me, a new life, get it?"

"I get it. It's been kinda hard to miss." He glanced at her midsection.

"You knew and didn't say anything?"

"Not for me to say. I knew you'd tell me when the time was right."

"Are you happy for me?"

"Are you happy? Then I'm happy." He stopped and turned to face his friend. "You know I'll be here for you, don't you?"

Andrea reached and hugged Tom. "I'm counting on it."

—⁂—

Anticipating Liz's arrival, Andrea browsed her favorite shops in Seahaven center. She bought apricot and honey hand soap and bodywash, and lavender scented sachets for the drawers in the loft. As she walked toward the True Brew to pick up fresh baked scones, the aroma of chocolate drew her into Seahaven Confections. The choices of fudge mesmerized her as she struggled between Cappuccino and Chocolate Oreo. "I'll take a half pound of each."

Assuring herself Liz would enjoy them, she picked up a two-pound box of dark and milk chocolates, with an assortment of Turtles, Caramels, and Chocolate Clusters. Her final stop was the True Blue, where she blamed it on her pregnancy when instead of her usual scones, she ordered three each of the eclairs, French macaroon cookies, and canoli.

As promised, Liz arrived the following morning. Andrea watched as a Lincoln Continental pulled into the clamshell driveway. A gentleman emerged from the car and opened the back door. He assisted a frail woman, head wrapped in a turquoise and pink turban, out of the car.

The sense of excitement faded from Andrea as she walked toward her friend. "Liz, at last. Welcome to my humble abode."

The raspy voice replied, "Take my arm, darling, would you. Riding over those dirt roads almost killed me."

The driver removed two large suitcases from the trunk of the car and followed Andrea's nod to the front door. "Place them inside the door, please. I'll take it from there." She walked arm and arm with Liz, a slow step at a time up the porch step and into the house.

"Take me to the sofa, will you, darling? I just need to recover. That was one long ride, and that backseat was hell on my bony ass."

Andrea took in the scene. Liz was a shell of herself, thin, hairless, her voice a hoarse whisper. She wondered if she came to die. She looked up at the loft. Her dreams of hosting her guest there ended. Liz could never climb the stairs.

"Close your mouth, Andrea, you're catching flies."

"What do you expect? You could have kept me up to date on your health all these months."

Liz crossed one thin leg over the other. "It's all good news, dear."

Andrea sat next to her friend. "Fill me in."

Liz peeled a fifty from her purse and handed it to Andrea. "Tip the gentleman, would you, darling? I'm too pooped to get up."

"Sure, then can I make you a cup of tea. Chamomile?"

"Ginger, it settles my tummy. And a few saltines if you don't mind. Then we'll sit and I'll tell you the story of my life. I'm sorry I kept it from you, dear. You know me, stubborn old bird that I am."

—◦◦◦—

"Cancer?"

"The breast cancer I had twenty years ago showed up in my lungs about six months ago. I'm not complaining. Twenty years is a good run. I thought it was a cold, but when I couldn't catch my breath, the doc did more tests."

"That's why you've been so scarce."

"Treatment, honey. It was brutal." Liz took off her turban. "I don't have a hair on my body, Oh, that's more than you wanted to know."

"What else?"

"Appetite's gone. I don't even have a taste for gin if you can believe that."

"Okay, so what's going on now?"

"Now, I'm here with my friend. The treatments are over. They say I'm in remission, but we know how that goes."

Andrea took Liz's hand. "Hey, that's good news. Take it."

"Sure. Anyway, I just need time to get my strength back. This has knocked the stuffing out of me."

"I'm already planning in my head." Andrea pointed to the loft. "There's no way I'm letting you climb up and down those stairs. There isn't even a bathroom up there."

"Oh dear, and I go every ten minutes."

"You'll take my room, and I'll use the loft."

Liz pulled her hand away. "There's no way I'm taking your bed."

"No arguing. It makes perfect sense. We'll get that appetite back. I'll cook pasta, the house is stocked with sweet treats. Oh, and ice cream. You could never resist a pint of Rocky Road."

Andrea looked over at Liz, who had rested her head against the back of the loveseat and drifted off. She took her favorite blanket and placed it over her. "You're home, now, friend. I'll take care of you."

LX

Restored

Good company and home-cooked meals helped restore Liz's health. She, Tom, and Andrea passed a warm October, often enjoying dinners together and spending evenings watching the stars and moon from Andrea's screen porch. Some nights they had thoughtful talks, questioning the meaning of life, and others, they poked fun at each other and told old stories. Liz and Andrea competed to get belly laughs out of Tom.

It was a warm Indian Summer evening when Andrea, blaming it on hormones, choked up as she thanked Liz and Tom. "You know, I was all mixed up when I came here. I needed to reconcile my losses, my dad, Paul, the life I thought I'd have. Instead, I focused on finding my dead relatives."

Liz inserted a crack. "That's called avoidance."

Andrea laughed through her tears. "You're right. I wasn't ready to do the pain."

"No pain, no gain, lady."

"Yes, Liz. There's always a heckler in the audience."

She sipped her martini. "Okay, I'll shut up. Continue."

"But it wasn't a waste of time." She looked around. "I learned my Grandma Rose was right. John Birch loved her." She swept her arm. "And look at this beautiful home, thanks to Tom. And I did find family." She rubbed her belly. "A baby, you guys. I've never felt more at home."

Tom sat on a rocker, an unlit pipe in his hand. "She's right. It takes more than a coat of bright red lipstick on a house to make it a home."

Liz sat up straight. "Is this about me?"

Tom grinned. "Gotcha there, Lizzie. Didn't I? But it's true." He turned toward Andrea. "You fixed a house and fixed yourself. Now you're really at home, and it's not because of all them dead relatives you found."

Liz inhaled the October air. "I know this house has been a godsend for me. I couldn't have made it this far without you two." A moment passed. "How about you, Tom. Did you fix yourself along with the house?"

Tom put the pipe in his mouth and wagged one finger. "Tom don't talk about stuff like that." He wiped his nose with his sleeve.

Liz sipped her martini. "This kind of talk is too serious. If it keeps up, I'm gonna sing *Kumbaya*."

"No, please, don't. I've heard you sing. How about a big dish of Rocky Road? The baby's hungry."

Tom jumped up. "I'm in. I'll serve on your Mexican dishes."

"Farmhouse." Andrea countered back. "And I'm eating for two, so make mine two scoops."

—◊◊◊—

When Tom suggested converting Andrea's small office into a nursery, she agreed, and was overwhelmed when Liz and Tom gifted her with a crib and rocking chair. "You two. I love you so much."

Tom blushed and stepped back. "I'll put these together tomorrow. Set them up in the nursery."

Andrea had ideas of her own. "I'll paint a mural on the wall. A rainbow with a pot of gold at the end."

Tom teased, "Yup. Can't let a kid come into this world without its own rainbow."

"And pot of gold." Andrea added.

"Yup."

It was getting toward the late afternoon. "You staying for dinner tonight, Tom?"

He put his coat and hat on. "Not tonight. Got errands to run. Whatcha cookin'?"

Andrea teased, "Nothing you'd care for, anyway. Just a roast pork with mashed potatoes, fresh string beans, that's all. Oh, and baked apples."

Tom had his hand on the doorknob. "What time?"

Andrea laughed. "We'll wait for you."

—⁂—

November turned cold, and Andrea and Liz hunkered down by the fire each afternoon and evening. They'd play Scrabble some nights, and when Tom came by, poker. As Thanksgiving approached, they made plans for a turkey dinner.

"Last year, I spent the day alone, and truthfully, I was sad." Andrea put her arms around her two friends. "This year I have a lot to be thankful for."

"Stop. You're gonna make me cry, and Liz doesn't cry."

Andrea snapped back, with a smile. "There's no time like the present…"

"After Thanksgiving, you're going to have to slow down. I'm stronger now. I can take over the cooking. You can put your puffy feet up."

"Thanks, Liz. I'm feeling fine. My only worry is climbing that stairway to the loft. I'm a little off kilter."

"She weebles, she wobbles."

"Yeah, yeah. But I don't want to fall down."

"Why not double up with me? After all, it's your room I've taken over."

"You mean sleep together?"

"I don't bite, you know. You're approaching the end and getting bigger. I can't let you keep climbing those steps. I worry."

Andrea's petite body grew to accommodate what her doctor predicted to be an eight-pound baby. "The bigger issue, no pun intended, is the bathroom. I'm up and down those steps all night."

"Then it's done. What side do you want?"

"The one closest to the bathroom."

—⁂—

It was an early December evening, close to their ten o'clock bedtime when Liz broached the subject. "It's been months, and you haven't said much about Brian."

Andrea shifted in her chair, trying to get comfortable. "Not much to say. I made a big mistake."

"Listen, you can't take all the blame."

Andrea's voice rose, "How could I have been that stupid? Did you know?"

"That Brian was married? Of course, I did. Or at least I knew he was up to something. Look, if a guy likes a woman, he doesn't leave her alone twenty-eight days of the month." She pointed a finger, "Unless, that is…"

"He's married." She calmed down. "Why didn't you tell me?"

Liz sipped her ginger tea. "Because, darling, you chose to ignore the obvious signs. You settled for what he was offering." She shrugged. "Maybe you thought it was all you deserved."

Andrea checked her watch. "It's ten. Am I keeping you up?"

She held up her teacup. "Still finishing. Keep talking. I know you've been thinking about him."

"You know, the past couple of years have been a blur. Let's face it, Liz, I've been a mess. I ran away."

"From Will?"

"From my life, or non-life, if that's a word. Look at me. I went from three years of taking care of my dad to marrying the wrong man."

Liz softened her voice. "Have you figured out why?"

"I always knew, deep down. I've told you about Paul, right?"

"A thousand times but tell me again."

"I know I didn't tell you I called him after my dad passed. I thought he'd beg me to move out West, be with him, start our lives together again."

"No, you didn't tell me."

"I humiliated myself. Told him I was planning a visit, didn't get the hesitation in his voice."

"Honey, you're not a mind reader."

"True, but I should have figured it out. He wasn't thrilled to hear from me, didn't even respond when I mentioned a trip out West. He actually interrupted me, stop me from babbling about old times together." She looked at her hands. "I could cry now, remembering." Andrea stopped. "He got married."

"Saw that coming."

"Well, I didn't. Between losing my dad and knowing I couldn't have Paul, I kind of went numb. I knew I'd never love anyone that way again."

"Have you ever thought maybe you glorified Paul in your mind? There are a lot of wonderful guys out there. And you're a catch."

"Yeah. I created such a perfect man in my head, I convinced myself there'd never be another one."

"So you settled for less than you deserved."

Andrea shifted in her chair. "You should have been a psychiatrist."

Liz put her cup on the table and curled her legs under herself. "So, tell me, what did you expect when you moved into this house?"

"I think I needed time to figure it all out. I thought I'd be around family."

"In the cemetery?"

Andrea smiled, "I hear ya."

"You gotta get your feet on the ground, kid, with a baby on the way."

"I'm getting there. It hurt, but I learned a lot about myself from the Brian debacle."

"Do tell."

"I can't say I loved Brian, but I learned I'm willing to try again." She patted her belly, "but frankly I'm in no hurry."

"There's plenty of love coming your way."

"I've been thinking more about what is best for me and the baby. Living here all year, first of all, is too isolating. It's deserted in the winter. I have no friends, no job. Now I'll be raising a baby all by myself…" She grabbed the grave marker she kept on her side table. Her voice cracked. "I don't want to be another Abigale Birch."

"Okay, okay, calm down. You don't have to stay here."

"I haven't told you everything about her, or the others. The Birches were a bunch of recluses." She didn't mention they killed people.

"What the hell is that you're waving around?"

Andrea looked at the jagged piece of flat stone. "This is Abigale. I found her old grave marker half-buried in the family cemetery. She's my great-great-great-grandmother. I keep her here for company."

"Andrea," Liz shouted.

"I told you I was getting nutty. Look, this is her pile of diaries. I've read them all, twice. I immersed myself in the lives of dead people, reading their diaries and journals to avoid living my own life."

"You were taking time to reassess after your divorce."

Andrea became somber. "Seriously, Liz." She held up the grave marker. "This woman was afraid to go out into the world. She spent most of her life sitting in front of this fireplace, reading her precious books. She thought she found love once or twice, but she was duped by selfish men who only pretended to love her. She died a lonely woman. I feel like I'm living her life."

"That's enough. I can't hear any more or I'll have to put you away. Talking to grave markers, reading diaries from reclusive relatives... walls lined with pictures of dead people you never met... you need a plan, girl."

It was late. "Right now, I plan to hit the sack. I'm tired and I've kept you up beyond your bedtime."

"Okay, I'm ready, but I'm not letting this go. You need a plan."

LXI

Special Delivery

As Christmas approached, the team, Andrea, Liz, and Tom prepared for the hospital run. "I got my truck, it'll get through a foot of snow."

"Tom, there isn't a flake on the ground. We haven't had snow yet this winter."

"Just sayin'. I'm your transportation. Liz will hold down the fort, here."

"This sounds like we're preparing for battle. I'm sure we'll have a nice, calm trip to the hospital on a crisp, dry day, and the baby will make his or her entrance with grace." She plopped onto her stuffed chair. "Let's just hope the mother has some grace."

Liz brought a plate of scrambled eggs and bacon to Andrea. "Do you want a bagel with cream cheese to go with that?"

"Why not? This body's shot to hell, anyway." Andrea tried to balance the plate of food on her lap and lean over her extended waistline to eat. She put the plate down. "This is impossible. I spill more than I get into my mouth."

"You're a cranky one this morning, missy."

"You'd be cranky, wicked cranky, if you had an eight-pound human strapped onto your hips."

"Why don't you take a nap?"

"It's ten o'clock in the morning." Andrea double checked her watch and held up one puffy foot. She hauled herself from the chair and lumbered into the bedroom. "Okay. Can't eat, might as well sleep."

Tom sat himself on the loveseat. "I got a feeling it's close."

"If being a grouch is any indicator, it sure is. She was due yesterday."

Less than an hour passed before Andrea called out to Liz.

Liz came out of the bedroom, eyes wide. "This is not a drill. Her water broke. She started labor. What do we do?"

"Calm down, Liz. You know your job. Get her bag from the bedroom and put it by the door. I'll walk her to the truck and come back to get her bag. Can you do that?"

"Seriously, I'm lightheaded."

"Okay, then sit, I'll get the bag into the truck and come back for Andrea."

"Okay, okay, I'm okay. I'll call the doctor and let him know you're on the way."

Tom was an abundance of calm. "You do that. Then stay put. I got this."

—◊—

Tom called Liz every two hours to keep her updated on Andrea's labor. "She's doin' fine. They let me in to see her every hour."

"Tell her I love her."

"Yup, she knows."

The phone rang at ten p.m. Liz was wrapped in a blanket and curled up in Andrea's stuffed chair.

"You got a girl. All pink and white. Big one."

Liz wept and sobbed. "Thank the Lord. How is my girl?"

"Andrea? She's a champ. Sitting up, drinking cranberry juice. Here."

"Liz?"

"Darling, are you okay? I've been sick with worry."

"I'm fine. Sitting in my bed with the cutest little one. Would you like to say hello to Elizabeth Abigale Birch?"

Liz couldn't speak for a moment. "You don't have to…"

"I want to. I'm going to raise her to be just like you, a mix of brains, sugar, and spice."

Andrea heard the crack in Liz's voice. "I'm tired tonight, sweets."

Andrea's eyes spilled tears. "Sleep well, my friend."

LXII

Beginnings and Endings

Seahaven, Massachusetts
March 2021

Elizabeth Abigale Birch proved to be a sweet, calm baby. By March, she weighed a healthy thirteen pounds, and cooed and giggled when Tom and Liz entertained her.

Liz did not thrive during the winter. Andrea noticed she'd lost the twelve pounds she gained in the fall, and though she now had two inches of stark white hair, she no longer wore eye makeup or her signature red lipstick.

"I have a doctor's appointment next week."

"No problem, I can drive you into Boston."

Andrea and Liz were having morning coffee. "The appointment is in New York, love."

Andrea put her cup down, noticing Liz's thin, white fingers wrapped around hers. "New York? What's up with that?"

"Darling, this has been wonderful. A gift, really. You, Tom, the baby. We've become a real family, watching out for each other."

"And, but…"

"It's time for me to leave. My sister and I have a plan. I'm going home. There's a clinical trial she wants me to get into."

Andrea reached for Liz's hand. "That's good news. A clinical trial."

"Truth is, I'm going home to die. The cancer's back. Never did believe that remission bullshit."

"But a clinical trial, that's hope."

"Andrea, I've always had a mind of my own, you know, I dance to my own drum."

"I know that, better than most. But this is life we're talking about, Liz."

"No, it's quality of life. Listen, I don't have a say that cancer is going to kill me, but I do have a say about how it kills me. And I'm not going to be vomiting, bald, and lying in bed, hooked up to IVs for my last months."

Andrea nodded in understanding.

"I'm gonna sit on the back porch with my sister and tell old stories, talk about our mother and father, all the good stuff in my life. Maybe have a martini if I want one. That's how I'm going out. You get it?"

Andrea wiped her eyes. "I do. Live on your own terms, die on your own terms."

"Thank you. That's why I love you so much."

"When do you leave?"

"My sister is picking me up at noon tomorrow."

Andrea slammed the table. "Liz."

Liz smiled. "Darling, you know I don't do long goodbyes. All the crying and wailing, it's not for me. But I'm worried about you."

"No need. I listened when you said I needed a plan. I enrolled in an online program and got my teacher's certification renewed. I have a phone interview for a position at a grammar school as an art teacher at the end of the week."

Liz raised her voice. "Perfect. Where? Someplace with people, I hope."

"Wellesley. West of Boston. I thought you'd come with us."

"Like I said, we took care of each other when we needed it. Listen, my condo is in Newton, a bordering town. Take it."

"Liz."

Liz was more excited than Andrea had seen her since she brought the baby home. "You'll be doing me a favor. I've basically abandoned it. There's no mortgage, just pay the monthly fee."

"But it's yours."

She clapped her hands. "I'll leave it to you in my will. My gift to my namesake. A home. Please, let me do this."

Andrea relaxed. "If it will get you to calm down, okay, for a while."

Liz jumped up but became dizzy. Andrea caught her and sat her back down.

"Let me get you the keys."

"Liz, sit, take some water. We'll take care of everything before the morning. Besides, I didn't get a job offer yet."

"I'm fine."

"There's another hurdle. Tom. How can I leave him?"

Color returned to Liz's face. "He's going to Ohio to live near his son."

"What? How do you know? You two are conspiring behind my back?"

"Maybe. But, darling, it's with love." She winked.

—⚹—

Andrea, with baby Elizabeth on her hip, and Tom watched as Liz's sister drove out of the driveway with their friend. Tom put his hanky to his face and blew his nose. "Cold comin' on."

Andrea sniffled. "Think I'm getting the same one." She offered Tom coffee. "We need to talk."

"Did that big mouth tell you?"

"I squeezed it out of her. Tom, I'm happy for you. This is what you've worked for."

He blew his nose again. "I won't leave unless you and Elizabeth are okay."

"We will be okay."

"Did ya get the job?"

"What?"

He sipped his coffee. "Liz may have mentioned it this morning when you were busy with the baby. Do you need a babysitter when you go for the interview?"

"Honest to God, you two, with your conspiring."

Tom stopped making cooing noises at the baby. "Don't worry about anything. I got the truck. I'll get you all moved into the condo."

"Wow, I guess you two had quite the talk."

"We gotta take care of each other, right? Right?"

Andrea nodded through her tears. She smiled at her chubby cheeked angel, "You hear that, Elizabeth? Uncle Tom's gonna get us all settled in our new home.

"What would we have done without you and Liz? We are so loved."

Tom didn't answer Andrea. He took Elizabeth in his arms and spoke to his Godchild, instead. "Yes, Mommy is right. We are so loved."

On a hot day in late August, Tom loaded his truck with baby furniture, clothes, and other personal items. "What a blessing Liz's condo is furnished. She had elegant taste."

"She was a classy lady, that's for sure." Tom looked around the main room. "You comin' back in the summer?"

"Absolutely. That's the beauty of a teaching job. Elizabeth and I will spend the summer on the beach."

"And tending the garden."

She agreed. "And tending the garden."

Tom pointed to a wall. "You taking any of those pictures of your dead relatives?"

"I get the point, Tom. And no. The relatives are staying behind." She stopped and bounced Elizabeth on her hip, "Except for the most important one."

Tom looked at his watch. "Better get going. Long day ahead of us."

Andrea was packing a last box. "You go on out. I'll be five minutes."

She piled the last of Abigale Birch's diaries in the box, planning to tape it up and store it in the loft. Andrea picked up the grave marker she kept on her side table. She was about to put it in her backpack.

On second thought, you need to rest in peace, Abigale Birch. She placed it on top of the diaries and sealed the box.

<u>Andrea Birch Family</u>

Andrea Birch
1984–

Elizabeth Abigale Birch
2020–

Tom Whelan
1954–

Liz
1949–2021

THE END

Thanks for reading **Her Family's Secrets**
You may enjoy other books by Joanne Parsons.
Historical Fiction
Kitchen Canary
Through the Open Door
Suspense/Mystery
Predator in the House

Please Leave a Review on Amazon

BOOK CLUB QUESTIONS

What is the metaphor in **Her Family's Secrets**?
Did any characters experience love?
Were the women characters strong or weak?
Why did Andrea marry/date bad guys?
Was Abigale a sympathetic character?
Was she justified in killing George Smythe?
Why was Catherine, Iris's daughter withdrawn?
Did Andrea find family?
Who was your favorite character?
Would you like to read a sequel?

About the Author

Author Joanne C. Parsons began writing novels after a long career in eldercare administration. Her first book, **Kitchen Canary,** is a historical fiction novel based on a family story. It tells the tale of two young Irish women who immigrate to Boston in the eighteen hundreds to work as nannies. **Kitchen Canary** won several awards for fiction and historical fiction.

Through the Open Door is a sequel to **Kitchen Canary** and follows the characters, freed slaves and Irish immigrants, and the challenges faced by their children, first generation Americans.

Joanne wrote her first mystery, **Predator in the House** in 2020. **Predator** features quirky characters, dark humor, and twists and turns as a Boston detective obsessively searches for an abducted girl.

Joanne lives on a pond on Cape Cod with her husband. Together they have five grown children and seven grandchildren who visit often.

She invites your feedback at jgparsons921@gmail.com and is grateful for your reviews on Amazon.com.

Please contact her if you'd like her to Zoom into your book club meeting or appear at a book signing, your library, or other book event.

Made in the USA
Middletown, DE
21 December 2021

56811178R00157